THE COTTON CHRONICLES
VOLUME TWO:
A GROWING SEASON

A COTTON PROFESSIONAL PRESS
PUBLICATION

BOOKS BY BETTY COTTON MCMURTRY:

The Cotton Chronicles Volume One:
A PLANTING SEASON

The Cotton Chronicles Volume Three:
A FALLOW SEASON
(Due October 2019)

BOOKS BY FORD MCMURTRY:

COTTON FIELDS

CARDIAC CATS:
THE GREATEST FOOTBALL STORY NEVER TOLD
(Due September 2020)

AGAINST A CRIMSON TIDE:
A PACIFIC WAR TALE
(Due December 2019)

A Growing Season

The Cotton Chronicles: Volume Two

Betty Cotton McMurtry

And

Ford McMurtry

DEDICATION

To my family and friends who have supported me along the way.
--Betty

In memory of Coach Thomas D. Jackson, a master story teller, who taught me never to give up and Coach Charles "Chuck" Barber, the first coach to believe in me.
--Ford

ACKNOWLEDGMENTS

Thanks to my children, Mary and Ford, for helping make this a reality. Thanks to Judy and Craig Johnson who encouraged me to "tell my story".

Thanks to Melissa Dunlap for her professional editing and for bringing an outside perspective to the characters.

Special thanks to Lois George for her numerous contributions to this book and The Cotton Chronicles series. We could not have done it without you!

Author's Note: This is a work of fiction. Outside of actual historical figures, any resemblance to persons living or dead is purely coincidental.

Cover Photo Credit:
United States Library of Congress FSA/OWI Collection

PROLOGUE

Throughout the decade of the 1930s, the Great Depression continued to have an economic impact upon most Americans. Those in the South fared better than many of their counterparts in other regions of the country because many Southerners lived in farming communities and were able to grow sufficient food for their families.

However, such was not the case for unemployed factory workers, shop keepers, and those whose jobs no longer existed. While many of these families were forced to load up their trucks or wagons and flee to other areas of the country in search of work, it was common for Southern families to plant their roots locally as tenant farmers or itinerant farm laborers, living in shacks located within the "Quarters" of the large farmsteads. There, they worked closely with their neighbors to share the bounty of the land.

In "A Planting Season," Walt Turner, an emerging businessman with interests in Angus beef, thoroughbred horses, cotton, and lumber, brought his young bride, Annie, to Geneva County, Alabama. With a shrewd mind for business, his farmstead grew exponentially as he diversified into other investments.

In short order, Walt found himself competing with the likes of Robert Ward, a native Geneva Countian deeply invested in cattle, dry cleaning plants, and nightclubs across South Alabama and parts of Florida. By striking a deal with the Southern Railroad to finance a spur track off the main line and into the town of High Springs, Ward Enterprises gained control over much of the economic and political scene in the Southeast. Having the exclusive rights to set carriage rates for use of his railroad spur created a revenue stream that made Robert Ward a wealthy man, often at the expense of farmers and businessmen in need of a means to ship their goods.

Through their various business interests, the Turners and Wards tilled the soil to scratch out a living better than most and then "planted" the seeds of their families. Afterward, they carried on with their enterprises and left the cultivating of their "crops" to their womenfolk.

.....

As was their custom, Walt and Annie Turner sat together on their porch watching the fading rays of sun over the landscape of their 3,000-acre estate known as High Point and talked of what they could anticipate as their future and that of their children and grandchildren. Annie opined their root stock was sturdy enough to survive the hard knocks she expected would be encountered as The Great Depression wore on. Walt agreed wholeheartedly. They were, by golly, Turners after all. Now, they glided to and fro in their rockers anxiously as they awaited the growth of the seeds they had planted.

CHAPTER 1

Rain pelted the window of Olivia Ward's bedroom. The dull staccato echoed throughout Mrs. Smith's house and reflected Olivia's dismal mood as depression crept over her. Nearly four months had passed since Jean had been born prematurely, and it distressed Olivia greatly for her newborn to remain at the Ward farm at High Bluff under her mother-in-law's care.

"It's unnatural," she thought. "The very woman who vowed to kill me and my daughter Kate has gone out of her way to insure life for my newborn baby, Jean."

Birthed using an experimental procedure, Jean required round-the-clock care including maintenance of a make-shift incubator to trick the tiny girl's body into believing it was still in the warmth and safety of her mother's womb. As Jean clung to life, Judy Ward refused to accept Dr. Charles James' prognosis for her granddaughter. Her persistence and determination to keep Jean alive were phenomenal, and she had enlisted an army of colored women from the farm's Quarters to provide assistance for weeks on end. It was Dr. James' expert medical opinion that it was Judy Ward's resolute determination, more than science, which had kept her granddaughter alive.

The procedure to deliver Jean and the excessive blood loss had left Olivia in an extremely weakened condition. Now, Olivia reflected upon her own battle she had fought to live. In the harrowing hours after Jean's birth Olivia clutched to a thin lifeline. Each time she had felt her grasp on it slipping, she recalled how her ne'er-do-well husband, John, had whispered his plea to her. At her lowest ebb she would recall his words, "Olivia, fight. I need you; we need you."

As the dark clouds raced across her window, Olivia accepted the truth of what Dr. James had told her. If she expected to have Jean brought from High Bluff to be with her, she must regain her physical strength and, moreover, overcome her depression. "So be it!" she thought.

On the first day of December 1932, Olivia rose from her bed, dressed and commenced on her road to recovery. It was time for baby Jean to come home.

.....

A few miles away, the rain created a symphony of notes as it struck chords on the tin roof of the hay barn at High Bluff. There was a mixture of 'baaah's and naaay's' from the "horn section" comprised of the adult and baby goats and sheep huddled together away from the open door. Pigeons cooed in the rafters as they preened and plucked their feathers.

Evelyn Ward, perched high in the rafters, ignored the cacophony of sounds as she doodled and scribbled a few lines in her journal notebook as the pigeons coiffed themselves. She was nearly ten years old now and had become accomplished in her writing. This was in no small part due to Olivia's working with her after school most days. A deep thunderclap scattered the fowl from their nests as Evelyn, deep in thought, penned her next line.

Before Jean's arrival, Evelyn's father Robert had made arrangements for her to take the school bus to Mrs. Smith's house to visit Olivia. Then, every evening after work, he retrieved her. The plan worked out well for everyone: Olivia had help with the household chores and minding Kate while Evelyn got to spend time with her sister-in-law, who she adored. Olivia had always been more of a mother figure to Evelyn than anything else. Robert, not to be left out, used the opportunity to dote on his granddaughter, Kate. That was the past, though.

Since her niece had been born three months ago, Evelyn had not been allowed to spend any time with neither Olivia nor Kate while Olivia was on the mend. She worried about 'Cotton' and the thought of Olivia being ill made Evelyn sad. She knew Dr. James had done what he could for her, but it seemed she had something the adults called 'a case of the vapors' for which there was apparently no easy remedy. Her daddy said the only cure was love and time; Evelyn had plenty of both to give if she could only find a way in to High Springs to see Olivia. There, she could do her own 'doctoring.'

．．．．．

Back in High Springs, a few blocks from Mrs. Smith's house, the rains were no less steady. The rhythmic pounding of hammers against nails kept pace with the raindrops tapping on the roof of the cottage Joe and Isaac Jackson were constructing for Olivia and John Ward. Fortunately, they had worked journeyman hours over the past three weeks to raise the roof which now afforded them a relatively safe haven for framing-out the interior rooms. Conspicuous were the burlap sacks which were nailed to the window openings to keep out the rain and critters. The window frames bought from a mill in Atlanta had been delayed by two weeks or they too would have already been installed.

Joe hollered to Isaac from the back room. "You 'bout ready to knock off and get a bite, brother?"

"Not yet. You and your stomach is gonna keep us from finishing this cottage on time for Miss Olivia and her babies. Stay with it! Mama said she would bring us something when she had a chance. We'll wait for her."

Joe sighed with mixed emotions. Working steady from sunup to sundown for three straight weeks had been hard work. Since Mister Robert had delivered the materials he had bought and the lumber which had been donated by Mister Turner to build Olivia's cottage, they had not taken a single day off as they worked at a feverish pace to ensure Miss Olivia could move in by Christmas. As he descended a ladder to load his apron with a few handfuls of nails, he surveyed their progress.

They had laid the footers and piers, installed the subflooring, framed the exterior, and shimmed the front and back doors. As he climbed the ladder to continue framing the front bedroom, he was satisfied with what they had accomplished.

"This is gonna be real nice for Miss Olivia and them girls. Yes, real nice."

"Don't you let Miss Olivia hear you say 'them,'" Isaac chided. "She'll put a heap of hurting on you if she thinks you are backsliding in your language."

"You know that's right!" Joe answered with a grin.

"Building this house for her is a start, but we can't ever repay her for giving us reading and writing lessons from Mister John's old school books," added Isaac. "Even when we thought we couldn't do it, she challenged us to do better. Now look at us."

"You are right, brother and we sure enough can't repay her for all those cakes she baked for us. I don't think she's keeping a tab on us but we sure would owe her a heap for them," laughed Joe.

The boys reveled in their own successes for a moment and then set about finishing their work. They had a tight deadline to meet and they were determined to keep their promise. Besides, Olivia's sister, Beth, was about due to stop in for her daily 'inspection' and neither of them wanted to be caught dallying.

.....

Olivia giggled as Beth updated her on the progress the two men were making on the cottage. "Come hell or high water," she said, "Isaac and Joe will have your cottage ready to move in on time."

Not only had Beth made known her expectations for daily progress on the cottage, she had also challenged Olivia to work to regain her strength so Jean could join her in the new cottage for the Christmas holidays.

Olivia was amused by her sister's behavior but she couldn't tell her how much it and how it parroted Judy Ward's when it came to pursuing her objective; Beth would have been mortified to be compared to Judy's often harsh methods. The truth is they were both effective and neither knew how to give up, even when a fight was lost. Olivia cautioned Beth her constant badgering of Isaac and Joe might not be productive, especially given their exceptional work ethic.

"It may be true I go overboard a bit, but you know what Papa says about the squeaky wheel getting the grease. I'm the squeaking wheel and I'm going to get what I need done!"

"I appreciate your tending to me and looking in on the construction these last few months, Beth. I'm still trying to find my strength to get around. It's so unlike me; I just can't seem to bounce back like I did after birthing Kate. I am worried more about you, though. With all of this time you've spent away from the cannery, is your job secure?"

Beth knew her sister needed her and any other consideration was a moot point. Family always came first. Twice when John was home during that time, Beth had gone to High Point to check on their mother, Annie, and to gather tidbits of gossip from town. Her best source, though, was Gussie Balcomb, the colored woman who ran the Turner's household affairs. Other than these times, Beth stayed with Olivia night and day, sleeping on the settee in her sitting room.

Often during the day, when Olivia felt up to it, they reminisced about good and bad times they had experienced over the past few years. Now, Olivia's depression concerned Beth greatly. In the past, she had countered Olivia's mood swings by relating the stories Gussie shared about John's rolling store stops at High Point.

John, along with backing from Mr. Adkins, had converted an old school bus into a traveling convenience store which made rounds to the outlying farms during the busy farming season. Once Olivia became pregnant with Jean, she could no longer keep Kate all day by herself so John agreed to take her along with him on his route. To say John, at twenty years old, was ill-equipped to manage a toddler was an understatement. Prior to their first outing, John had never even changed a diaper on his own. Thus, hilarity often ensued.

"It was unfortunate," Olivia thought. "Maybe John would have been happier if he had succeeded. He really enjoyed interacting with the farmers."

The store was successful by any measure, but it had ceased operation in October when many customers could not afford to pay cash for their goods. Compounding matters, the amount of credit John had extended prevented him from being able to restock the store. Most disappointing to Olivia was that John had not ceased gambling away his earnings at the dry cleaners as he had promised her and his father. It became unsustainable and consequently, the venture died on the vine.

"It wasn't all a loss," Olivia said. "Taking Kate on the route with him had brought John closer to her."

Beth agreed and reminded Olivia of the time John stopped near the pasture down by High Point where horses were grazing. He had gently lifted Kate up on the fence rail to nuzzle with Butterscotch and Taffy, Olivia's childhood horses. Kate took great delight in the magnificent thoroughbreds, especially their velvety noses which tickled her chin.

"And, you will have to agree we've come a long way together in bringing Papa around," Beth reminded Olivia.

"You're right. I painfully remember the longest time when the girls and I were not welcome at High Point. Gussie worked out a signal so John would know when Papa was away so he knew it was safe to stop at the main house. While Kate enjoyed her visit with her Mama Turner, John peddled his wares in our Quarters."

"I'm so glad Papa finally relented," Beth said.

"Well it wouldn't have happened if you hadn't stood your ground with him. I'd still be banished for life had you not taken up my cause."

"You're kind to say so. And yes, I did stick up for you. But, something else changed Papa's mind. I don't know what it was and truthfully, it doesn't matter. What matters is Kate has brought Mama a heap of joy where there had been none for years. Needless to say, we are all happy you're back."

Regular talks with Beth were the best tonic Olivia could have had; they made her happy. More so, according to Gussie, John had finally come to show a hint of love for Kate.

"Dat man sho 'nuf dotes on that young'un. There ain't no question she be the apple of his eye."

With John's tentative acceptance of Kate as his daughter, and Beth's optimistic encouragement, Olivia continued to improve at a rapid pace. She looked forward to having Jean home with her soon and she kept a watchful eye on John. She prayed his love and newly demonstrated affection for Kate would continue to grow. She was ever mindful of John's precarious role in ensuring Kate had a name and the resulting opportunities to live a normal life in a small town where gossip and innuendo had spoiled many a pot of stew. "If I can just keep him on the right path," she thought. "I know John can learn to abide a life that includes his daughters, if not one that includes me."

· · · · ·

The Saturday afternoon sky was overcast. Olivia sat at the kitchen table sorting out strips for her rugs while the girls napped and John listened to the 'swap and shop' show on the Phillips radio. Outside, she heard a car stop and two doors open. Olivia pulled back the kitchen curtain to reveal Paul Gunderson and his wife, Sandra had arrived.

"John," she said in a stage whisper. "It's Paul and his wife. Were you expecting them?"

"Yes! He just moved back to town to take a job at the bank with his father. I saw him on the square the other day and I invited him to stop by this afternoon with Sandra for coffee. I so look forward to spending time with him and catching up on old times. I guess I forgot to tell you. I'm sorry. "

Olivia hid her dismay as she quickly cleared the table and put filled the percolator with water and haphazardly spooned coffee grounds into the strainer. John answered the knock at the door and raucously greeted his friend while stepping aside and inviting them inside. Paul stepped inside and nodded a greeting to Olivia who had appeared in the hallway while desperately wiping her hands on her apron. Olivia smiled and nodded in return. "Hello Paul," she said softly. "Hello Sandra," she said a little louder.

Paul smiled and turned with an outstretched arm to usher in

Sandra who remained on the porch. His smile quickly dissipated as his eyes met hers and she stepped back away from the door.

"Paul, this is a mistake. We should not be here. We should have listened to your mother."

Sandra turned and hurried to the car. And, on her way she resorted to feigned dismay, expressing her incredulity. "How could you expect me to associate with people who live in quarters meant for domestics?"

Paul looked at John in dismay. "I'm sorry about this, John. Maybe you and I can meet some time at Jerrell's?"

John nodded but said nothing as Paul backed slowly away and then turned to catch up with Sandra who was waiting by the car for him to open her door. He closed the front door and stood staring at the back of it for what seemed to Olivia to be an eternity. Then, he turned to her with an expression Olivia would never forget. It was a look of undisguised hatred.

"There goes my best friend whose wife can't abide his friendship with me, a loser. Why, Olivia? This is your fault. Why didn't you stop my advances upon you that night in the barn? Because of your weakness, I have to live every single day paying for your mistake!"

.....

Christmas should have been a joyous time but it wasn't. Although Jean had finally come home to her mother and they had moved into their new cottage, it was a time of intense anxiety. John could not hide his resentment of Olivia. Most nights he did not come home; and when he did, his behavior toward anyone in his path was ornery and cruel. He was moody and brooded nearly every waking moment. Not only did he not speak to her, he withdrew from the girls. His latent anger simmered under the surface and while he didn't say anything to her, Olivia feared he might lash out at her physically. She lived in constant angst but was resolved to take whatever steps necessary to protect Kate and Jean.

"John can do whatever he wills to me and I'll take it," she thought. "But, he can ask Judy about what happens when animals are cornered. He best not harm my girls."

CHAPTER 2

On New Year's Eve 1933, Olivia rocked as she sat tying a rug from scraps of flour sacks. She hummed a church hymn as the church bells tolled the beginning of a new year.

"It's a shame," she thought. "Those beautiful bells only chime for church services, weddings, Independence Day, and New Year's Day. I wish there were other occasions. People must certainly enjoy their melodious tones." As she thought more about it, she realized she had only heard the bells ring one time outside of those events: the end of The Great War."

After tying four rugs, she checked on the girls. She thought she heard Jean whimper but it was a false alarm; both girls were sleeping soundly. She retrieved her hair brush from the vanity and on her way back to the kitchen; she passed the bedroom and noticed her reflection in the full length mirror. She nearly dropped her brush in shock. Despite the facts she was only a few months past her 26th birthday, she saw before her the image of a tired and desperate 'old' woman. Child birthing and dealing with John's errant ways had certainly taken its toll on her.

A few minutes later she found herself mindlessly brushing her hair while staring at the kitchen cabinets. She pondered what she could do to alter John's behavior toward Kate. She realized the truth of her situation and admitted as much. She could not change him but perhaps she could stop indulging in self-pity and forego her tendency to consider the 'what ifs' about her life. Instead, she would concentrate on her blessings and 'what is.'

It would be somewhat of a change for her but she knew she could do it. She just needed to stiffen up her backbone. As much as she hated to admit it, that was one of the qualities she admired about Judy. She was tough as nails and as much as she had tried in vain to eliminate Olivia and Kate from her family, she had fought for Jean when it counted. She only wished she could have been a fly on the wall when Judy had confronted Dr. James about Jean's prognosis. According to Flora's account of the incident, Judy had been "hell on wheels" when dealing with the doctor shortly after Jean was born.

"Missus Judy sho 'nuf is a mighty force," Flora had bellowed. "She meant nobody, no how, would interfere with her keeping her Baby Jean alive. She done got Dr. James' goat. He come to check on Jean and whilst he was there he done made a big mistake when he said her efforts wasn't 'nuf to save Jean. She was as mad as a wet setting hen. Ifn you coulda' seen how she exploded; it was like somebody done poured gas on a fire. As he tried to skedaddle outta that there house, Missus Judy done kicked him in his britches and shouted fer him to get his sorry ass out with his hogwash. She said she done promised her son his daughter would live, and by God, she would!"

Olivia yawned several times as she rose and prepared for bed. When she lay down, she was fitful and unable to fall asleep right away. Despite her best intentions, she could not escape the miserable thought of a life wasted by being spent with John.

Aside from his irresponsibility with money and his drinking, she could not dismiss the thought of Paul and Sandra's aborted visit and the implications Sandra had made regarding her seeing Olivia as nothing more than a house maid and not fit to be good company. He seemingly blamed her for everything afoul in his life: his father's decision to refuse giving him a job at Ward Enterprises, having two daughters, missing an opportunity for love with Margot Brown, and his being forced to drop out of school. To John, Olivia represented an impassable road block to his happiness and was the root cause of his perpetual misery.

"When will it ever end?" she thought. And then she answered her own question: "It won't. He's a lost cause."

She turned on her side to ease her mind, but she did not succeed as his increasing discontent and belligerent behavior continued to play in her mind. Sleep eluded her and eventually, she sat up and turned up the bedside lamp. Its eerie light flickered through the clear glass bulb causing shadows to dance on of the walls of the cottage. She stared at the images while waiting for her eyelids to grow heavy. They did not.

The clock struck two o'clock and John had not come home. Olivia was glad. She had dreaded his arriving home drunk after celebrating the New Year and her likely being subjected to his verbal abuse as she often had in the past several months.

Three days passed without any sight of him.

· · · · ·

On the fourth day the owner of the cannery, David Anderson, came around in the early afternoon asking about John's whereabouts. He said John had not been to work since the last few days of December. Ever the dutiful wife, Olivia did her best to cover for John while telling Mr. Anderson she would have John contact him as soon as he came home. There wasn't much else she could say; she didn't have the faintest idea.

About an hour and a half hour later, John came home to the cottage and stumbled into the kitchen. He staggered to the bedroom and flopped across the bed. Olivia closed the door behind him, hoping he would sleep off his drunken stupor. At the same time, she lamented his backslide. She did not look forward to returning to the living conditions she had endured when he had moved into the shack in the Quarters with her several years ago and now she was determined to shield the girls from such debauchery.

She occupied the girls with some Nabisco crackers so they would remain quiet and not wake their father. At the same time, she wondered, "What can I do to help him? Nothing. He has hit rock bottom... again!"

. . . . .

After David Anderson left the cottage, he went directly to Robert Ward's office to inform him of his rationale for firing his son. Robert had invested heavily in the opening of the cannery and, although he had largely remained a silent partner, Anderson knew full-well Robert's influence across the Southeast and wanted to ensure he did not end up on any Ward Enterprise 'black list.' When he arrived, Robert ushered him into his private office.

"I have come to tell you in person why I had to fire John today. His unreliability and drinking on the job gave me no choice. In these difficult times, there are simply too many men in High Springs who need a job and will report for work each day. We have a line ten-deep every morning looking for daily work. I don't know what has happened with him. Since he came back to work for me, he has been an excellent employee up until the past month or so. Lately though, I don't even recognize him and, frankly, he seems not to give a damn."

Robert mustered his patience and apologized for John's behavior. He thanked David for taking John ahead of many deserving individuals with families to feed. Typically, John had squandered the opportunity. As soon as David left, Robert closed his office door and put his head down on his desk.

"What has happened to cause my son's behavior to change so drastically?" he asked staring at the floor beneath him. "Damn it all! Has he slipped back into his old ways? Good Lord, why didn't I put two and two together when I've found him constantly away during my visits? One way or another I'll get to the bottom of this." He left his office and drove directly to Olivia's cottage.

CHAPTER 3

The afternoon air in the countryside surrounding Dothan was a brisk 38 degrees as Paul Gunderson opened the trunk of his automobile and withdrew a thick leather flying jacket and satchel bag. As he closed the lid, he nearly dropped the two three-foot rolls of paper he had been balancing under his chin. Fortunately, he caught them before they blew away.

Passing by three large pole barn structures containing several bi-planes, he entered a tiny two-room building adjacent to the grass airstrip and headed into the planning room which doubled as a makeshift kitchen. There he stowed his hat, overcoat, and suit in a wooden locker, and changed into coveralls. He pulled on the brown leather jacket and rolled out the navigational charts on the table. After scribbling a few notes on a small pad, he checked his watch, and rolled up the charts. As he did, he heard an automobile pull up outside. Shortly, the front door opened.

Heinrichs Friedman was a husky man who was nearly as tall as Paul and sported mutton chop sideburns. When he spoke, his accent was decidedly German, but yet not as thick as Paul had remembered from the phone call. He shook Paul's hand, and got right to the point.

"Thanks for meeting vith me, Herr Gunderson. As we discussed on zee phone, I head a group of local investors who vant to capitalize on the growing popularity of aeroplanes for civilian and military use. In investigating financing with your father, he tells me you have a flying background dating to your days at zee University of Alabama.

Is that true?"

"Please sir, call me Paul. Yes, it is true. After The Great War, the Army sold off much of its inventory of bi-planes to civilians for sport and training purposes. The Flying Club in Tuscaloosa purchased four of these to use as trainers for their club members. Since then, they have purchased newer planes as funds have allowed. As a sixteen-year-old boy in 1927, I, like many adults and youths across America, was inspired by Charles Lindberg's solo Trans-Atlantic flight. Although the field there at the time was not much more than a pasture like this one, when the opportunity presented itself, I took full advantage of learning to fly from a few of the Old Timers who flew in France."

"Wunderbar!" Friedman exclaimed. "You may not know but after zee var I immigrated here from Germany vith my family and have made a good living repairing motors for tractors and farm equipment. Although many of my friends fled Europe, a few remained. These are individuals engaged in advising several countries of zee benefits of aerial spotting, transport, and leisure travel. There is a market for business trips, forecasting zee weather and delivering mail. Trained pilots are in short supply and several competitors have begun offering pilot training. I am involved with a group of investors who vant to position themselves to take advantage of any opportunities which may arise here in Alabama and the surrounding states."

"How does this involve me?" Paul asked. "It sounds like your business is with my bank, not me."

"Ah, right to the point. I admire that in you. Vhile vee have negotiated financing for an aeroplane through your father's bank, vee have no means of ferrying it here from Vichita, Kansas, where it is being built. Your father suggested you might be interested in doing so."

"Kansas? That's certainly a long way away."

"Ja, it is," belched Friedman. "Of course, you vill be paid for your time. And...," he paused. "You vill have the opportunity to fly zee Stearman C-3B."

Paul was surprised. He had heard about the peppy little plane but he had never imagined he would have the opportunity to actually fly one.

"Well that is certainly an attractive offer for an enthusiast such as I. But I must ask, why me? Surely someone else is more qualified?"

"As you can imagine, zer is a dearth of qualified pilots in zee area and vee have been unable to find a suitable candidate. Your father has assured me you are of impeccable character and that your discretion in such a matter can be relied upon by my associates. Do we have a deal, Herr Paul?"

Paul did not need any time to consider Herr Friedman's offer. While at the University, he had accrued more than 160 hours in bi-planes which were inferior but functioned similarly to the C-3B. He probably had more time in these planes than he had in the automobile parked outside. Perhaps his abundance of confidence was getting the better of him, but he expected no trouble in being able to fly the new plane.

"Believe it or not, I've flown a similar plane and I'll have no problems ferrying it home for you. We've got a deal. When will Wichita expect me?"

Freidman enthusiastically shook Gunderson's hand. "Wunderbar! I vill deliver zee necessary documents for transfer of zee plane to your office tomorrow along with petty cash for your fuel and expenses along zee way." For the first time, Friedman noticed Paul was dressed to fly. "You're going up today I zee?"

"Yes, sir. I needed to get in a few hours this month to maintain my sharpness. Now, it is even more important!"

"Safe landings, *mein freund*," Friedman said as he patted Paul firmly on the back and shoulders. "I vill see you tomorrow."

Thirty minutes later, the young pilot bathed in the turbulence of air rushing over the windscreen of the Curtiss Fledgling Model 48. As the wind cascaded off his helmet and goggles, he reached his cruising altitude and airspeed. Then, he throttled back the power, checked his fuel mixture setting, and held the control stick steady and slightly back which gave the bi-plane a slightly nose-up attitude. The Wright J-5 Whirlwind engine whined like a sewing machine as the Curtiss cut through the wind, soaring across the Houston County line into Geneva County.

As he entered a lazy, wide-sweeping, banked turn to return to the airstrip, he mentally calculated the flight time, distance, and fuel he needed to complete the nearly 900-mile trip from Kansas to Alabama. All totaled, he figured he would be gone nearly a week.

"Sandra won't be happy to have me away," he thought. "But lately, she has made a lot of demands of me and I've come to feel like I've lost sense of who I am. The time away will do us both good. Absence, they say, makes the heart grow fonder. We will see how fond of me she is upon my return."

CHAPTER 4

The knocks on the door were rapid and resounded throughout the cottage. Olivia opened the door to find Robert standing there. Her heart sank as she dreaded the questions she knew were coming. "The girls are asleep," she cautioned. "Please keep your voice low."

Robert was nearly out of breath. "Do you know David Anderson fired John this morning?"

Olivia's expression spoke volumes and she motioned for him to come with her into the sitting room. Jean cried out and she quickly left him for a moment to tend to her. From the back room, Robert heard John yell at Olivia in a slurred banter.

"Get the hell out of here and leave me alone, woman. No, I won't be quiet, so what if I wake up those brats? Are you so stupid? Do you not understand I can't stand the sight of them or you?"

A loud thud reverberated through the wall and was followed by a softer thud and a yelp from Olivia who appeared in the hallway holding John's boot. Robert was enraged. He knew where his ne'er-do-well son was now and he was determined to drag his sorry ass out of bed and set him straight.

He moved past Olivia, who put up an unsuccessful effort to stop him, and continued down the hallway. His anger grew with each step as the words "those brats" rang in his ears. John reeked of the smell of alcohol and Robert's first thought was that he wanted to beat the immature little cad to within an inch of his life. However, his cooler side prevailed and he stopped in the doorway.

"Son, I do not believe what I have heard. Never would I have considered you capable of hitting a woman and certainly not one who is the mother of your children. What do you have to say for yourself? Have your mother and I raised a fool?"

John, face-down on the bed, raised himself up on his elbows and looked at his father. "It's not enough to have a nagging old woman harass me, now I have to put up with you, too. Well, take a good look at this no-good son of yours. Like Old Man Gunderson and most people in High Springs, you think I am no good, don't you? You sure as hell don't think I am good enough or smart enough to work for you. You saw my success with the rolling store but you won't even give me a chance." John turned and flopped onto his back while covering his head with a pillow.

Robert's anger evaporated with a measure of some guilt as he observed his son's sobbing. Neither a scolding nor a beating would benefit either of them in this moment. It was apparent John's hurt came from deep within him and it had probably festered there for some time. Robert moved across the room and sat on the edge of the bed while placing an arm over his son's back. He could not ignore the truth of what John had said. Robert had long-recognized John was good enough to work for Ward Enterprises; but until now, he had refused to present him with the opportunity on some misguided principle.

He thought back to the time when John and he had discussed the possibilities available to him if John were successful in his venture with Mr. Adkins. They had agreed he could earn a shot at working for his father. When the route failed two months ago, Robert immediately recognized it was not John's fault but had never considered taking him on board to work for him. Now, he knew he should have and he wondered if it were too late to salvage his son.

"John, hear me out. You are smart enough and good enough to work for me. If you can get yourself sober by morning, come to my office and I will make you a proposition."

John did not respond. Robert, however, sensed he was listening. "I understand your actions here today were out of frustration. Perhaps I am to blame for some of them. But I will tell you that you need to consider the high standards I hold in my business dealings and decide if you are prepared to uphold them."

John still did not respond as he continued to hide his face in the pillow to hide his disgust. Robert gently patted his son on the chest twice and decided to leave him be, for now, to soak in what Robert had told him.

Robert emerged from the hallway and found Olivia in the sitting room with a cold cloth pressed against the back of her head. He could tell John's physical abuse had pushed her to the limits of her tolerance of him.

"Does he generally sober up by morning? If he does I need to talk to both of you. I'm sorry you and the girls are going through this. Don't worry, Olivia. You have been through much at the hands of my wife and son. We will get through this together."

With that Robert left and Olivia experienced an emotion foreign to her. Her feelings of contempt for John had left her and were now replaced by those of hatred. She had an overwhelming feeling of needing to get out of the house and she gathered up the girls and walked with them over to Mrs. Smith's.

·····

A few minutes later, she arrived at Mrs. Smith's where she was greeted by Carolyn Gates, a dear friend of her mother, who immediately noticed Olivia's distress. They sat down with Mrs. Smith in her sitting room. Rachel Green, the teenage daughter of the local midwife Janie Green, was there helping with some light housekeeping and she agreed to entertain the girls in their old rooms while the adults talked.

"What has upset you so?" Carolyn asked.

Olivia, although ashamed to admit what had happened, shared the details and her ill feelings and ensuing fear of John. Both women gasped.

Carolyn regained her composure and asked, "Do you think his behavior is because of his exclusion from the Gunderson's party? As you probably have heard, the social snub by Paul's parents of his best friend has been the prime topic for the town's gossip mill."

"It could be. I just don't know."

Although it was common knowledge among the gossip mongers on the square, Carolyn sensed Olivia was unaware of the circumstances of the Ward-Gunderson falling out. So, she told her, replete with examples, of Jack Gunderson's long-running feud with Robert Ward and his desire to damage him socially, politically, and financially by heaping shame and embarrassment upon both John and Olivia.

The most despicable act, she said, was what Mr. Gunderson had done to have John's football scholarship offer at the University of Alabama withdrawn. As she listened, her attitude toward John changed for the better and she felt like she should give him another chance to find a degree of contentment, if not happiness, working for Ward Enterprises. She hoped his meeting with Robert the following morning would prove fruitful. As she considered the possibilities for John, she thought, "It must be if my daughters and I are to have any peace."

. . . . .

Beth was waiting for them when Olivia and the girls returned to their cottage. Olivia settled the girls with their toys and told Beth about John's being fired and all that had transpired once Robert arrived. Beth was concerned about her sister's ability to survive financially and offered to help.

Olivia explained John's loss of his job would make no difference to them since he had never given her any part of his earnings anyway. Beth was shocked and angered but she did not want to belabor Olivia's distress so she dismissed her feelings.

"That's all water under the bridge, Beth. Enough about what has happened with John; tell me about Mama. The last two times I've visited her, she seemed withdrawn. Do you think there is something wrong with her?"

Beth said she was unable to figure out what was going on with their mother. She seemed to be happier than she had been for a long time, but at the same time, something wasn't quite right with her and she behaved as though she were depressed.

"I've watched her closely, but I haven't detected anything except that she is forgetful at times and sometimes has trouble completing a sentence. Yours's and the girls' visits are like a magic elixir for her well-being."

Olivia nodded in agreement. She knew her mother looked forward to seeing the girls, especially Kate. "You know her forgetfulness is probably the cause of her depression. At sixty years old, it must worry her to realize she is already losing her ability to recall what she intends to say. But I don't think her behavior is caused by her age; I think it is something else."

"Olivia, you are the only one Mama will listen to. Will you please try to persuade her to see Dr. James?" Beth waited for Olivia's assurance but none was forthcoming. Olivia was distracted, even agitated, and not paying her full attention to her.

Abruptly, Olivia's eyes met Beth's and she sternly addressed her sister. "Beth, what I am about to tell you I mean in all sincerity. If John returns while you are here today, you must leave immediately. Don't argue with me, just do as I say because he is out of sorts with me right now, and I'm afraid of what he is capable of doing."

Beth could read between the lines; she knew John had caused her sister some physical harm. "Olivia, if he is a physical threat to you or to Kate and Jean, let's quickly gather up a few of your things, and all of you come with me to High Point. Will you do that?"

Olivia was tempted but she knew she, alone, would have to deal with John when he eventually came home. However, she could not risk Papa's reaction. His temper was fearsome and Olivia worried what Papa might do to John if he knew he had laid hands on her. Besides, she knew John had carried a pistol with him on his rolling store. She didn't dare risk allowing Papa and him to get into a physical altercation. In John's state of mind, there's no telling what he might do on an impulse.

"Beth, go now. The girls and I will be alright. Please do not tell Mama and Papa about this. Mama must not have any more on her mind than she already does and Papa must not become involved for his own safety. Promise me."

Beth wanted to argue, but realized Olivia was resolute in her decision. She agreed to honor Olivia's request for secrecy.

CHAPTER 5

It was well past midnight when Olivia went to bed. At dawn she woke to find John had not come home yet and she was afraid he probably would not arrive by the time Robert stopped by in a few hours. Just before six o'clock Robert knocked and she hurried to greet him at the door. Immediately, he asked if John was up and was infuriated when he learned he had not come home the night before.

"Damn it, Olivia, he knew I was coming today. He could not have misunderstood my intent to help him." Robert sat down and dropped his head in his hands and mumbled. "Who am I kidding? John doesn't care! Hell fire, Olivia, am I a fool to continue to try to salvage him?"

How could she answer? For that matter, she was unsure if he really expected one, so she remained silent and let him vent his frustration.

"For the past three weeks, Judy and I both wondered why John was never home. We also wondered why he didn't attend the reception for Paul and Sandra. After witnessing his behavior toward you last night, I don't think I even know who my son is anymore. If you have any ideas, please share them with me."

"Mr. Ward, John did not attend the reception because he was not invited."

Her response did not register with Robert. He was too engrossed in deciding what to do. "I guess he can't be helped if he can't be found. You say he didn't come home last night? Has this been his regular behavior?" He paused for a moment before her answer had registered. "He wasn't invited? What are you saying?"

There was no need for her to lie. "No sir. I believe Paul's wife, Sandra sees me as nothing more than a housemaid and John as a business and social liability for Paul so she scratched him from the guest list. Now as to John, you should know that before Jean was born, John stayed out some nights and he would come home just in time to pick up Kate and make his rolling store runs. During that time, he was never drunk or abusive but now he rarely comes home and when he does, he is usually drunk."

Olivia took a breath. What she would tell Robert next might cause Flora and the Jackson boys harm, but she could not conceal John's vagary any longer.

"Mister Ward, Isaac and Joe told Flora they overheard some men talking about John when they were waiting at Gates' Feed and Seed. He spends a lot of his time in the back room of the dry cleaners where gambling goes on. That is probably where he is now."

He held up his hand to stop her. "Wait a minute. Are you telling me John is in a poker game at my dry-cleaning plant at this very minute? I can't believe it, especially considering I specifically instructed Herbert Franklin to steer John clear of any games in town."

Robert grew angry as he recalled his promise to fire Herbert and make certain he would be unable to find other work in High Springs if he allowed John to gamble at the cleaners. Surely Herbert was too smart to risk his livelihood for the little he and Wallace Gleason's boys could take from John. Robert gathered his hat and coat and left without saying a word.

Olivia wondered whether he would go find John or would wash his hands of him.

. . . . .

Robert drove to the dry-cleaning plant, pushed his way past Billy Jones manning the front counter, and burst into the smoke-filled back room. The smell of sweaty bodies and open bottles of rot gut liquor nearly choked him. He scanned the room and located the target of his wrath.

John was facing the other direction, bending over the table placing his bet and never saw his father walk in. It was obvious he had been wearing the same clothes for several days and he looked like the bum he was fast becoming. Robert stormed past John, stopping only when he reached Herbert Franklin. There he grabbed Herbert by his jacket collar and jerked him upward and out of the chair. Herbert's arms flailed and his cards flew through the air. Then Robert released his grip while letting him slump down to the floor.

"Get up and get your ass out of this building you low-down piece of dung. Apparently, you didn't believe me a year ago when I warned you what I would do if you allowed John to gamble here with you and your card shark friends. Well, Mister Franklin, I am here to collect. Get out now before I throw you out."

Herbert got up from the floor and faced Robert. "Mister Ward, I tried to keep John out of here, but he kept coming back. He got so far in debt to Wallace and the boys that he had to keep playing in order to whittle down his markers. In fact, he got in so deep he had to start hauling...." He tried to stop but it was too late. He glanced quickly at Wallace Gleason across the table. Wallace grimaced at Herbert's gaff.

"Hauling? Hauling what?" Robert asked as he violently shook Herbert by the collar. Herbert trembled; he knew his goose was cooked now. Robert tossed him to the floor, and Herbert fell over himself as he stumbled away and out the front door. Robert told John and the other men to clear out and leave the pot and their earnings on the table.

Accordingly, each man hastily left his chips and stacks of bills in exchange for getting out while the getting was good. They knew Robert Ward's power and didn't want to incur his wrath by crossing him further. As they filtered out, Robert turned his attention to Wallace, who outweighed him by fifty pounds.

"Not you, Wallace." Wallace hung his head and stopped near Robert, and off to one side. "Hauling what, Wallace?"

Wallace shook his head in disgust and turned an eye toward the ceiling.

"Tell me now, Wallace, or your fat, sorry ass along with your wife and kids will be out on the street by tomorrow morning once I evict you from my rental property."

He couldn't dodge Mr. Ward any longer. "Moonshine," he said softly. "The boys and me have been making some 'shine out in the woods and Johnny Boy here has been delivering for us to pay off his markers. We knowed you was tight with Sheriff Otis Miller and the other lawmen 'round these parts and we knew none of them would touch him for fear of your preventing them from gettin' re-elected."

Robert was incensed. While his juke joints in Florida skirted a tight line between lawful and illegal, he had been careful to ensure his business ventures did not go so far astray that public backlash would force the local constabulary to take public action against him or his businesses. Manufacturing and distributing liquor violated the 18th Amendment of the United States Constitution. It was simply too much for Robert to stomach, even despite what he secretly knew was going on in Washington D.C. as they spoke.

The kind of activity Wallace and his cronies were involved in bypassed the scrutiny of local lawmen and tended to draw the attention of the 'Federal Boys' from Washington. Not only that, it stood to jeopardize handshake agreements with the fellas in Chicago, New York and Miami who had their own operations in full swing. As long as Robert Ward tended business in his own backyard and didn't stray too far, they would look the other way. News of Wallace's business venture was the kind of trouble Ward Enterprises did not need.

"It ends today, Wallace. Do you hear me? Today. No more! Now get out your sorry ass out of here too."

Despite giving up several inches in height and the weight disadvantage, Robert had no trouble shoving Wallace in the general direction of the door. Now that they were alone, Robert turned his attention to his son.

John was too drunk to do more than watch as his cronies had made their rapid exits. As Robert raked the cash and written markers into a garment bag, John sat down and slumped over face down on the table and closed his eyes. Seeing his son was in no condition to hear the 'Riot Act' at this moment, Robert walked to the front counter and ordered Billy Jones to close up the place for the rest of the day. He also told Billy to come see him the following morning if he had any interest in following his instructions to the letter in the running of the plant. Billy enthusiastically said he did and he would.

Now that the illicit gaming in the back room of his dry cleaners had been brought to an end, Robert realized that being angry at his son at this juncture would be fruitless. He returned to the back room and slung his son's nearly unconscious body over his shoulder. Then he carried him outside to the corner of the building to a rain barrel where he dunked him head first and left him there, upside down.

John sobered quickly in the freezing water. He thrashed about violently as soon as he realized he was drowning. Robert pulled him out and tossed him aside into the mud-colored puddle accumulating beside the barrel.

"Son, I'll give you two choices. You may wallow there in the mud where you have been mired for years or you can raise yourself up and out of your miserable existence so we can talk about your working with me."

Robert then turned toward his car without looking back. Behind him, he could hear John's boots squishing out rancid water as he shuffled along trying to catch up. When he finally did, Robert turned to him. "Get in the car and I'll deliver you home."

·····

Within a few minutes they were back at the cottage. When they arrived inside, Robert assuaged Olivia's fears and asked her to put on some coffee. Robert, it turns out, had a good bit to say.

"Go wash up and put on some clean clothes. I can't abide your stench, and it grieves me to see you look like the bum you seem to want to become. Once you are cleaned up we can discuss a job you might consider. If you accept my proposal, you'll begin work in my office on Monday morning."

John returned shortly and in addition to smelling and looking more presentable, he had sobered up significantly. Robert motioned for Olivia to join them with the coffee. As John approached the table, she poured coffee for the men but noting for herself.

"I'm all ears, Dad."

"On Monday you'll begin work in my office. It's not a cushy job; you'll work long hours, seven days a week for at least six months." He waited and observed John's reaction and continued.

"You'll provide project management for the construction of two nightclubs in South Florida. The work on the club in Miami will start the first week of June, and work on the second club will commence about two weeks thereafter. Time is money so a strict timeline for construction must be maintained. Additionally, there are several other projects closer to home on which I'll need your assistance."

John grinned as he listened but neither he nor Olivia said anything so Robert continued.

"What I am about to tell you is strictly confidential and I am entrusting you with this information on the assumption you are mature enough to handle it appropriately. My contacts in Washington have advised me President Roosevelt is going to take the first step in repealing Prohibition. Soon, importing, manufacturing, and selling alcohol will be legal pursuant to the whims of each state and county."

"Really?" John asked. "I can't believe it."

"Yes. It's a matter of tax revenue. Prior to Prohibition, a large chunk of federal, state and local taxes was derived from the sale of alcohol. When the stock market crashed in '29, tax revenue dwindled and federal and state governments nearly collapsed. Someone got smart and realized millions of dollars in tax revenue were being lost to the illegal manufacture and sale of the 'Devil's Juice.' Your pal Wallace would know a thing or two about that."

"What?" Olivia asked with a puzzled look.

"Not now," John waved a finger to dismiss her question as Robert continued.

"In the next few months, I am told Roosevelt will introduce legislation to allow the manufacture of beer and wine and will determine if the decision to fully repeal the Prohibition should be decided at the state or national level. If everything goes as planned and Roosevelt can get the votes to repeal the amendment in 38 states, then counties in the individual states will likely hold referendums to vote on whether to be 'wet or dry.' A vote for 'dry' means no alcohol sales will be allowed. In Florida and Alabama, I believe I have sufficient influence to sway the vote in counties in which we have clubs to become 'wet.'"

John sat back and ran his fingers through his slick black hair in amazement. "Dad, that could mean hundreds of thousands of dollars in profits."

Robert smiled. "No son, it could mean millions of dollars in profits. And, my decision as to whether I will open a new juke joint near the Alabama-Florida line will depend on two things: whether Holmes County is voted as wet or dry, and if it becomes dry, the outcome of the Holmes County sheriff's race."

He paused so John and Olivia had time to digest what he had said. "Aside from your responsibilities as my project manager, I will need you to work to have our preferred candidate for sheriff in Holmes County elected."

Although John had numerous questions, he did not raise them at this time. If his father was correct about Roosevelt's ending Prohibition, there would be a lot of business headed their way.

His head was still not fully clear from the scene at the dry-cleaning plant a few hours ago, but he considered his gambling debts with Wallace forgiven. Still, some time away from High Springs would allow Wallace to have a cooling off period lest he decide to recoup his markers through other, less pleasant means.

At last, John was excited about the prospect of working with his father. But, to be honest, he questioned his ability to handle all of the responsibilities of the job his father had described.

Robert observed John's concern. "Son, I would not risk the investment I am making in these clubs if I were not sure you could handle the job. I've arranged to have an experienced project manager mentor you. He will teach you the intricate aspects of setting up and running our businesses. In addition, I've got some ideas as to how we can shore up your political and social skills."

Learning he would have someone to mentor him in running the business eased some of John's concerns, but he was still unsure of what his father meant when he alluded to another skill he would need to develop.

Robert turned to Olivia, who had largely been silent. The whole thing was a bit overwhelming for her, especially since she had been ready to literally kill John a few hours ago.

"Olivia, I know when your mother, Annie, was not well, you served as hostess when Walt entertained influential politicians. He, as do Judy and I, entertain with the purpose of gaining concessions from political operatives. I am confident you have witnessed how the game of 'you scratch my back and I'll scratch yours' is played. Could I impose on you to teach John how this is deftly accomplished? Will you agree to teach him 'the game?' "

Her response was a resounding, "No!" Before Robert could react, she continued. "John has made it clear by his actions that he has no respect for me or his children and I'll not allow myself to be humiliated further by his disdain for us. He has shown time and time again he has no use for anyone but himself. Let him figure it out on his own."

She rose to return to the kitchen, but Robert stopped her, asking her to stay and hear how John felt about her teaching him. John remained silent.

As he waited for John to speak Robert thought, "It would be a mistake to put John in this critical position without the requisite skills, especially those associated with gaining political support or concessions. But the stakes are too high and I simply cannot trust anyone else. Hell, I can't even find anyone to run an honest dry-cleaning establishment."

The more he thought, the more troubled Robert became. "If we are to succeed in obtaining state liquor licenses for the clubs in West Palm Beach and Miami, we'll need the political support of local and state officials. It will be imperative for you, John, to cultivate this support via whatever means necessary. Can you put your loathing for your situation aside long enough to allow Olivia to help you if she will agree to do so?"

Robert looked at Olivia woefully. Surely, she understood what was on the line. She must agree to help him. Olivia held her emotions in check. She still wasn't convinced John would be receptive to her guidance, but out of respect for Robert and all that he had done to thwart Judy's attacks on her and Kate, she decided to hold her decision a little while longer. She remarked that there were occasions when she had assisted Papa in his quest for political support and with a willing student, she could teach him the ins and outs of 'the game.'

"Papa taught me what was necessary to succeed. According to him, success depended on the extent to which the person he needed to support him was willing to play the game. You are right, though; if John doesn't understand every nuance of how the game is played, he will stand no chance in gaining concessions."

She paused and then asked what she considered an important question. "Are you experiencing legal complications which will require you to rely on political accommodations? If so, would bribes be involved? I ask because bribes are illegal but are often used to gain political concessions. If bribes are involved, would John be at risk from a legal standpoint?"

Robert did not reply, but grimaced slightly. Olivia picked up on his expression and thought, "I have heard of Robert Ward's skill in bending the rules wherever he encounters opposition. Now, it appears he will expect John to engage in such activities. No, surely not. The outcome could be disastrous for him."

She noted her concerns and spoke of her father's admonition to all his children. "He insisted we always look before we leap. According to him, if we look first, we can minimize bad outcomes. John will not accept my advice, but I offer it, anyway. John, in this situation you need to follow Papa's advice to me, and take a long, hard look before you leap into what appears to me to border on involvement with illegal activities."

John looked stunned and turned to her. "What are you talking about? Do you think it would be a mistake to accept my father's proposal?"

Before she could answer, Robert tried to take a different approach, but Olivia would not be silenced. "Before you agree to your father's plan, clarify exactly what you are willing to do for him."

She could tell John had tuned her out but she continued anyway. "Your father has perfected the art of avoiding the consequences of his actions. He has learned how to navigate the fine line between making ordinary political contributions and committing illegal bribery. Be careful in carrying out your father's directives." Again, she stood and prepared to leave.

Robert ignored her comments. The word "illegal" caused him to wince but he continued speaking as though she had not spoken.

"Olivia, don't leave. Some of my plans for John will impact you and the girls. Let me go over with you John's schedule. Except for brief, infrequent visits of not more than a day or two, John will not return to High Springs. This is what I shall expect of him, provided he acquires the skill to perform the work I have described."

John interrupted, "Olivia said she could help me learn the skills you refer to, and you have said you have hired a mentor for project management. I promise I'll be a dedicated student and, based on what she taught me about running the rolling store, I know Olivia will be a more than satisfactory teacher."

He turned to Olivia, but she didn't commit. She would wait and see how she felt about the whole business come Monday.

Robert addressed her. "How do you feel about the prospects of John's lengthy absences?"

That point had caught Olivia's ear and she did not hesitate to let him know she relished the idea of being free of John's presence. "Mr. Ward, John has been absent from our lives for years, so yet another prolonged physical absence will not be noticed. In reality, it will be a welcomed relief."

"Okay, fair enough," he said. "You two must have a lot to talk about so I'll take my leave and see you on Monday morning, Son. Right now, I need to go hire a dry-cleaning staff."

Olivia let Robert out and walked in the kitchen to find John. "Olivia, I need this chance. Will you help me? Considering how I have behaved, I would understand if you refused."

She laughed. "Did I hear you correctly? Are you asking for my help? I guess Beth was right, pigs can fly!"

CHAPTER 6

During the nearly four months Jean had remained at High Bluff after her birth, Judy became attached to her granddaughter. The fact was despite Judy's history of treating Olivia and Kate poorly, Jean would not have survived without Judy's tireless care. Olivia understood the bond between them and she acknowledged how much she had to be grateful to Judy for. Thus, she tolerated Judy's frequent visits and tried to ignore Judy's rejection of Kate as her granddaughter.

During the first week of May 1933, Judy's behavior became the 'straw that broke the camel's back' with Olivia. Judy, along with Evelyn, had stopped at Olivia's to pick up Jean to carry her to High Bluff. While they were at Olivia's, Evelyn reminded her mother Kate's 2nd birthday was the following week and she asked about their plans for a celebration.

"Why do you ask about Kate's birthday, Evelyn? If you had not mentioned it I'd not have even remembered the date, and I certainly have made no plans concerning her. Stop talking such nonsense, girl. I'm sure Olivia has made plans for the child's party. We need not be involved."

Meanwhile, Kate paused playing with her alphabet blocks. She was perceptive beyond her years and sensed a hostile tone in her grandmother's voice and resulting attitude toward her. Her usually cheery smile turned to sullen frown. Olivia observed the hurt expression on Kate's face and vowed she would not continue to tolerate Judy's neglect of her oldest granddaughter.

It was not just Judy's behavior that was ill-tempered, John's rejection of her broke Olivia's heart. Over time, Kate's defense was to withdraw from those around her. Most significantly, she no longer interacted with her grandfather whom she had affectionately called Daddy Ward. Instead, she withdrew from him even when he attempted to read to her, an activity she had always enjoyed immensely. Olivia knew she had to intervene so she decided she would ask for John's help when he arrived home that evening. Upon his arrival, Olivia noted how tired John looked and debated whether she should approach him. But, she decided she must.

"John, before you begin your studies, do you have a minute? It is important."

John glared at her and seethed.

"No, Olivia. I don't have a minute for you unless it is about my studies. Get it through your head, even if I did, I'd not use it listening to your drivel. Is it so difficult for you to accept I don't give a damn about anything you have to say? Leave me alone!" he shouted as he moved past her and dumped his things on the kitchen table.

John steamed inside but his thoughts had a certain clarity about them. "If only she could do as I ask of her, we could find a way to get along. She won't though. She thinks she can just 'will' me into a 'family' with her and I will have none of it. I don't want that. I never have and I never will."

Olivia would not be deterred. Kate's well-being was far too important so she persisted.

"John Ward, while I am immune to your harsh words and pointed rejection, your daughter Kate is not and she yearns for your attention. At one time you enjoyed interacting with both girls, so why do you now treat them as non-entities? Kate's 2nd birthday is just around the corner and I plead with you to relent and join her to celebrate."

Her plea fell on deaf ears.

. . . . .

With little fanfare from her grandmother or father, on May 9th, 1933, Kate celebrated her second birthday with her mother and young sister. They had a modest party and the air was filled with giggles and soap bubbles from a bottle Olivia had made for the girls to share. Later in the evening, Robert brought Evelyn by the cottage to present Kate with their gift. Unlike the year before, Robert did not bring a gift purported to be from her father, John.

. . . . .

The road was narrow and rutted and Walt Turner took his time as he navigated his way across a creek to deliver a pair of trotters to the Deveraux plantation nestled deep in the swampy, cypress trees of the Louisiana Bayou. As his truck juggled its way across the smooth stone creek bed, his thoughts were with his granddaughter Kate and he was sad he was not with her to celebrate her special day.

He had every intention of saving the date on his calendar but the economy continued to grind at a snail's pace and he simply could not bypass the opportunity to sell the trotters, even with the stipulation they be delivered immediately. Ordinarily, he could have put off the buyer, but he was struggling to keep his businesses in the black while meeting his mother-in-law's demand to fund his erstwhile daughter Ann's upkeep during her extended stay in Savannah.

After delivering the trotters and collecting the much-needed cash payment, Walt sat on the porch of a boarding house in Tupelo, Mississippi, and thought of the conversation he had with Annie the day before he left High Point. Thinking about the loving woman he was fortunate to have as his bride brought a smile to his face.

He recalled Annie's words, "Walt, I worry your constant travels may cause you to become ill; the distances you travel and the businesses you handle are stressful for a young man, and Walt, you aren't a young man anymore."

He harped on her for suggesting the two of them no longer possessed the vim and vigor of earlier days and he insisted he had not reached the age of his dotage. Now, he smiled thinking of how she had pleaded with him not to work so hard. Typically, Annie had told him, "Don't you know you are all I need? There is nothing I want except for you to be by my side."

Walt had not offered Annie an explanation for his increased frequency of travel. He simply did not want to worry her with their financial woes, especially since they involved Ann. And besides, any explanation would have exposed the greed of her own mother, Amelia, whose demands from him were tantamount to blackmail.

Without increasing the amount of the payments required to sustain Ann, Amelia made it clear that Walt would be more than welcome to fetch Ann and allow her to most certainly return her to her slovenly ways in Alabama. Walt had only to recall John Ward's dire prediction for Ann's ultimate fate to motivate him to find the way to meet Amelia's demands.

Despite her ongoing infatuation with him, John had successfully convinced Ann he would never marry her. He did not want to hurt her feelings maliciously, but he wanted to her to understand that the manner in which she carried herself would only endear her to men who were looking to her for a good time and not those of refined upbringing who could afford her the lifestyle she so desperately craved. He went on to tell her she had exhausted her options in Geneva County where she was regarded as little more than a 'good time' by the men there.

When Walt asked John how he had achieved what he and her

mother could not, John's words stung: the people of High Springs regarded Ann as 'white trash' and as such she would suffer a fate worse than Olivia's. No man worth his salt would consider marrying her and even then, it might only one who would simply use her and discard her when he was finished.

Walt took a deep drag on his pipe and slowly exhaled its misty vapor into the cool Mississippi night. "For too long I refused to admit how Ann deliberately flaunted her disregard for cultured behavior. Now, I am ashamed of my treatment of Olivia's unintentional transgression which produced by beautiful granddaughter Kate, who reminds me so of her grandmother. Shame on me for not seeing both of my girls for the people they truly are."

CHAPTER 7

The Kansas sky was nearly cloudless with unlimited visibility and the sun was at the ten o'clock position. The conditions were perfect for flying. Paul Gunderson had been cruising around 7,000 feet for about an hour before he needed to adjust his course south.

As he prepared to enter a slight bank to his right, he applied positive throttle, but he accidently pushed the lever too far forward. The Model 75's Continental R-670-5 radial engine sputtered twice, its propeller slowed to a stop, then reversed two half revolutions in the other direction. There was a belch of white smoke, then near silence. The only sounds the pilot heard were the air rushing over the windscreen and his heart beating in his leather flight helmet.

His airplane had stalled.

Paul immediately realized his error and stared intently at the Model 75's altimeter as the nose of the bi-plane dipped forward. As if going backward in time, the needle began to wind downward faster and faster.

He felt his stomach in his throat. He was losing altitude and the engine was off. In a moment, his wits returned to him.

"I've gotta level out," he thought.

With both hands gripping the stick, he nudged it back to the center position and brought the nose slightly up. This, he knew, would slow his descent and put him in level flight. He was cautious not to over-react lest the plane drop like a rock from the sky.

Slowly, the left wing dipped and he leveled the stick. His thoughts turned to the throttle. It was still in the forward position. He reached for it and pulled it back into the idle position. The wind was rushing by faster now, and the nose dipped again. He checked the altimeter.

Four thousand..., three thousand, five hundred..., three thousand....

"This is not good. Not good at all," he thought as he reached for the starter button and jammed it home twice.

The engine barked once and the prop spun twice. A large plume of white smoke sputtered. "Too much fuel in the carb," he thought. He punched the starter button again causing another belch of smoke.

Two thousand, two hundred fifty..., two thousand..., one thousand, seven hundred fifty...,

"Come on, baby. One time for me, you sweet girl," he implored the engine, firmly jamming the starter button nearly through the firewall in front of him.

POOOFT... CRAAAACK... the engine reported as it roared to life. Clear smoke puffed from the exhaust and the Continental's cylinders whined as if begging for gas.

Gunderson nudged the throttle forward painfully slowly and the thirsty engine guzzled its life-sustaining elixir. Sounding stronger now, the engine purred and he pulled back slightly on the stick while sliding the throttle forward into the three-quarter position.

Nine hundred fifty..., nine hundred.... Eight hundred seventy-five... nine hundred....

Paul gasped. He was flying level now. He looked over the side of the cockpit and the cows in the fields and grain silos of Southeast Kansas appeared far too close for his comfort. He caught his bearings and corrected his course while minding not to throttle too far forward this time.

As the plane climbed back through five thousand feet, Paul became conscious of the temperature in the cockpit and in particular, his seat. What once had been comfortably warm was now unbearably cold; the product of the pungent liquid which had accumulated in the crotch of his coveralls. "Great," he thought. "I'll never live this down with the ground crew."

.....

Around three o'clock in the afternoon on the second Wednesday in June 1933, John completed his six months of training with Olivia and his project management mentor, George Shultz, a highly regarded industrial contractor from Birmingham who owed Robert Ward a favor. It was one of the few days when he arrived home early and did not remain at work until supper time. Olivia would later recall the bittersweet memory of that rare pleasant evening shared together with John and their daughters.

Upon his arrival home, John promptly offered to feed the girls and give them their baths. Olivia could not believe she heard him correctly. For months he had engaged in only the bare minimum of interaction with them and, as for his attention to her, he had refrained from communication outside of the tutoring she had been giving him.

To her amazement, his behavior mirrored that of the time of his 'Meet Jesus Day' with her when Olivia had stood up to John and forced him to acknowledge the path to ruin he was on in his ways. That was before Jean was born, though and since then he had generally acted with a measure of civility toward her and the girls right up until Paul and Sandra Gunderson's unexpected visit.

Now, his attentiveness to the girls overwhelmed her. In order to give him some time alone with his daughters, Olivia left them in the sitting room and busied herself in the kitchen. She smiled as she listened to Kate's laughter as he tickled her and she jabbered non-stop to her father.

Shortly, he brought Jean into the kitchen for Olivia to dry her and put her in her night clothes. A while later, he returned with Kate and asked if it was too early for him to put the girls down for the night.

"I'm sorry I forgot to tell you before. I have been invited to Paul and Sandra's home for supper tonight, and I'll need to leave before too long. I won't be late."

Olivia nodded and bade him a pleasant visit. He noted Jean was almost asleep and he took her from Olivia to place her in her crib. Then he gathered Kate, sat in the rocking chair, and read to her. Before he finished the story, she was sound asleep. Closing the book softly, he rose, placed her in her crib, and stood there for what seemed an eternity watching her soft curls wiggle under her heavy breathing.

With the girls down for the night, John announced he had good news to share: he would be leaving to work on a project for Ward Enterprises in South Florida on Friday morning. He went on to say that given the magnitude of the project he didn't know if he would have time to call regularly, and he certainly had no idea when he would return.

Olivia beamed. "This evening has been wonderful for the girls. You have given them a wonderful gift of your attention which has made them happy. Thank you."

John nodded but avoided eye contact with her as he continued dressing himself. Olivia continued.

"I'm happy things are working out for you. It must please you to renew your friendship with Paul."

John glanced at her and managed a brief smile. "It seems like old times with him and I regret I'm leaving. It will be good to spend this evening with him before I leave."

Olivia smiled meekly and wondered what it would be like to have been treated as John's legitimate wife and to have been included in the Gunderson's invitation. Yet she faced the stark reality of her situation and acknowledged this would never be the case. As John tied his shoes, she took his valise from the top of the closet and began laying out his clothes for his trip.

As he slicked back his hair in the mirror, John took notice and thought, "Why does she have the capacity to make me feel like such a heel? For the past six months, she has worked every night preparing me for this opportunity with my father and not once has she complained or asked for anything in return."

John squeezed a large dollop of paste from the tube of Colgate Rapid-Shave Cream into his hand and smeared it on his face. Then, he carefully guided the Gem razor over the contours of his jaw line as if an artist sculpting a masterpiece. With each stroke, guilt edged its way into his thoughts.

He recalled Ann's suggesting he was incapable of loving anyone. At the time he did not contradict her, but he should have. He had loved Margo Brown enough to want to spend his life with her. Were it not for his immature behavior, which had led to his seduction of Olivia and its consequences, perhaps he would have seen Margo packing his suitcase for his trip and he would have felt warmth toward her.

But, it was not to be. Because of his effort to spite both Ann and Olivia, he had lost his chance to make Margo his wife. Even so, she still occupied his heart and, as a result, there was no room for Olivia. Realizing the futility of his ramblings, he pushed his feelings aside and went over his itinerary with Olivia.

"As I mentioned before, I have no idea when I will return here to you and the girls. I know I'll be in Tallahassee for Thanksgiving and Christmas but considering the time table for the construction and staffing of the two clubs, I'll be away most of next year. I guess I'm saying you will know I'm coming when you see the whites of my eyes."

Olivia said she understood and wished him success in his work. Inside though, she felt joy knowing she would have a reprieve as the object of his intermittent hostility. She was anxious for Friday to arrive so that she could undertake plans to improve life for her and her daughters. Having John away for an extended period of time was a salve to her emotions. At last she could focus on the girls and herself without fear of setting off John's fragile temper. She felt happier than she had in years.

After John left for supper with the Gunderson's, Olivia retrieved her hidden stash of money she had squirreled away. She had dared not risk having John find it lest he gamble it all away. In a way, she felt a bit guilty about the money. It was, after all, his.

What John did not know was that Robert had given Olivia the money and markers he had raked up from the table when he booted John and the other gamblers out of the back room of the dry-cleaning plant. Robert said she had earned it for putting up with his irresponsible son for too long. In her hands, he was confident the money would be used for good.

She was determined to make her newfound windfall count for something and she had saved it waiting for the right opportunity. With John out of the picture, she planned to use it to develop her daughters into well-mannered and refined young ladies who would one day be capable of taking their places in any echelon of society. They had an advantage: they had Annie's thoroughbred blood pumping through their veins, even if it was diluted a bit by that of a grade stallion.

· · · · ·

Olivia and the girls slipped into their usual routine without John around. She wanted to ensure the girls grew up in an atmosphere conducive to their taking a station in life that would attract suitable gentlemen callers. Therefore, she planned to make improvements to her cottage to reflect the elegant environment her mother had created for the family at High Point.

To wit, Olivia relied upon her mother's guidance to achieve her objective. Her funds were limited so she would choose carefully so as not to squander her money on cheap fabrics, furniture and china. Eager to get started, she packed the girls up in the car after their morning nap and made her way to High Point to visit her mother.

Once she arrived, the girls ran off with Gussie while Olivia looked over patterns with her mother. Together they chose fabrics for the draperies and chair coverings, and Annie offered Olivia several pieces of fine furniture in need of refinishing she had acquired over the years and stored in one of the barns.

After a productive day with her mother, Olivia and the girls returned to High Springs. While she was tired from an afternoon of decorating, she could not afford to rest. There was much to do. The time was upon her to begin her canning and preserving of fruits and vegetables for the coming winter. Feeling a bit overwhelmed at all that was before her, Olivia sat down with her calendar to lay out a plan to juggle all she had do accomplish.

First, she would ask Isaac and Joe to collect the pieces of furniture Mama had given her. Although she knew the boys were busy, they could refinish the pieces at their leisure so they would be ready when she finished canning in a few weeks.

In addition to the renovation and canning, she knew she could not ignore her commitments to sew outfits for several customers. She also had to bake cakes for Mr. Adkins' weekly standing order at the mercantile. Even with all of this to complete, she still needed to find time to braid rugs. "There is no rest for the weary," she thought as she pressed onward day in and day out.

· · · · ·

Before she knew it, Olivia realized John had been gone for nearly a month. She wasn't surprised when she heard nothing from him. He had said as much would be true. The Fourth of July was fast approaching and she intended to ask Beth to go with her and the girls to the High Springs annual celebration. While she was certain John's continued absence would be a topic of conversation in the small-town gossip mill, she was resolved not to hide at home and deny her children an enjoyable day.

· · · · ·

Throughout John's time in South Florida, Robert visited him often to review progress on the construction of the clubs and John's efforts in cultivating political support for Ward Enterprises' interests. Despite the training and mentoring he had arranged for him, he continued to question his decision to give John responsibility for so great an undertaking.

Upon Robert's return to High Springs, he did two things: get a report on John's progress from George Schultz and check in on Olivia and the girls.

Schultz had worked with Robert on several projects in Birmingham. To Robert, he was a trusted ally and Schultz felt the same way in return. When Schultz's construction company ran into some trouble with an outfit out of Kansas City, Robert obliged him with the name of a contact in New York to quell the unrest. To his delight, Schultz's troubles disappeared virtually overnight and he now owed Ward Enterprises an enormous debt of gratitude. Schultz's reports on the project in West Palm Beach and John's work there were favorable. Thus, Robert ignored his niggling doubts, allowing John to remain in South Florida as originally planned for the remainder of 1933.

As soon as he concluded his business with Schultz, Robert made it his priority to visit Olivia and his granddaughters. He and Olivia had a tacit, unspoken agreement they would not discuss John. However, after he had returned from his visit with John during the last week of June, he had inadvertently mentioned John was going to spend some time in Holmes County campaigning for the candidate Ward Enterprises backed for the office of county sheriff.

Despite her inclination to the contrary, Olivia abandoned her usual acceptance of John's prolonged absence without comment or objection.

"Will he come to High Springs and be with the girls and me for Thanksgiving?"

"Olivia, I don't expect John to return to High Springs for either Thanksgiving or Christmas. Rather, I suspect he will spend them with Judy and me in Tallahassee. We have a lot of work to do in cultivating the support we are going to need in the near future, and John has an integral role in accomplishing this. When the three of us spoke of John's new job, I made it clear as to the necessity for his prolonged absence. Even so, I am bothered; I have kept him so busy that on the two times he has been here in High Springs, there was no time for him to spend with his daughters."

Olivia didn't comment on Robert's revelation. She had mixed emotions. On one hand, life was simpler and was shrouded with less drama when John was away. On the other, it hurt to learn he had secreted away to High Bluff to see his parents without making even a smidgeon of an effort to see his daughters. So it was no matter, regardless of his newfound responsibility, he had not changed one iota. As far as she was concerned, the physical and emotional distance from John was beneficial to them all. He could stay away indefinitely for all she cared!

Robert left shortly thereafter, and he couldn't dismiss Olivia's apparent lack of concern with the news he imparted. As he drove towards High Bluff he thought, "John has lost any regard Olivia ever had for him; he has become a nonentity in her life."

· · · · ·

Beth was a regular and welcome visitor who kept Olivia abreast of all that was happening at High Point. Bolstered by Carolyn Gates' weekly visits, Olivia was able to stay ahead of the speculations concerning John and his prolonged absences. On one of her visits, Beth had mentioned a remark Papa had made about one of his recent trips to Holmes County to deliver lumber to a builder.

"According to Papa, the sheriff's race is a heated one, and the scuttlebutt is that John has been dispatched to help sway the race in favor of a candidate Ward Enterprises is backing. He overheard two men talking at a local café and the speculation was the Wards were backing the wrong horse. He asked me if you knew anything about John going to the Holmes County seat in Bonifay. Papa didn't mince words: John had best be careful lest he get himself in a heap of trouble there. In addition, Papa said he should be horse-whipped for abandoning his wife and children."

There was nothing Olivia could share with Beth except that she suspected John would come to High Springs later in the summer or early fall, but she did not expect him to visit her and the girls.

"I prefer that we not discuss a situation over which I have no control, nor do I desire to have control over."

What Beth did not understand was how Olivia, for the first time in a very long while, experienced contentment alone with her daughters. The overwhelming anxiety she endured while never knowing how John would behave or the extent of his hostility was replaced with a sense of peace.

.....

Through the end of August, Olivia continued to leave on the back burner the projects she had been neglecting. Although she continued to devote her time to baking cakes and braiding rugs for Mr. Adkins, she decided it was time to tackle the cottage. With the help of her mother and Olivia's part time help Martha Cox, they began cutting and sewing the material for the draperies and chair covers.

Despite running into several obstacles, Olivia was able to finish the week before Thanksgiving. When Isaac hung the last pair of draperies, Olivia and Beth placed the final pieces of furniture Annie had donated. Then the two sat and admired their handiwork. It was even more splendid than Olivia could have imagined.

.....

Thanksgiving Day arrived and Olivia prepared a special meal to celebrate the day. Although it was only she and the girls, she set a majestic table as she positioned the girls to experience the holiday in style. To her surprise, Evelyn arrived from High Bluff and Olivia set a place for her, and the four of them enjoyed their time together. As laughter ensued, only Jean appeared to miss her father.

.....

On December 5, 1933, the Congress of the United States passed the 22nd Amendment to the Constitution which repealed the 18th Amendment. The Prohibition Era was officially over. As such, each state and county had the freedom to decide their position on alcohol. Their legislature could to be 'wet' and allow alcohol, or 'dry' and prohibit the manufacture, sales, and possession of same.

Ward Enterprises had a lot to gain by ensuring the counties in which their nightclubs and juke joints were located in Florida voted to become 'wet' and Robert set his plan in motion to ensure this was the outcome. He hoped, against all odds, that his grooming of his son John was sufficient to successfully execute the plan over the coming months. There was a lot at stake.

CHAPTER 8

In the early spring of 1934, Olivia worked with Isaac and Joe to turn the soil in virgin ground to enlarge the vegetable and herb gardens. Once they had finished, she started working to get seed and plants in the ground by mid-March. By the last week of April, she had worked sun up to sundown to see to it the tasks were complete. Then she turned her attention to preparing for Kate's third birthday in the first week of May.

.....

On Kate's birthday, Olivia's cottage was filled with joy. Beth had been able to get Annie over her doldrums and out of the house to attend. Evelyn, now ten years old, and her father Robert were among the first to arrive. Additionally, Martha Cox, along with Carolyn and William Gates joined in celebrating this special day with Kate. All were entertained watching Jean's attempts to open her sister's presents much to Kate's chagrin.

After opening presents, everyone enjoyed cake and ice cream. Although it was on everyone's mind, no one mentioned John's absence until Robert and Evelyn prepared to leave. Before they departed, Carolyn asked Robert the question no one had dared to ask.

"Robert, I can't help but notice John's absence at his own daughter's birthday. Do you know if he ever intends to return to his family? We understand he came to High Springs several times this past year, but as far as we know he neither stayed with nor visited Olivia and the girls. You'll have to admit this causes those of us who care for Olivia and the girls to wonder if he has abandoned them."

Robert was taken aback with Carolyn's assertion, but he responded nonetheless.

"John is very busy in Tallahassee taking care of my business interests. He will return to High Springs and his family when he completes the tasks he's been given, and not a minute sooner. There are time sensitive issues of a confidential nature I simply cannot discuss. Even so, you may rest assured John is here for Kate's birthday in spirit, if not in person."

Robert cut his eyes to Olivia hoping she would intervene and move the party along without further discussion of John's whereabouts and the intimation that he didn't care about his children. Olivia understood John all too well and she had come to terms with it. He had no intention of returning home. The lifestyle of a single man with no encumbrances suited him well. Now that he had achieved this coveted status, he was not going to forego it.

There was a pregnant pause and Olivia noticed the look that passed between Annie and Carolyn. She could tell both felt compassion for her. She only wished Carolyn would not continue her line of questioning of Robert. Carolyn did, though, and what followed was nearly more than Olivia could stomach.

"To be honest, John has all he can say Grace over right now. I hired a professional mentor to assist him with the logistics of managing my construction projects and he performed well. On the other hand, he has been perceived in some key social and political groups as either a country hick or a jock. Thusly, he has failed miserably to ingratiate himself into those circles vital to our success. It's my fault, really. I should have known it would be nearly impossible for John to pull this off without the help of an insider. Olivia is as smart as a whip and there is no question she has the social skills to complement John's efforts; but, she does not have connections to gain entry into the desired groups and without them she would have been a liability to him. John required an acceptable hostess to augment his efforts to influence elected officials. Once Judy and I understood what he faced, she took the initiative to solve our dilemma. Judy was impressed by a delightful young woman who had accompanied several influential politicians to social functions at our home. Once Judy learned she was available to act in the capacity as John's hostess, Judy hired her."

Olivia seethed, hearing Robert's explanations. Annie, who could hold her tongue no longer, was infuriated.

"Does John Ward think we are idiots to accept this hog wash?"

The adults gasped at her outburst. Normally, quiet and reserved, this was very much out of character for Annie. While many assumed she had simply reached her limit, Olivia wondered if there were something more going on. Annie turned to Beth and told her she was very tired and asked her to take them home.

Martha, Carolyn and William departed at the same time causing yet another awkward moment of silence leaving Robert and Evelyn alone with Olivia and the girls. Robert asked Evelyn to attend to Kate and Jean while he spoke to Olivia.

"I had no intentions of hurting you, Olivia," he said.

Although she was both angry and hurt at Robert's suggestion that she lacked sufficient social graces, Olivia felt sorry for Robert. John had repeatedly disappointed him and it was apparent Robert had attempted to put the best face he could on the situation.

"Thank you for trying to lessen John's latest insult to me. Please take Evelyn and go home. The girls and I will be fine. There is no need for you to have any further concern for our well-being."

Upon Robert and Evelyn's departure, Olivia spent time with her daughters and thanked God that Papa was not at the party. She envisioned what spectacle would have taken place had he heard Robert's admission John's new partner was a woman.

CHAPTER 9

The Depression lingered throughout the nation and at this point in 1934, there was no region of the country which did not feel some adverse economic effects. Discretionary funds were in short supply for most families, even those regarded as being from 'old money.'

Because of this situation, Walt had nearly exhausted his ability to market his trotters even to long time customers. Money simply was not available for them to invest in the thoroughbreds. Because he was desperate to generate funds he needed to cover Ann's increasing expenses and Amelia's unrelenting demands, he traveled far afield to develop opportunities with whomever he believed could afford their purchase.

The pressure upon him was acute, especially knowing how his absence palpably affected Annie. He could not tell her of the situation with her mother; it would distress her too much. However, at times when Annie pleaded with him to remain at High Point, he was tempted to divulge the ultimatum Amelia had issued. He either paid what she stated she needed to finance Ann's stay with her and Aunt Pearl, or he must fetch Ann and take her back to High Springs where she would certainly resume her crass ways.

Every time Papa returned, Beth shared with him her concerns about her mother. Beth's message was the same each time. When he was away, Annie suffered from acute depression. She withdrew into her suite and refused to have interaction with anyone, including Olivia.

Walt did not need Beth to enlighten him about Annie's condition;

each time he returned home, it was evident that she had lost some of her vitality. When Olivia came to High Point to discuss the situation with him, he found he needed to share the reason for his behavior. He had to share with someone his worries about being financially able to meet Aunt Amelia's demands.

"Olivia, do you think for a moment I am ignorant of your mother's condition? Surely you do not! To the contrary, I am conscious of the changes in her and that I hurt her with my absences. It breaks my heart. Understand why I continue to be away from her. I'm going to share with you what I cannot with Annie."

Walt went on to explain the expenses associated with keeping Ann with her grandmother and aunt.

"According to Amelia, Ann is behaving herself. Although she continues to be exceedingly selfish and demanding, she is well received among Amelia and Pearl's friends and has a host of would-be suitors. Based upon Amelia's letters, it is probable Ann may find a respectable husband provided she does not revert to any of her old ways."

As Olivia listened, she realized Papa was truly 'between a rock and a hard place.' Her grandmother had not taken in Ann out of love and concern for her. Rather, she allowed her to remain with her because of the money she would receive from Walt as Ann's caretaker.

Walt sighed as he concluded his explanation, "Amelia would turn Ann out in a minute if I failed to meet her demands. She knows I will come through somehow because Ann cannot return to High Springs."

"Papa, have you written Ann to explain you cannot continue to subsidize her extravagant lifestyle? She must understand there is a limit on what Amelia may spend on clothing and entertaining on her behalf?"

Walt shrugged and, without responding, he turned from her and left to prepare for his trip by train to Maryland where he had located a buyer for a pair of trotters. Olivia had her answer. He would continue to do what he must to keep Ann away from High Springs and what he imagined would be her ultimate undoing.

. . . . .

Throughout summer of 1934, John spent his time between South Florida and Bonifay. While there, he oversaw construction of the clubs in Miami and West Palm Beach, hired the staff to run them and prepared for their openings. But this was not the full extent of what Robert expected from him.

John also needed to cultivate the class of patrons who had the discretionary funds to enjoy the nightlife and gambling the clubs had to offer. Additionally, he needed to woo the appropriate political figures who would ensure that gambling and the sale of alcohol were legal in counties in which Ward Enterprises operated.

Thus, John was a frequent traveler on the train from South Florida to Bonifay where the political campaigning for the new Holmes County sheriff was fierce. Plans for opening juke joints near Bonifay depended, in large measure, on the outcome of this election.

While John proved to be exceptional in his setup and organization of the clubs, he quickly realized how lacking he was in the finesse necessary to effectively influence the election without resorting to frivolous donations which could later be declared illegal bribes. What he understood was that despite Olivia's best efforts to teach him and warn him of the pitfalls, it required considerably more experience than he possessed while operating as an outsider in a local arena.

In Tallahassee, John's charm and persona as a sophisticated young businessman carried him far in establishing social contacts and political support. But Bonifay was firmly entrenched in a 'good old boys' culture which was not accommodating to a young man perceived to have been born with a silver spoon in his mouth. Unbeknownst to him, plans were already afoot by prominent individuals to bring him down once the election was over. In the meantime, they bided their time to watch, take notes, and prepare for their subsequent actions.

.....

On one of Olivia's visits to High Point with the girls, Annie was the first to recognize that Kate would make a splendid equestrian. Although she was only three years old, Kate sat upright on a trotter and did not waiver as Walt and the trainer, Gabriel, led her around the riding ring. Shortly thereafter, Walt acquired a gentle pony he knew would be just right for Kate as she commenced formal training under Gabriel's watchful eye.

From the time Walt brought the pony to High Point, Olivia arranged for Beth to pick Kate up on Friday afternoons to work with Gabriel who coached her on her riding form and control of the pony. When he was not away on business, Papa lent a firm hand.

Once, Olivia had overheard Papa's telling Kate about the first time he saw her grandmother Annie riding high in the saddle. Olivia laughed so hard she snorted as her amusement with her father's exaggerated Scottish accent hit a crescendo. While it had largely been diluted into a traditional Southern drawl, the syrupy brogue returned even thicker than ever as he further embellished the story with each subsequent retelling.

"Kate Ward, you may be just but a mere tyke as to your age, but certain it is you've a Scottish love for horses. And it is certain I am that you'll grow up just like my beloved Annie; you have her seat and her love 'o horses."

• • • • •

While John was away from High Springs, Olivia's life changed little. After Jean's difficult birthing, Rachel Green had filled in for Olivia while she recovered. Since then, Olivia had mended and now continued to care for Mrs. Smith at her house. Every day, Olivia took Kate and Jean with her as she prepared meals and shared time with her. When Mrs. Smith and the girls napped, Olivia used the time to bake her cakes in the large kitchen with double ovens and a large table for cooling and frosting the finished products.

The Depression affected Olivia just as it did others and she struggled to provide for herself and her daughters. Her saving Grace was Mrs. Smith's generosity in allowing Olivia to use her kitchen and Mr. Adkins' willingness to trade or barter for staples which allowed Olivia to continue her cake and rug sales. Otherwise, she had no cash to continue her efforts.

In addition to the rugs, she had a standing order for cakes with him along with orders from two stores in Dothan. However, in this economy, cakes were a luxury some could not afford and she worried constantly that customers would not have the discretionary funds to sustain her business.

It was pleasing to Olivia to know she could share her time with her dear friend without being badgered with questions about John's lack of involvement in their lives. Mrs. Smith was a wise woman who understood all too well the hurt Olivia continued to endure because of John's actions. Therefore, she refrained from discussing him.

This was not the case with Flora. Whether Olivia wanted to hear about John's visits or not, Flora promptly reported to Olivia whatever she knew about them. This was especially true when he brought home the woman Judy Ward had hired to serve as hostess for the social functions they sponsored in South Florida and Tallahassee.

"I know you doesn't want to hear about what Mister John done brought to High Bluff for supper, but I aims to tell you anyhow! That woman introduced herself to me like I was white; she told me her name was Ingrid Schonen.

I show 'nugh didn't know what to say 'specially when she told me her people done come to here by way of Austria, whatever that meant. I tell you she was a tall one; I'd say 'bout tall as Mister. John. They done told all 'bout where they been going and that they gonna be back here in February for Valentine's Day."

Olivia listened intently as Flora paused to catch her breath and continued, "I overheard Missus Judy tellin' one of Mister Robert's banker friends how pleased they was with her. She went on tellin' of her 'peccable tastes in dressin' and her social graces. I ain't never heard so much talk 'bout someone like that. It was like they was sellin' a prize sow. I had to chuckle though. That lady does resemble Missus Judy something fierce!"

Olivia smiled at Flora's comparison of Judy to a sow. She realized Flora was trying to help by keeping her apprised of John's whereabouts. Therefore, she gave up attempting to discourage Flora's reports and simply listened without commenting. Still, she dreaded her next visit to Mr. Adkins' store, knowing the gossip John's visits would create and the pleasure many in High Springs would take in hearing another tidbit to humiliate her.

. . . . .

When Robert Ward was in High Springs, he visited his granddaughters often. Olivia appreciated deeply the fact that Robert, unlike her girls' own father, had always shown a consistent interest in both children. It meant the world to her that they could share a connection with their grandfather. He had even arranged for either Isaac or Joe to bring Aunt Evelyn to spend several days at a time with them.

Robert's visits were not always just about the girls. He kept Olivia informed about John's whereabouts and of his progress in Florida. But, he did not care to discuss John's absence during the holidays with Olivia's family. Just recently, on two separate occasions, he had the misfortune of encountering two of Olivia's brothers. Each time, he was given an earful about John's deplorable behavior and Robert's failure to do anything to rectify it. They were fit to be tied. Now again for the coming holidays, John would not be spending time with his wife and children. Robert felt the need to provide some cover for John and Olivia and he would begin with Olivia.

"Olivia, right now, there are critical issues in Florida facing Ward Enterprises that require delicate handling. As we continue to push our agenda there, Judy and I will hold several galas throughout the holidays and John's presence will be required to ensure our success. Just as your father is often called away on business, I hope you will make this clear to your family so hopefully they can understand John's need to be away."

As Robert droned on, Olivia listened respectfully to the 'hog wash' Robert spouted, all the while thinking, "Save your breath. Thanks to Flora, I know the real story and all of your excuses will not change the fact your son is doing exactly what he chooses; he is living the life of a single man without any thought of his children."

·····

As he had predicted, John remained away from High Springs through Thanksgiving and did not communicate with Olivia. Like previous years, she planned to spend Thanksgiving at home with the girls. They even invited Evelyn to spend a few days before and after with them. Although times were tough and they didn't have much to spend, Olivia prepared a delicious meal for them with a turkey her brother Thomas had harvested from his farm.

As they sat around the table to say Grace, Olivia was mindful of the many blessings they had received over the year and she was grateful for each of them. First, she had two beautiful, healthy daughters whom she loved dearly. She was especially grateful Jean had recovered with no lasting ill effects from her premature birth. She was also grateful for Evelyn and her unconditional love for her nieces.

Although she often found herself at odds with Robert, she was thankful for his efforts to support her; and she could not dismiss the fact that his donation of the materials and labor to construct the cottage under whose roof they now ate had made it a reality. For the first time in Olivia's life, she owned the home in which she lived. It was truly a miracle.

She had special words for Flora, Frank, and the boys. They had made her life easier beyond measure and she asked God for special blessings for them. Finally, she was thankful for her family.

Beth had been a Godsend for her. When her own father had sabotaged Olivia's ability to worship in church by petitioning the elders to withdraw their fellowship from her, Beth had championed Olivia's cause in front of the pastor, the congregation, including Papa, with an impassioned speech on her sister's behalf. Furthermore, Beth had brazenly defied Papa's command not to carry Mama to Olivia's side when she was on her deathbed on the night Jean was born. All concerned agreed: without Beth's brave actions against her father, which were not typical of her gentle personality and the cultural norms of the times, Papa would never have reconciled with Olivia.

She ended her prayer with her realization, "Lord, I have often espoused the notion that through you all things are possible. I have believed that where there is a will, there will always be a way through your Son, Jesus Christ. This year has only served to reinforce those beliefs. Thank you, Father, for your blessing. My girls and I have been truly blessed beyond our needs."

·····

The week after Thanksgiving, Olivia had a surprise visitor. Beth appeared at her door clutching an envelope. Olivia quickly opened the folded paper and tears rolled down her cheeks as she read the note from Papa. He, along with Mama, invited Olivia, the girls, and Evelyn to spend Christmas Day with the Turner Clan at High Point. Olivia turned her eyes upward. "Yet another blessing in a year of many blessings."

·····

On Christmas Day 1934, Kate sat proudly atop her pony, her glee was something to behold as Papa Turner led her along the fence line and allowed her to rub the velvety nose of each horse as they passed. For a moment, Olivia thought back to a simpler time when she often stopped at the railing to treat Butterscotch and Taffy to bits of rock candy she had purchased at Jerrell's. Perhaps one day Kate and Jean would share the love of horses she once had.

From her bedroom window, Annie watched attentively and was happy to witness Kate's perfect posture in the saddle. It warmed her heart to see Papa with the girls, especially since there had been a long period of time when neither Olivia nor Kate was welcome at High Point. With Annie's pleading, combined with Robert's offer of free railroad carriage for Walt's lumber and cattle, Walt had relented and allowed Olivia and Kate to visit again.

"Regardless of the circumstances of her birth," Annie thought. "Kate possesses all the traits of a thoroughbred. She is like Olivia in her nature and in the way in which she carries herself. I only pray she has an easier go at life than my Olivia has encountered thus far."

MCMURTRY

CHAPTER 10

The New Year arrived and Jack Gunderson was busy at work. In his role as president of the bank, he monitored daily deposits and the balances on the accounts of its depositors, and he had noted the steady decline of most accounts throughout the year. Few customers were able to replace funds they withdrew and most were living hand to mouth. The hardships associated with one or more aspects of the Depression continued to abound throughout the community and affected everyone to some degree.

In contrast, John Ward was one of the fortunate few who had increased his deposits throughout the past year. In early January 1935, the balance of $141,000.17 which John maintained came to Jack's attention. He had been engaged in a long simmering feud with Robert Ward over what he considered to be his immoral, if not illegal activities and as a result, he kept close tabs on both John and Robert's accounts.

As he thumbed through the last few month's cash deposit tickets for John's account, he noted they totaled more than the amount he had paid his own son for an entire year's work at the bank. and he brought it to Paul's attention. "Hasn't John Ward been working for just a brief period with his father's company? How could he have accumulated so much money in such a short time? This cannot be!"

Jack knew Paul had no knowledge of John's activities, and as he mulled over the balance in John's account, he became angry and thought, "Damn it! Again, I have to witness my son falling short of matching John Ward's achievements. Something shady is going on and I will not have my bank become a party to some illicit scheme of Robert Ward's design."

Jack speculated that John had earned his money by questionable means, but he had no evidence to support these assumptions. Needing someone closer to the situation to dig a little deeper, he decided to call upon his banking friends in South Florida and the Panhandle.

Paul interrupted his father. "Dad, I'm proud of John's success. He's my best friend and, although we've had our differences over the years, we have always put any ill feelings aside when the other was in need. I miss him and I would welcome his return to High Springs on a permanent basis."

Jack was incensed at his son's lack of recognition of John as a social pariah. "John Ward is not fit company for a vice-president of this bank. Son, you will discount any notion of renewing your friendship with him; I will not tolerate it. Am I being clear?"

"Dad, what do you have against John?"

Jack's face reddened as his anger increased. He snorted as he attempted to calm himself. "I tolerate Robert Ward because I have to due to his power and influence with the bank's board of directors. It pains me to say it but if he chooses to do so, on a whim, Robert Ward can call for a vote of the bank's directors and have me removed as president. He has stacked the board with men who are indebted to him; and because he holds mortgages on most of their properties, if they have to choose between us, I won't last five minutes."

Paul stared at his father in disbelief. "Has Robert Ward indicated in some way his displeasure with your performance? I've never heard you mention your job could be in jeopardy. Why do you think he would sack you?"

Jack attempted to help his son understand his situation. "Son, no one understands how Ward Enterprises accrues money. Most who know Robert Ward suggest he possesses the Midas touch, considering that every one of his business ventures continues to thrive and produce considerable profits despite the lagging economy. By either some stroke of luck or dirty hand, he lands nearly every contract he bids on in Alabama and Florida under Roosevelt's plans to rebuild the country."

"So, Robert Ward is a successful businessman, and you are unable to determine his sources of income. Why does it matter? Why is his success a threat to you? I've seen no basis for your fear."

"Son, you don't understand. In addition to his financial hold over them, some members of the bank's board of directors' fear Robert may open another bank completely under his control. If he does, it will become our primary competitor for our customers who still have money to put on deposit. Then, our bank would fail. Therefore, I have no option but to publicly voice my 'respect' of him."

Paul detected some paranoia in his father's statements as well as a degree of jealousy.

"Dad, I hear what you're telling me, but your fears appear to be irrational and certainly are insufficient to affect my relationship with John."

Paul then remarked he had work to accomplish and he returned to his office. His father followed him. He could not afford to alienate Robert, but he was determined his son would not associate with John.

"Wait and listen to me. I tolerated your association with John Ward throughout your high school years because you participated in school activities and sports together. But, when you both were selected to play football together at Alabama, I vowed this would not be the case with your college years."

He paused for a moment as he considered how much of his actions he should reveal to his son. Determining he had passed the point of no return, he continued.

"When I had the opportunity, I coaxed the University of Alabama's administration to force Coach Wade to withdraw his offer of a football scholarship to John. I succeeded you see. John was cast away without a second thought in an embarrassing manner and, as a result, I eliminated the continued comparison of your accomplishments to those of John in this community."

Paul was dumbfounded to learn of his father's dishonorable actions. Finally, he understood why his best friend had been treated so unfairly.

"How could you have done such a thing?"

He found it difficult to describe his utter disgust with his father's actions which he now knew were motivated by his jealousy of Robert Ward's accomplishments and standing within the community. He decided he would not let his father's jealousy of Robert Ward's success sabotage his relationship with his best friend.

CHAPTER 11

On Valentine's Day 1935, John quietly returned to High Springs for two days to meet with his father to go over plans to construct another juke joint in Holmes County, Florida. Once again, Ingrid Schonen accompanied him and, as in the past, John made no attempt to contact or look in on Olivia or his daughters. His visit did not go unnoticed to at least one set of eyes. Flora was 'hell bent and devil sent' to keep Olivia informed during John's visits. As she made her way to Olivia's cottage, she was bursting at the seams to share the latest news.

"It was plum' disgraceful how Missus Judy and Mister Robert done behaved. I done seen how Missus Judy treated that dark haired Jezebel that John brung home." Flora squealed. "I might only be the hired help, but I knows what I knows. The way this here woman carried on with John every night was like she done be his wife. She sho 'nuf was mo' than any friend I e'er seen."

Olivia had enjoyed her relative peace with John away and attempted to steer Flora from the subject by inquiring about the well-being of the folks in the Quarters. Flora told her they were 'jus fine' before continuing her soliloquy.

"As I told Frank, they's done seemed to be fogettin' right from wrong; John has hisself a wife and young'uns right here under they nose. I can't stomach none of that there business, Miss Olivia."

Olivia had heard enough and she intended to squelch the gossip she suspected would spread quickly in High Springs.

"Flora, I am well aware of John's arrangement. In August, Mister Ward told me John would require a female employee to serve as his hostess for some of his social obligations. Having the woman visit them at High Bluff is their way of showing their gratitude for her assistance. It concerns me not in the least and I would appreciate your mentioning nothing more of it."

As Olivia ushered her to the door, Flora shook her head and told herself how plum ignorant Miss Olivia was. But she could not know how her tale of John's bringing home a lady friend hurt Olivia. For a long time, she had been the butt of cruel jokes about the old maid seducing a boy and ruining his future. Now, she would be the subject of the more hateful gossip: John Ward had forsaken his wife and children and brought another woman home to High Springs.

Olivia returned to her baking. She did not have time to worry about maintaining John's name and some two-bit floozy he had hired to parade in front of politicians. She had received some good news she hoped would give her and the girls more financial stability. On her next visit to the mercantile, she shared her good news with Mrs. Adkins.

"As you may remember, I tutored college-bound students for a few years. According to Miss Metcalf, I prepared them well. Not long ago, I ran into her again and she suggested I consider becoming a teacher. All I need to do is obtain a temporary teaching certificate. Although I don't have a degree, I am confident I could obtain a provisional certificate."

Olivia detailed the actions she took to complete the required forms and mail them, along with a recommendation, to the Alabama State Board of Education. She hoped to hear of their decision within a month or so.

Mrs. Adkins beamed pride. Olivia, however, was not as joyous and added, "There is one obstacle I must overcome. The local school board has exacting stipulations regarding its moral standards for teachers. Given the gossip around Kate's birth and my age difference with John, it is unlikely I will meet this standard to be allowed to teach in High Springs. I will simply need to seek a position in a nearby town where my past is unknown."

Mrs. Adkins reassured Olivia that any community would count themselves lucky to have her as a teacher for their children. She indicated they would pray for her and would hope for the best. Olivia thanked her for her unwavering support and hugged her as she left to meet Beth at Jerrell's Drugstore.

. . . . .

As she measured the depth of the NEHI Grape soda bottle with her straw, Beth expressed in worried tones her concern about Mama's deteriorating health.

"Olivia, you have witnessed a few of these changes in Mama's behavior and seen how frail she has become. Haven't you?"

"Yes, I have. After her continuous bouts with depression coupled with her uncharacteristically angry outburst at Kate's party last year I became concerned and I have been watching her closely. I spoke with Dr. James and he insists there is a problem he does not have the experience to correctly diagnose. She needs to see a brain specialist in Birmingham, but Mama is reluctant to do so. He has asked me to convince her to change her mind."

"Oh, Olivia, she is so stubborn about her own health while she has doted on all of us over the years. Papa and I have worried while watching her undergo these changes. Lord, I never imagined anything so serious. By the middle of next week, Papa should be home. As soon as he returns, we'll get him to persuade Mama to see the specialist Dr. James recommended. Papa is the only one who holds any sway over her."

.....

Walt was unsuccessful in his initial attempts to get Annie to agree to go to the specialist. It was not until late July 1935 when she finally agreed. After driving to the depot from High Point, they took the train from Dothan to Birmingham and stayed overnight.

The specialist informed Walt that Annie had a slow growing tumor in her brain, and it was inoperable. He further explained it was the tumor pressing on a segment of the brain which was the cause of her headaches and changed behavior. There was nothing he could do other than prescribe pain medication to keep her comfortable.

He spoke candidly, telling Walt it was impossible to gauge how rapidly the tumor would grow. He thought it was one with a slow growth pattern, considering Annie had had symptoms for a while and she continued to live. This would not have been the case with a rapidly growing tumor. Hopefully, it would not become life threatening for a year or more, but her changes in behavior might become more pronounced.

Walt nodded his appreciation and shook the doctor's hand while thanking him for his candor. As Walt turned to fetch Annie from the waiting room, he paused to quickly dab both eyes with his handkerchief. "Stiffen up ol' boy," he thought. "Annie needs a strong draft horse to pull her through this."

As they boarded the train, Walt held Annie's hand firmly as he helped her to her seat for the long ride back to Dothan. Once they settled in, he ensured she was comfortable and he remained oddly quiet. He felt the need to encourage her, but he could not find the words to do so. In the doctor's office, Walt had realized Annie's mortality for the first time and he questioned how he could go on without her.

CHAPTER 12

One evening in late August, Olivia worked diligently on a stack of flour sack pillows in the sitting room while listening to the Philco Model 90 radio situated nearby on a side table. As she carefully stitched the seams, she listened intently as the announcer on WDTN out of Dothan set the tense scene. Chicago White Sox pitcher Vern Kennedy was carrying a no hitter into the eighth inning against the Indians. Her concentration was broken by what she thought was a crack of the bat on the radio. But as she craned to listen for the announcer's call, she realized the sound had come from her screen door.

She turned to see John enter. As he passed the sitting room, he slowed down only long enough to say that due to delays in construction in Florida, he would be home for a while. He then retreated to the bedroom and unceremoniously closed the door behind himself.

Olivia was surprised to have John back under their roof. While she was concerned about the impact his sudden reappearance would have on the girls, she also worried how it would affect her. Since Jean's birth, John had not demanded intimacy with Olivia. He had made it clear that he detested being in the same room with her, but this did not necessarily mean he would not use her to assert his marital 'rights.'

She was mindful of Dr. James' warning that another pregnancy could prove fatal for her. Her greatest fear was that in his lust, he would inadvertently make her pregnant again. So, she refrained from going to bed until she was certain John was already asleep. Fortunately, he slept soundly until early the next morning when he dressed and left without as much as a goodbye.

.....

Paul Gunderson checked in at the tiny airstrip near Dothan. Since he ferried the Stearman C-3B bi-plane from Kansas nearly two and a half years ago, he had accrued the highest number of hours of all the pilots on the airfield's civilian roster. Although the plane was still serviceable for beginners, it would not meet Triangle Aviation's increased demand for advanced training. That, in conjunction with the fact there had been only a limited production run of C-3B models, meant there were few spare parts to be had. The airplane was still solid, but it was aging. In short, they needed a new one and the Model 75, which was similar in design and function to the C-3B, would fit the bill nicely.

Paul called Heinrichs Friedman at his hotel and they agreed to meet at the pavilion at High Springs Lake the following morning before work. Friedman made a strange request before he hung up.

"Herr Paul, you must be sure you aren't followed. Do you understand me?"

The following morning, Paul took a circuitous route to Lake High Springs where he found Freidman waiting for him in his car. Paul sat in the passenger's seat and they discussed their plan. The Triangle Aviation board of directors had agreed to fund the purchase provided Paul could guarantee them a favorable rate from his bank.

Then, as before, Paul would ferry the plane to Dothan from Kansas. This time however, he vowed to use a light hand on the throttle. Flying eleven hours in wet underwear had made for a long day he had just as soon not repeat!

Although Paul was used to bank transactions being confidential, he sensed something odd about his dealings with Heinrichs. He had not said anything and had adhered to Friedman's requests up to now but they parted, Paul's curiosity got the better of him.

"You mentioned my being followed. Is there anything I should know?"

The German laughed. "Ahhh, no mein freund. It's just that one cannot be too careful these days."

Friedman had clearly underestimated Gunderson and he realized it in that moment. He trusted had trusted him so far; he might as well bring him into the fold now. At least a little bit more.

"Herr Gunderson, you are too smart for an old man like me to toy vith your sensibilities. Vhat I tell is strictly confidential. You agree, no?" Paul nodded. "Zee vord from the Fatherland is that there are people there vith an unnatural interest in zee progress Americans are making vith aviation. Within the past few months, several German 'tourists' have been caught snooping around various airfields. I just think vee should be cautious about vhat we are doing here. That is all. I will let you know if you need to be concerned."

The two parted ways with Paul agreeing to set up the financing with his bank and ferrying the plane to Dothan from Kansas. The financing would be the easy part. Explaining to Sandra he would be leaving her alone again was a different story. After the last time she had not welcomed him in her bed for nearly a month.

·····

It was a beautiful fall day near the end of September 1935 and Olivia decided to forgo the car and gathered the girls in their wagon and pulled them uptown to purchase material at Mr. Adkins' Mercantile. As she strolled, she picked up bits of gossip from passerby and shopkeepers. She was surprised to learn of John's establishing himself as a respected businessman across Alabama and parts of Florida. Even Mr. Adkins was effusive in his praise.

"After his initial success with our rolling store, I have held him in high regard. It certainly wasn't his fault the economy floundered and it now pleases me to witness his regaining respect even from among those who previously would not associate with him."

It was with a touch of bitterness that Olivia thanked him as she had spoken with others who had expressed similar sentiments. People easily forgave John or dismissed his part in her own fall from grace but did not accord her the same forgiveness or opportunity to redeem herself. It was a source of perpetual frustration for her.

• • • • •

John stayed at the cottage during the week but could be found at High Bluff with his mother and Evelyn on the weekends. He passed the time as he awaited word from his father on their resuming construction in Florida. Meanwhile, he became increasingly more and more frustrated as he remained in a constant state of limbo. He had worked hard to advance himself to prove his father justified in extending him this opportunity, and the delays in construction were thwarting his momentum.

He much preferred the lifestyle of a carefree businessman to that of the 'family man' role he was forced to play with Olivia and her children. He enjoyed traveling via luxury club car with an attractive assistant, dining in the best restaurants, and staying in opulent penthouse suites associated with his stature at Ward Enterprises. So, he was disappointed he could not return to Florida right away.

But being in High Springs meant he had some time to spend with Paul when he was free from his duties at the bank and not flying. The last time they had seen each other, Paul mentioned he wanted to meet for lunch to discuss an opportunity he felt John would find beneficial. John had accepted and anxiously awaited hearing more. He was pleased Paul now saw him as a legitimate businessman rather than a loser who had been forced to drop out of college to live in the Quarters with his 'old maid' wife and her children.

Meanwhile, Olivia refused to spend time dwelling on John's activities. Papa had apprised her of Mama's health and now, facing the uncertainty of her longevity, Olivia's view on life had changed. It caused her to reflect on the extent to which she had allowed herself to be controlled by the opinions of others. She accepted an irrefutable fact. In the grand scheme of life, the opinions held by people in High Springs weren't worth considering. "I'll not let others dictate how my daughters and I live our lives," she thought.

A few days later, as she pulled the girls along in their wagon on her way to see Mrs. Gates, she paused to admire the window display. With her back to the street, she was startled to hear her name called. She turned to find Sandra Gunderson standing before her.

Forcing a smile, Sandra greeted her, "Olivia Ward, how are you? Paul and I were disappointed you were unwell and unable to join us for supper with your husband, John."

Olivia initially thought to accept Sandra's fake expression of regret and let it die, but she remembered her resolve. "By crick, I am through pretending!" she thought.

"Sandra, you need not be concerned about my health. It was not any sickness that kept me from accompanying John. The truth is the tragedy of his being married to an old woman like me and being saddled with children at a young age is simply more than he can bear and he did not extend your invitation to me. It seems we are nothing more than an inconvenience and embarrassment to him, and you and Paul would be best served to kindly exclude me and my children from any future social considerations."

Olivia stood resolute as she observed Sandra's expression of disbelief. And then she continued. "While I thank you for your invitation, however insincere, please express my regrets to Paul."

Pulling the wagon, she went on her way as Sandra stood rooted to the same spot. Olivia was giddy with excitement and had she not been in the middle of town, she would have let out a shout of joy. Instead, she decided to treat the girls to a soda at Jerrell's.

Shortly, they arrived at Jerrell's and Olivia pulled the wagon inside. Then she found a table and lifted the girls into their seats. Kate was a perfect little lady sitting in her chair, but Jean was determined to visit with those around her.

Olivia did not notice John when he came in with Paul a few minutes later. John saw her but did not acknowledge them. Paul did, however, and he went over to Olivia's table and greeted her and the girls. It was then she realized John was with him.

Paul remarked on his disappointment that she was unable to accompany John for supper. Olivia bit her tongue; certain he would get the whole colorful story from Sandra later. As he returned to join John, Paul felt a bit awkward. It puzzled him how John did not acknowledge his wife and daughters sitting two tables away from them.

Once they finished their soda, Olivia loaded the girls into their wagon and pulled them past John and Paul's table without so much as a glance at her husband. Kate, however, announced to one and all, "Mama, there's Daddy."

But Olivia never paused as she headed out the door and homeward. When and if John ever came home, she expected there would be repercussions from her encounter with Sandra Gunderson. She was not wrong. She had poked the bear of John's emotions.

CHAPTER 13

A few hours later John returned home. But, unlike his nightly routine, he did not go directly to the bedroom. Instead, he stormed into the kitchen where Olivia was tying a rug. He screamed at her like a banshee while standing directly over her with his arms akimbo.

"What in the hell do you mean embarrassing me with Paul and Sandra? Did you tell Sandra you were not sick and that I declined to take you to their home? What were you thinking?"

Olivia felt John's anger and she feared him but was determined to remain calm and not to show it.

"John, the girls are asleep so you will kindly lower your voice," she said matter-of-factly. "Yes. I told her the truth. Don't you agree it is better she know before she is forced to put on a false façade of friendship in front of me in the future? Now she will know an insincere invitation for me to join the three of you for dinner is neither expected nor appreciated. At least now she knows that you and I are nothing more than two tragic individuals who occupy a cottage together. Now leave me alone. You repulse me!"

Olivia's harsh words astounded John. He could not believe her dismissal of him and he wondered what had come over her. Heretofore, he had been the one to dismiss her, but now the tables were decidedly turned. It was bad enough she made him out to be a liar when she spoke to Sandra, but Paul's words of censure over what he described as John's 'childish behavior' at Jerrell's was worse. But Paul's candid remarks about Sandra overwhelmed him even more.

Paul said John would never face with Olivia what he faced with Sandra on a daily basis. He went on to say that with her gracious manners and kind ways, Olivia was an absolute jewel compared to Sandra who was mean-spirited and had no consideration for others unless they could do something for her. Although it pained him, John felt strongly these were words he would be wise to consider.

Later that night as she entered their bedroom, Olivia could tell John was not asleep. She approached her side of the bed and lay as close to the edge as she could without hanging off the mattress. The stressful events of the day had taken their toll on her and she was almost asleep when she heard John whisper.

"I have been so wrong about you. Please forgive me."

She lay still without reacting. She had determined that never again would she open herself to the hurt and humiliation John was capable of inflicting upon her. Any chance they might have had to co-exist had evaporated with his behavior at Jerrell's. He had failed to publicly recognize her and his daughters for the last time. Having the Ward name to lend legitimacy to her children no longer held any advantage for her. She was, after all, a Turner. That's all she needed to make her way in life.

. . . . .

The following morning, Judy and Evelyn came to visit but found Olivia and the girls were not home. At Evelyn's suggestion, they drove over to Mrs. Smith's house where they found Olivia at work baking in the kitchen. Judy wondered if Olivia and the girls had moved back in with Mrs. Smith since they were here so much of the time.

"Olivia, may Evelyn and I plan Jean's third birthday celebration for next week at High Bluff?"

Evelyn pulled on Olivia's arm and excitedly exclaimed, "Cotton, we've already made some plans; you must agree."

"Oh, Rabbit, how can I refuse? Of course, you may plan the party."

Olivia cautioned her that Mama and Papa Turner and Aunt Beth would not be able to attend. Mama Turner was ill and Aunt Beth would need to stay and care for her while Papa is away on a business trip.

Judy commented, "I wasn't aware your mother was ill. What ails her? Perhaps I should pay her a visit."

Tears formed in Olivia's eyes and she was unable to respond. Mrs. Smith broke in, "Annie has an inoperable brain tumor and the specialist in Birmingham told Walt that her outlook is guarded. He could not say with any certainty how long she will survive. We are all in a state of shock at the news and we are taking it day by day."

Judy was stricken with a deep sadness. Knowing how close Olivia and her mother had always been, it grieved her to learn of Annie's condition and to realize how it affected Olivia. In spite of their tumultuous history together, Judy Ward had experienced an epiphany with Jean's birth nearly three years ago and she had grown to regard Olivia differently since.

"Why don't Evelyn and I take Kate and Jean with us and I'll bring them back before their bedtime. This will allow you time to finish these batches of cakes. Will this help you?"

Olivia was surprised and paused to clear her thoughts. "You are going to take Kate, *also*?"

Judy nodded as Jean squealed her delight while Kate remained withdrawn and quiet. Jean loved visiting High Bluff where Flora always had fresh pecan pie on the ice chest in the dining room. And playing with Evelyn was always fun.

"Why yes, of course Kate is welcome."

Seeing this new side of Judy touched Olivia and she realized that, even with all her faults, Judy meant what she had said. If it came down to it, Olivia could rely on her for assistance. However, she was concerned about Judy's obvious favoritism between the girls and prayed it would not hurt Kate. She hugged and kissed the girls goodbye.

As she watched the '30 Ford back out of the driveway, Olivia was grateful. With all that she had on her plate with Mama's health, John's surprise return, and the girls, she certainly had no energy to deal with a spiteful Judy. She only hoped it would last. If forced to choose between her son and his wife and children, she knew where Judy's loyalties lay.

CHAPTER 14

On Monday evening, Olivia lingered in the girls' room until she heard John go back to prepare for bed. Once he had time to fall asleep, she tip-toed to their bedroom to try to ease into bed without disturbing him. He was not asleep though and turned to face her. Quickly, she backed toward the door but was not quick enough. John raised himself and asked her to come and sit beside him.

"Today Dad told me I am to prepare to return to South Florida at a moment's notice. He expects Dade County to vote to be a 'wet county' any day now and, from the gist of his comments, it appears I'll be living in Miami for the rest of this year and next. Considering what Dad shared with me, I'll be working to gain political support for our liquor licenses. Since I have no idea how long this will take, I don't know when I may return to High Springs."

Olivia was apathetic. "So, go then. Why are you suddenly concerned with getting my approval after you have so callously dismissed me and our daughters for so long?"

John answered abruptly, "You don't have to tell me how terrible I am as a father and husband. I'll remind you that I never wanted to be with the likes of you. I was perfectly happy to fetter away the summer in Ann's company while I prepared for college. I am not asking for your forgiveness or anything of the sort. What I want to share with you has nothing to do with you and me, or our daughters."

He rubbed his face in his hands as he considered how to convey his innermost feelings. "I realize the specialist refuses to speculate on how long your mother may live and I just want you to know that I wish I had the wherewithal to ease the pain you both suffer."

John's voice cracked; he had to get his emotions in check before he could continue. "I hope that Kate and Jean will grow up to be like your mother because she is the epitome of all that is good and kind." Slightly embarrassed with his emotions on display, he turned from her to settle his lingering thoughts about Olivia.

Olivia was surprised. John's words were potent and seemed to express his genuine regard for her mother. They touched her deeply as they pushed against the protective wall she had erected against him. She realized the congenial feelings they both felt in this moment would be short lived. Olivia reached over and patted John's hand on the bed beside her. Then, without saying as much as a word, she quietly retired to the sitting room where she spent the rest of the night reading her Bible on the settee.

. . . . .

Having talked shop with John at Jerrell's a few days earlier, Paul landed upon an idea he felt might benefit John's efforts to advance his political standing. Paul was a member of the Masons, a fraternal organization which espoused high morals in its members. As a result, it was an exclusive club which consisted of many highly regarded members of the community.

"Surely John would benefit from the associations he would garner as a member of my Masonic Lodge," Paul thought.

There was only one catch: John's history of drinking and carousing, along with the circumstances of Kate's birth, had at one time provided fodder for the town gossip mill. While Paul felt enough time had passed for those indiscretions not to be an issue, he could not say so for sure. Besides, John had more than proved his business acumen with his successful launch of the rolling store with Mr. Adkins, who was also a Mason; and John's management of several large construction projects in Florida for Ward Enterprises.

Paul recognized that the Masons was a voluntary organization; anyone who desired membership had only to petition and receive a unanimous vote of the membership. Therefore, Paul hoped that given the chance for members to meet the 'new' John Ward, they would see him as a valued member of their brotherhood and grant him the required unanimous vote.

Thus, Paul invited John to meet him for a Coca-Cola at Jerrell's where he asked John if he had an interest in pursuing membership. John recognized the benefits he could accrue from associations within a countrywide brotherhood, and he was honored by the fact Paul had confidence in him. So Paul asked if John could attend the next meeting to be held in High Springs at the Tulip Theater. John agreed to attend to get a feel for how the members would welcome him and if right, he would submit his petition for membership.

. . . . .

The night of the meeting was upon them and John waited for Paul to arrive outside The Tulip. When Paul pulled into the parking lot, he hurriedly greeted John and ushered him inside. John noted Paul was not his usual easy-going self and seemed preoccupied.

Inside, Paul hastily showed John around. He was greeted by a number of members whom he did not know personally but he recognized as movers and shakers across Geneva County. Most greeted him with nods of the head or brief waves of approval. However, one was noticeably detached.

Jack Gunderson was obviously perturbed at something. He neither greeted him nor made any overture to acknowledge John or Paul as they made their way around the room. And John thought it odd that Paul seated John and himself across the room from his father during the meeting.

John felt a lump forming in his throat. Jack Gunderson's distancing from him coupled with Paul's preoccupation could only mean one thing: Mr. Gunderson would not be supportive of John's petitioning for membership.

"How is it Paul intends to sponsor me as a member here when it is clear his father cannot abide me? While I will forever be grateful for Paul's confidence in me and his risk in voicing his support for me publicly, I shall not petition for membership. It is more than enough to know my best friend wanted me to become a Mason with him; but this is a lost cause for me."

Around eight o'clock, the meeting ended and Paul thanked John for coming; he immediately left through a side exit leaving John standing by himself. After trading a few hurried handshakes and pleasantries with well-wishers, John exited through the same door. Thinking about his situation with Olivia, John chose to delay going home until he thought she would be asleep to avoid facing her again.

He made his way across the square and walked the five blocks to his father's office. He wanted to tune in to the radio there for news of the election in progress in Holmes County. He also wanted to review several reports on the status of the delays in construction at the clubs in South Florida.

As he rummaged through a stack of correspondence, he noted a letter outlining the process for securing licenses for the clubs. His attention was drawn to an attached telegraph containing the outcome of the election for the position of the Holmes County sheriff.

"Dammit," John cursed loudly. "Our candidate lost. How did this happen? We shelled out a lot of money to ensure he would win by a comfortable margin."

He sat in stunned silence for a few minutes. There was no question that this was a significant setback for both him and Ward

Enterprises, and he thought, "Heads will roll. I'll talk to Dad about it in the morning and get his instructions."

.....

Jack Gunderson was vociferously opposed to John Ward petitioning for membership in the Masons and he said as much. Still, Paul hoped his father's fear of Robert Ward's influence over the bank's board of directors would throttle him. Robert Ward had the wherewithal to start his own bank just to spite Jack Gunderson and the threat of such should be enough to cause Paul's father to cast a white ball in the ballot for John's membership. His casting a solitary black ball would finish John's chances.

Now the meeting was over, and father and son faced off in the alley at the rear of the Tulip Theater.

"You expect me to cast a white ball in support of John Ward's petition? Not on your life! Based on what I've told you about him and his father's business dealings, what in the hell ever gave you the idea I would ever support that bastard?"

Paul was surprised at the vehemence in his voice. While he understood the extent to which his father was prepared to go to cause Robert Ward harm, he had never expected it to go so far as to impact his son. As his father had put it, he would 'bring them both down mightily.' By 'both,' it was now obvious he meant Robert and John.

Jack continued his rant as he boasted of turning over the damaging information on John's finances to authorities in Dade and Holmes Counties. There was an unmistakable paper trail of deposits, withdrawals, and checks which would probably result in criminal charges against John, and with any luck, his father. If not, explaining away John's carefree spending would certainly tie them both up in a lengthy investigation, much to Jack's amusement.

Once the district attorney reviewed the documents and determined an investigation should be launched, the Wards would be knee deep in manure. So, as long as John or Robert did not find out about Jack's involvement and intervene in the next day or two, there would be nothing they could do to stop an indictment. He would revel in their downfall as the Gundersons had the last laugh.

.....

The rows of pecan trees silhouetted against the clouds on the horizon as Paul Gunderson raced toward High Bluff in his black sedan. He could not allow Robert and John to be blindsided by what was about to befall them.

"Perhaps it is not too late," he thought. "I can't imagine what a lengthy investigation and possibly jail time will do to John. I'm not sure he can survive it."

Although it was late, Flora ushered Paul into the study. Robert arrived shortly and Paul outlined how his father had been monitoring John's pattern of withdrawals at the bank. His father then used his banking friends in Miami, West Palm Beach, and Bonifay to gather incriminating information on Ward Enterprises. To top it off, Paul said Jack had shared this information with election authorities and law enforcement in those towns.

"Mister Ward, we both know Florida folks don't take kindly to outsiders meddling in their elections. From what I've learned from my dad, they are coming after John and maybe even you. You've got to protect him before it is too late."

Robert acknowledged the gravity of the situation and indicated he would alert John right away. Then he would sequester him somewhere out of sight until he could handle the situation.

"Judy and I will get John and the three of us will leave early on the train for Miami. Thanks to you, I may have the time I need to curtail these serious legal actions against John."

Paul understood the urgency of the matter. So when Robert stated they would travel by train to Miami, Paul reminded him he was a competent pilot, and could fly them to Miami.

Robert mulled over Paul's offer and decided against it. He reasoned it unwise to alert others, especially Jack Gunderson, of their actions. Robert felt Paul's flying them down on short notice might arouse undue suspicion. He thanked Paul, saying he might take him up on his offer in the future. Seeing he could do no more, Paul headed back to High Springs. He could not escape the uneasy feeling about his best friend's future.

As soon as Paul departed, Robert awoke Judy and hurriedly brought her up to speed on Paul's visit. She ignored her first impulse to tell Robert to drag Jack Gunderson out of bed and settle this as men. But her cooler side prevailed, and she agreed they must get John out of sight.

"Judy, I'll return as soon as I find John. Meanwhile, you begin packing and be prepared to help me lay out our best strategy to handle this situation upon my return tonight."

As Robert took his hat and coat from Flora at the front door, the clock on the mantle struck eleven o'clock. The crisp October air whistled through the window vent as he barreled toward High Springs. He would roust John shortly, but first he decided to stop in at his office to pick up papers he would need to help exonerate John. Then he would head over to Seventh Street to Olivia and John's cottage where he suspected they had already retired for the evening.

·····

John sat alone in his tiny office at Ward Enterprises and reflected on his accomplishments in the past two years. He performed well the tasks his father had assigned him for the construction of the two clubs.

He thought, "I've succeeded in shedding the image of a school bus driver and I am regaining a high regard from the townspeople in High Springs. Even so, I am surprised at the results of my efforts."

Then he stopped his wool gathering about the Holmes County election. He glanced at the clock on the wall and realized it was past eleven. Thinking Olivia would be in bed by this hour, he prepared to close up the office to head to the cottage.

As he searched for his keys to lock his office, he heard a noise and saw his father entering through the front door. He was startled at the lateness of his appearance, and he hoped nothing had gone wrong in Miami or West Palm Beach. Why else would his father be in the office at this time of night? Robert was equally surprised to see John in the office at this late hour. He was also relieved he would not have to spell out John's predicament in front of Olivia at the cottage. He wasted no time summarizing what Paul had told him.

"John, Paul warned me about an ongoing criminal investigation and pending indictment against you in Holmes County. He had no knowledge of any of this until this evening when his father alerted him of his plan to ruin us both."

Robert explained the circumstances that led up to Jack Gunderson's actions and the mean-spirited jealousy behind them. "Frankly, if Jack had not become so enraged, Paul would not have learned of the extent to which his father had attempted to sabotage us."

John looked at his father in disbelief. "What does all this mean, Dad?"

"What it means, Son, is that you did not follow my instructions. I told you to keep your deposits and withdrawals to a minimum to avoid suspicion, to carry your walking around money in cash bundles in a waist belt, and to avoid intermingling the money earmarked for campaign contributions and 'other considerations' with your personal account. The one hundred forty thousand dollars you left in that account attracted attention of the worst kind and you also left a paper trail of incriminating withdrawals across Florida. They are coming for me through you, Son, and you have made it easy for them. The Holmes County district attorney will likely indict you anytime now, issue a warrant for your arrest, and seek extradition from Alabama. I can't change the past, but with Paul's information I hope to change your future. Your mother and I will head to Florida tomorrow to fix your mess. You stay here, and, for God's sake, stay out of sight."

John was flabbergasted; he slumped into a nearby chair with his head in his hands.

"There's another thing, Son. You owe Paul a debt of gratitude. Because he dared defy his father tonight, we have a chance to act quickly to save our business, and hopefully save you in the process.

MCMURTRY

CHAPTER 15

While Robert was away, Judy worked through much of the night and early morning at High Bluff to perfect their plans. Meanwhile, John sat at the cottage contemplating what he could face if he returned to Florida. Admittedly, he was frightened as he considered what his father told him about Paul's warning.

Thinking of the personal risks Paul had taken by confronting his father, John wondered if he would have done the same for Paul. He hoped so, but he was not at all sure. Given Paul's display of courage, John had a new respect for the depth of their friendship, especially now that he more fully understood Old Man Gunderson's strong dislike for both him and his father.

Eventually, sleep overcame him and his final waking thoughts were his gut feeling that all he had accomplished over the past few months was slipping away and he was powerless to halt it.

.....

It was nearly three in the morning by the time the crossroads at High Bluff were in sight. Robert pulled into the side yard where his headlights landed on a sleeping Rufus, who lifted his head briefly and then rolled over on his side. The old hound's watchdog days were in his past.

In a jiffy, Robert was inside where he found Judy at the kitchen table. As he had asked of her, she had a plan in mind, and together they went over it. First, they addressed what they could do to protect John in Holmes County, and then they discussed a new issue that had arisen in the clubs in South Florida.

Based on reports Robert had received within the past two days, there was an issue that put their ownership of the clubs in jeopardy. Over the next few months, they would have their hands full in Florida.

"Judy, there is no doubt John's inexperience has allowed a mole to work his way into our midst in the clubs. Over the past few weeks, Chicago-based mobsters have worked to establish their hold on a few of our dealers, pit bosses and cage managers. Once they grease the right palms, the dealers allow card counters and other cheaters to infiltrate the games and score big. Then they move on before the honest pit bosses become wise to them. I've been told that this 'hit and run' strategy has proven quite effective in other clubs. John did not properly vet some of the out-of-town high rollers who were, in reality, mobsters. That being said, the larger issue is that their mere involvement in the running of our operations will jeopardize our clubs. Dade County law enforcement will not sit idly by and allow racketeers to take over their cities."

Judy stared back in astonishment but did not respond. Robert could tell she was thinking of John's poor decisions and their untimely impact on the situation.

"Yes, John made some unwise decisions in hiring some men I have learned are members of a powerful Chicago crime organization."

Judy shook her head in disgust. Robert then continued by telling her he feared John had allowed his drinking, womanizing, and gambling habits to create the situation they were now facing.

"I warned John of the consequences we would all suffer if law enforcement ever suspected any involvement of racketeers in our clubs."

Robert knew what he must now do. The gate was open and the horses were already out of the barn; he had no choice but to take on the criminal organization and drive its men out. Doing nothing meant losing a multi-million-dollar investment in the two clubs.

With a solid plan to mitigate their situation in the clubs, they then turned their attention back to protecting John in Holmes County. It would not be easy, and he knew he could not count on his usual allies. The old sheriff had turned a blind eye to activities in the juke joints, for a price.

The new sheriff, however, had run on a platform of squashing organized crime and driving out gambling and drinking from the community. Robert's friend in the D.A.'s office phoned Robert and advised him that the new sheriff had considerable support in Tallahassee and it would be a political liability for the D.A. to offer Robert any help with John's situation at this time. In short, John was on his own.

Judy offered Robert an alternative plan. "I am not worried about clearing out the riff raff in our clubs. Our friends in New York will handle them just like they did for your friend Schultz when he was having trouble with the Kansas City mob. My girl, Ingrid, will establish contact with her benefactors in New York and start the wheels in motion. However, I am concerned about leaving John here unattended and to his own devices. I would feel much better having him with you and me where we can keep an eye on him. If he is indicted in Holmes County and a warrant is issued, there is no guarantee Jack Gunderson will not work diligently to discover his whereabouts here and guide the police to him for his arrest and extradition. Why don't you and John go on down and wait for our Yankee friends to crack some skulls in Miami? In the meantime, I'll go to Holmes County where I have a reliable man who'll help me handle the situation there."

Robert was relieved to have Judy on his side. She was as smart as she was cutthroat in her business acumen. She had more than proved her worth years ago when she built what would become Ward Enterprises while he was hunkered down in the forest of the Ardennes and exorcising his demons in France for two years after the war ended. She was truly an asset to him and he wondered if he had ever given her the credit she deserved for their success. Now though, he was exhausted, and he led her to bed. They had only a few hours before they would set out for Florida via rail.

.....

As the sun came up over the tree tops outside Olivia and John's cottage, Robert and Judy Ward sat in their car waiting for the first sign of life inside. The windshield had a hint of dew, causing the morning rays to cascade in a prism throughout the car.

Soon, a light flickered on and Robert approached and entered the front door quietly without knocking. Within a few minutes, he had rousted John and apprised him of their change in plans. John quickly packed to leave. He was careful not to wake Olivia or the girls, so he just grabbed the bare essentials. He would buy what he needed when he arrived in Florida.

As John started to sling his valise over his shoulder, he stopped to retrieve an object wrapped in a gray handkerchief from his top dresser drawer, slipped it inside, and latched the buckled strap closed. Then he thought of Olivia and the girls and whether he should say goodbye. He hated to admit it, but he realized he might not ever see them again. This was especially true if things either went bad with the Chicago mobsters or his pending indictment.

"It's probably best to just go," he thought.

CHAPTER 16

The Chicago mob was made up of some of the most dangerous individuals with whom Robert and Judy had ever tangled. They were both keenly aware of how they had infiltrated other clubs and knew it was nearly impossible to reclaim an operation once they took over. Reports from both clubs confirmed that they were not totally successful in recruiting the entire staff but were diligently working to solidify their position. Those who would not be bought were roughed up and run out of town.

Thus it was clear; Robert and Judy had to fight fire with fire. They would need to use brute force to repel the takeover attempt. Judy placed a quick call to Ingrid Schonen who assured her she knew just the crew for the job. They agreed upon their compensation and Ingrid wired the trio of headbangers money and train tickets for the following morning. Judy then reported back to Robert that the wheels were in motion. He was relieved help was on the way and moved on to the next order of business, protecting John.

"Judy, you go on to Bonifay and make certain your man there understands what is needed; then get on to Tallahassee for the final piece of the puzzle."

She knew what she must do and assured Robert she had it under control.

"Put this worry out of your mind, dear. I completely understand there must be different approaches to sway the old and established families in Tallahassee who, until recently, have been the powerbrokers of Florida politics. I'll arrange to entertain the Governor and his wife along with a few of our mutual friends there. In South Florida, the people of influence have acquired their wealth not from their families but from their investments and smart business deals. Most in this group enjoy a 'rip roaring' good time. No boring dinner parties for them. By the time I'm done with them, they will have to check their calendars to ensure they haven't been transported in time back to the Roaring Twenties."

Robert was pleased she understood she could not take a 'two birds with one stone' approach. "That's brilliant, dear, but can you accomplish this in such a short time? Do you need additional assistance to pull off your soirees?"

Judy thought for a moment. "For the South Florida shindig, I'll give them a show replete with fast-paced entertainments. I have a contact in Key West who can pull this off in her sleep. As to the events I shall stage for those in Tallahassee, I'll provide classically highbrow and dull events. I loathe them, but the locals swoon when they receive my invitations."

Robert was impressed with her quick planning but he was still concerned about John.

"I've thought of that. Don't worry. I've set up a plan to get a message to John as to our status and any actions he must take. I'm concerned Jack Gunderson or law enforcement may be watching and monitoring him closely so I will code the messages so they will seem inane to anyone who doesn't have the code key. In return, he will respond with a few simple phrases to confirm he has received and understands my directives."

.....

There were whispers that there would be snowflakes by noon as

Delfino "Diamond Del" DeLuca, Vinfrido "Vinny Two Fingers" Veltri, and Aratone "Tony Basher" Bassi left a two-story brownstone in Brooklyn headed for New York's Grand Central Terminal to board the Atlantic Coastline Railroad's "Havana Special" to travel from New York City to Key West, Florida. They each carried overcoats over their arms concealing bulging train cases in one hand while carrying pasteboard valise suitcases in their other hands. As they reached their sleeper car the colored porter offered to stow their bags, but they politely declined.

"Dis here's precious cargo," DeLuca barked as he shielded his train case from prying eyes.

"Yeah, precious cargo," echoed Veltri in a thick Italian accent. "You no touch."

The men secured their bags in a locking closet and prepared to snake their way through the passenger and sleeping cars to the lounge car for a drink before the "Special" left the station. Poised at the door, DeLuca cracked it and checked the passageway both ways before looking back at his henchmen, Bassi and Veltri.

Two Fingers pulled open his coat jacket with a pair of badly mangled digits revealing a Colt 1911 automatic pistol tightly nestled in a leather shoulder rig. He removed the pistol, gently pulled back the slide, and let it go. As it snapped forward, it skinned a .45 caliber bullet off the top of the seven-round magazine and slammed it home into the breach. Basher followed suit and both nodded that they were ready for business. Now for the two-and-a-half-day trip to Miami. The boys grinned in anticipation of the job that lay ahead.

MCMURTRY

CHAPTER 17

It was a crisp October morning in High Springs and fall was upon them as Robert and John arrived at the train depot. As owner of the Southern Railroad spur from High Springs to Dothan, Robert enjoyed several perks. One of these was use of an engine pulling a tender, baggage car, and private club car for their business and personal travel. The private train was dubbed "The Ward Whistler" by railroad men along the line. Inside, a Southern Railroad employee served as their host to see to their comfort. He ensured a spread of food and a well-stocked bar was available to them. The luxurious furnishings created a pleasing ambiance while fostering a relaxing and carefree journey.

Today though, these amenities were lost on both men as their focus was on getting John out of town as quietly as possible. As the porter entered with a tray full of a selection of delicacies, Robert waved him away. They could not cloud their thinking at this juncture; too much was at stake.

The heavy velvet drapes and the plush rugs masked the sounds of the train's wheels running along the track. While John was oblivious to the opulence of his surroundings, he pulled back the heavy drapery and gazed out the windows framing the covered platform at the end of their car. The crops and livestock made up the passing landscape until they reached a junction at Marianna, Florida. It was here the landscape changed to incorporate masses of scrub trees.

Several hours later, the train neared Tallahassee and John moved to the covered platform and gazed upon the gated compounds in which were nestled stately antebellum homes. The people residing in these mansions were those who had controlled Florida's politics and social circles for generations. He viewed the panorama of wealth and symbols of elitism and considered his mother. She would work to gain entry into these homes and gain from their owners the political accommodations they needed.

Here, his thoughts returned to Margo Brown and he wondered what it would have been like to have her meet him each evening with her welcoming embrace. He chided himself, acknowledging that such thoughts were of an impossible dream, "The men residing in these homes are fortunate to return at the end of each day to their treasured families." Turning from the platform to join his father, John silently invoked a plea for solace. Instead, he experienced a feeling of envy of those who had that which he longed for.

This feeling would have vanished however, had he known the plight of the occupants of these palatial homes with their manicured lawns, wrought iron fences, and gate houses. What he did not realize was that many faced financial ruin along with a steady erosion of their power and influence. Because of these circumstances, some of them granted Judy and Robert entry into their elite circles.

These power brokers had influence in the politics of the state. Thus, they sold inside information and access in exchange for the Ward's and others' financial contributions which enabled them, for a while longer, to maintain their status quo. With the emergence of the new rich, the old rich played with deftness the game of 'you scratch my back and I'll scratch yours.' Some were very good. Others were very, very good John would soon learn.

.....

The next afternoon, "The Whistler" slowed to a stop at the Miami, Florida, main terminal and the colored porter collected Robert's and John's baggage. Before Robert could descend the three

118

metal steps to the platform, the telegraph operator met him at the door with a wire. As they settled into the limousine for the short drive to the Flamingo Club, Robert read the telegraph wire silently. Once he finished, he folded it and tucked it into his pocket and told John they had a lot of work to do.

At the club, bellhops unloaded their bags and a concierge escorted them to the lavish, three-bedroom penthouse apartment they would occupy during their stay. As soon as they were settled, Robert roused John and together they ventured downstairs club to scope out the lay of the land of the club. After they got their bearings, Robert had bigger fish to fry.

Robert felt it was important to visit local law enforcement personnel right away to gauge their level of interest in the goings on at the club and determine if they were aware of the presence of the Chicago mobsters in town. But before doing so, he needed to quiz the club's staff to gather as much information as he could to assess the overall situation. He did not want to speak to the sheriff before he knew what was going on. Therefore, Robert had John accompany him as he made his rounds of the club's front-end operations.

What he found was a group of anxious and loyal employees who feared that the Chicago mob would soon take over the club. It was reassuring to learn not one of them had been questioned by law enforcement concerning the presence of mobsters. In each case, he reassured them he was on top of the situation and they had nothing to fear. He would rid the club of these interlopers as soon as possible.

As it turned out, not everyone was happy within the club. As John and Robert made their rounds, they found several disgruntled employees who were either insubordinate or indifferent in their attitudes. Although the job of dismissing these disloyal curs would have traditionally fallen to John in his role of general manager, Robert bypassed him. He wanted to send a message: he was taking back control of his clubs.

Word spread quickly and as they continued their rounds it was evident Robert's rapid action to eliminate uncooperative employees had the desired effect. Those that remained knew he meant business and they were confident he would root out the infiltrators.

Robert quickly concluded the front-end was under control and that law enforcement had not exhibited any undue interest in the club's operations. They likely knew the Chicago mobsters were in town, but as long as things stayed quiet, the 'coppers' would let well enough be.

·····

As they visited each law enforcement precinct, John began to understand the effectiveness of his father's strategy. During their visits, Robert left senior officials with assurances he would eliminate the threat of a take-over by out-of-town mobsters. Of course, for the captains, sergeants, and officers who seemed amenable, Robert had John write down each officer's name and home address to add to the Ward Enterprises' 'Christmas card' list. Robert explained the scheme to John.

It was simple, really. Around the second week of December, the dry-cleaning plant manager, Billy Jones, would pick up several dozen pounds of dry ice at the High Springs ice plant. Then he would pack and address a few dozen boxes, each containing a turkey, bottle of liquor, and various delicacies to be delivered to those on the list Robert provided. Nestled deep inside each turkey were bundled the makings of a highly anticipated Christmas 'gravy,' a roll of twenty-dollar bills to brighten the holiday season for those who looked after the interests of Ward Enterprises. Robert could tell John did not understand fully how his strategy worked.

"John, it's like the 'you scratch my back' strategy Olivia explained to you before. Key officers look the other way and we ensure they have a fruitful Christmas. As for those few who don't want their back scratched, they investigate mob activity at the club, find nothing, and go home empty handed. So far, they have been unable to discover any connection between our clubs and the mob. It's our job to ensure we have the right people in place to make sure they don't ever find that connection.

"I think I understand, Dad. But how can we ever be sure?"

"As the Greeks said, Son: *res ipsa loquitor.* 'It speaks for itself.' If they had been successful in finding even a shred of evidence, they would have already closed our doors."

John accepted the fact that his father had a way to continue operations with the tacit consent of the local authorities. Listening to his analysis of how to react to the visits of the police and sheriff's deputies, he was convinced he did not have the experience required for the job his father had assigned him. He was in way over his head and had been for months. With the issue of the local police behind them, Robert declared it was time for them to deal with the bad asses in the back rooms.

"Before I face off with these mobsters you must acquaint me with the extent of your involvement with them. Understand, John, this is a fight to keep our club open. It is critical that I not be blindsided by any advantage they have because of your past associations with them."

It was then John faced the gravity of the situation his past behavior had created and he was ashamed of what he must disclose. Olivia's warning flashed across his mind. She told him, "With your brains and personality, you can succeed at whatever you chose. But to do so you must mature and become responsible for your actions."

How right she had been. "Dad, I'm really sorry. For nearly two years I performed better than you expected as I built, managed, staffed, and arranged successful openings of the clubs. Moreover, I achieved sustained patronage. But, all I accomplished I threw away when I allowed the goons in the back rooms to get me over a barrel." John paused as he waited for the hammer to fall. But, it did not and so he continued.

"Take whatever steps are necessary to win this battle. It is true I'm in a mess, but there is nothing they have on me which will impact your actions. I was a fool and these men took me to slaughter like a lamb. The truth is I never learned my lesson from Wallace in the back room at the dry cleaners. The men here used their pretty women and booze to lure me into gambling with them. Several times I realized I needed help, but my pride overrode my common sense. I allowed these clever thugs to browbeat me into raising the house limits and when I did, they cleaned house."

Robert asked why the losses did not appear in the monthly reports he received from their accountant. John explained how he had covered most of the losses with his own savings. But he had made a costly mistake in bargaining with them to erase the balance in exchange for giving them access to the staff in the back rooms.

"As soon as the men I dealt with gained control, they brought characters into the club whose mere presence in the front rooms scared off our preferred customers who ceased patronizing the club."

The cause of the hostile takeover was clear to Robert now. John had opened the door with his immaturity and gambling debts. He put his arm around John's shoulders. "Son there is no need to commence flailing yourself with a 'cat 'o nine tails.' You have told me nothing I didn't already suspect. The only things in question were the cause and the amount. So if this is the extent of what has led to their temporary success, the corrective action I need to take will be easy to initiate and quick to conclude. And, for the record, you have done a hell of a job with these two clubs. You were savvy to gain entry into the most elite circles of influence; and these accomplishments, alone, far outweigh what you have allowed to happen with these Chicago thugs."

John looked at his father in disbelief. "You mean you are not going to cast me adrift as I was before? I'm not destined to be a bus driver again?"

Robert had no intention of setting his son adrift, but neither did he intend to repeat his mistake, a colossal one, with John. "You'll not be without a job within Ward Enterprises. Moreover, in the future I'll make certain you are not burdened with overwhelming responsibilities. Considering this, let us agree we are equally to blame. Now, let's proceed to the back rooms and kick some butts! I'll tell you what I'm going to do. All you need to do is cover my back, Son."

. . . . .

Evelyn balanced herself against the wooden beams supporting the roof of the hay barn at High Bluff. She had dropped her colored pencil and was gingerly trying to pick it up with her toes without surrendering her position nestled between several bales of hay. The October wind was cool and crisp as it rattled against the tin roof.

"This will just have to do as it is," she whispered as she abandoned her quest to retrieve the pencil. "Brother John will just have to have a cat with no scarf."

She folded the white art paper three times and inserted it into the brown envelope with a letter she had written him. Then, as was her weekly custom, she addressed the envelope and retired from the loft in search of Rufus. She whistled and called him and he appeared from beneath the main house. Together, they walked out to the main road and waited for the postman to stop at their box. She was too short to reach the lid so she stood on a milking pail to carefully place her letter in the box. Then she sat on the pail with three pennies for postage. Rufus waited patiently with his head resting on her knee.

"I hope John will be proud of my grades in school," she thought. "But I really hope he likes my pictures I drew of the farm and the new kittens."

Shortly, she heard the sound of the postman's truck coming up the road from High Springs. She leapt to her feet to flag him down. "Important mail going out," she yelled as he stopped. "I'm a sending news to my big brother."

The postman laughed as he counted out the pennies in her outstretched hand and applied the appropriate postage. As he pulled away, he cast his hand up in a wave goodbye. As Evelyn watched until the truck disappeared over the horizon, her beloved cur, Rufus, began his long walk back to his hiding place under the porch.

CHAPTER 18

"What's your plan to deal with these 'rough customers' from Chicago, Dad?" John asked.

"It's a simple plan, Son. With the help of Ingrid, your mother has hired a few 'rough customers' of our own from New York to give us the leverage we will need to push all of the Chicago gang and the dealers, pit bosses, and cage workers they have bribed out on their sorry assess. The New York boys are well known and you can be certain some of these Chicago mobsters will recognize their names. I will let the ring leader know things are about to get dusty, and if they have a lick of sense, they'll pack their bags and get out tonight."

John was in awe of his father who, he often felt, acquiesced too easily to his mother's demands. He was surprised his father did not appear to fear the men they were about to face. Robert's plan confirmed what John already suspected; his father's bravado was based, in part, on the telegram he received as they had exited The Whistler confirming that the New York boys were on their way.

For his part, John was not nearly as confident as his father. He knew the Chicago mobsters had a bad reputation and were not normally to be trifled with. As such, he had purchased a nickel-plated Colt .38-caliber revolver with mother-of-pearl stocks from a hardware store downtown a few months ago. "God created man," John thought. "And Samuel Colt made them all equal." John wasn't leaving rough play with the Chicago mob to chance. He would be prepared. He unwrapped the gun from the cloth he had packed before he left the cottage.

An hour or so later, Robert and John entered the backroom and waited for the reaction of the six pit bosses directing the betting activities and manipulating house limits at the poker tables. Two more men were dealing blackjack at adjacent tables. After observing them for a few minutes, Robert picked up how each was cheating. He also noted they made no attempt to hide their actions.

He moved to one of the tables and bought chips to play. Within two hands, Robert stopped the play and declared the dealer was a cheat. He reached across the table grabbing the dealer by the collar and pushed him toward the door. He then moved table to table ousting the offending cheaters, loudly proclaiming to all that were in earshot, "These sorry bastards are fired. They have cheated you for the last time." He then returned the chips to the befuddled 'honest' players and closed down the games.

As he cleared the last table, a big, burly Italian standing around six and a half feet tall and weighing well over three-hundred pounds moved swiftly from his look-out post in the cage to see what the commotion was about. As he drew closer, he spotted John and angled toward him.

"Hey, what's with your old man? You best tell him who is running these games. He needs to back off if he doesn't want to get hurt."

Robert heard the rotund man's warning and before John could respond, Robert moved to stand chest-to-chest with the Italian.

"I'm sorry. Who did you say is running this operation? Last time I looked, my name was on the deed to this club, and I don't recall selling it. So, if you know what's good for you, you and your cronies best clear out of here and not come back." Robert allowed the Italian and the other men to recover from their shock before he continued.

"What do you think you are going to do 'little man'?"

"Well first, I'm going to kick your ass out of here, then I'm going to unleash my boys on the rest of your gang. You ever hear of 'Diamond Del' DeLuca, 'Two Fingers' Veltri, or 'Basher' Bassi? No? Well if you all don't leave tonight you'll meet them when they arrive from New York City on the noon train tomorrow. They are exceptionally skilled in persuading reluctant persons to vacate a place where they're not wanted. *Capiche?*" Robert asked, looking for any indication the big man understood. He paused for effect.

The Italian squared his shoulders. "Yeah we know all three of 'em. So, what? You think you can scare us by dropping the names of these meatheads. Well, think again cause we ain't buying your bluff. Understand?"

Robert smiled as he removed the folded telegram from his breast pocket and pushed it in the face of the Italian. "I suggest you read this wire, if you can read, and then decide if I'm bluffing."

The Italian read the message and turned to Robert. "So, you got some big guns on the way. Maybe John here should explain why this ain't gonna change nothin'. He owed us big money... and he made a bargain with us to settle his debt. The arrangement we had... stands!"

Robert didn't budge. Rather, he stood steadfast while maintaining a confident grin. John stood by quietly while fingering the trigger of the Colt nestled in his jacket pocket. By the tone of the Italian's voice, Robert could sense the weakening of his resolve; he wasn't so sure he could continue to enforce the bargain his bosses had made with John. Moreover, he understood what they would be in for once the hired guns from New York arrived. They were well known for shooting first and asking nicely later.

The air was thick with cigar smoke and by now, anyone who had not already left the club had begun to gather around at a safe distance. John decided he needed to contribute his two-cents worth.

"I've been told you can't get blood out of a turnip. Well, consider me a turnip and understand there is no more money coming from me. I am not the owner of this or any other club. You have two options. You can find me later and rough me up and afterward have nothing except a visit from three vicious men. Or, you can scram and get out of town now while the getting is good. So, it is time. You must choose."

The Italian's cronies didn't wait for him to answer. As they mumbled amongst themselves, they headed for the door. Not one of them felt they were paid enough to tangle with the soon-to-arrive New Yorkers and collectively decided to give up the ship without a fight.

Robert felt a wave of relief and announced to all within earshot that the games were closed for the evening, but would resume the following night with honest dealers. In the meantime, the drinks were on the house in the front rooms. He signaled to several security staffers to usher the patrons to the front and close the backrooms while he and John entered the cage to reconcile the cash and chips.

Later, as Robert and John walked back to the front rooms, John could not hold back a hearty chuckle. "Now I see how a pro does it. Do you think we'll ever have trouble from them again?"

"Not only will we not have trouble with them here in Miami, neither will we have any trouble in West Palm Beach. As soon as the Italian notifies his boss in Chicago about the presence of the New Yorkers here, they will ship out right away. They don't want the kind of attention dusting up with the New Yorkers would entail."

With the Flamingo Club now free of cheaters, they meandered throughout the front rooms mixing with patrons to establish calm. With deft charm, Robert and John were successful in enticing their customers to consider the Flamingo Club a place to enjoy themselves without fear of being cheated or untimely law enforcement visits.

• • • • •

Annie sat on the side of her bed and peered out at the sun sinking behind the pecan trees on the horizon. It had been only a short while but she had come to terms with what the specialist had told Walt and her. She was dying. He didn't know how long she had, but his prognosis was simple. She needed to get her affairs in order.

She wasn't worried about the children. Except for Ann's usual shenanigans, the rest of their children were faring marvelously. Even Olivia, steadfast as always, continued to find ways to thrive and provide for her children. Although she was grateful Walt had finally relented and welcomed Olivia back to High Point, Annie never disclosed to him her offers to help Olivia financially. Olivia simply wouldn't hear of it. She had matured into every bit the woman Walt had known she would become when he ordained her to run the farms at High Point when she was only ten years old.

Since the day he and her father had nearly come to blows over his courtship of her, Walt Turner had been everything in a provider she could have ever hoped for. Sure, he was a little rough around the edges at times and he could be as stubborn as a log, but she loved him dearly and he doted on her the way every girl wished for attention from her Prince Charming. Now he would be faced with life without her and she worried he could not adapt. Her piercing thought was that she must not give up. That, she thought, would be Walt's undoing, knowing she did not fight to survive to spend every living breath with him. Thus, she solidified her resolve. Her concerns were with Walt.

• • • • •

It was apparent to Robert his son was gaining an appreciation of how to maintain an unchallenged operation of the club. However, he still questioned whether John could, or better yet, would forego his drinking and gambling.

"John, if I eliminate some of your responsibilities, such as the management of the Dolphin Club in West Palm Beach, will you be able to handle management of the Flamingo Club for the next couple of years? And, if you affirm you can, are you prepared to forego gambling and drinking?"

"But, Dad. What about Holmes County?"

"Until we have more information, we'll not know what to expect. It is a waiting game there. In the meantime, though, you need to continue solidifying the contacts you have developed there. It is important for you to look for opportunities to gain support and concessions from the people you have cultivated there."

Robert thought for a moment and continued. "Considering all the hard work you have put into restoring it, we need to protect your reputation in High Springs. I fear the situation in Holmes County could undermine what you have achieved in High Springs so your mother and I will plant information there about your schedule in South Florida. We will float the premise that you are so busy you will be required to stay here in South Florida for an indefinite period of time. This will serve to answer questions that are sure to arise as to why you are unable to return home. Thus, if the criminal investigation Jack Gunderson has triggered develops to a point where you are arrested and held, your absence will not arouse suspicion with Olivia or the townspeople. How did you leave it with Olivia?"

"She understands I'll not come home for a while. There's nothing to worry about there."

Robert patted his son on the back and lauded him for a job well-done. As they walked back up to the penthouse, they both laughed at the big Italian's quivering voice. Then they parted ways to head to their respective rooms; each needed to be alone to address his separate issues. They agreed to meet for breakfast in the morning.

.....

Olivia couldn't put her finger on it but something wasn't right. After several weeks where her baking, sewing, and tending to the girls had gotten the better of her free time, she had stopped by to visit with Mrs. Smith. While she was there she had a recurring thought: something was different. It wasn't anything obvious. It was just the tone. Mrs. Smith seemed tired. She struggled to stay alert, her words trailed off noticeably when she spoke, and she tended to ramble a bit.

"Perhaps she was having a bad day," Olivia thought. "I'll be sure to check on her more frequently in the next few weeks. "Or, maybe it is just my imagination. I'll ask Carolyn Gates for her opinion. Surely she will have noticed something where I have not."

.....

Robert was busy in his suite concentrating on how best to handle the Holmes County problem. To open a juke joint on the Alabama-Florida state line required the cooperation of the Holmes County Sheriff. While the prohibition amendment to the Constitution had been repealed, it was left to individual states, and sometimes to individual counties whether they would be 'wet or dry.' Only 'wet' states or counties permitted the legal sale of alcohol, and currently Holmes County was 'dry.'

If Robert opened a juke joint in Holmes County, he would rely on liquor sales, though illegal, as the joint's primary source of revenue. A lot of money had been spent in support of the candidate for sheriff who did not win. Thus, there was not only the loss of capital, which hurt, but also the loss of vital concessions from the deposed as to the strict enforcement of the county's liquor laws.

Moreover, Robert's heart was heavy. What he had not told John yet was that his efforts to influence the election had failed miserably; and worse, John had left a paper trail right back to himself which the

131

newly elected sheriff had traced. As Robert prepared for bed, he was bothered as he considered John's situation and admitted he had erred in asking his son to handle what he was not prepared to do. He battled sleep as he thought, "What have I done?"

CHAPTER 19

Closing the Flamingo and Dolphin Clubs to stage the galas was more successful than Judy had dared to hope. The Miami Herald society editor enthusiastically described the events, labeling them in her column as ones never equaled in the past. The picture she painted suggested that anyone who was not invited or failed to attend had missed their once-in-a-lifetime experience. The full-blown coverage and pictures of guests resulted in a goodly number of those considered to be the new rich clamoring to find a way to be on the guest list for the next event.

Robert wore himself out traveling between Miami and West Palm Beach to serve as his wife's co-host, but he didn't mind. These events proved successful as a way to garner commitments of support from key individuals. This was a significant outcome as one individual had considerable influence with the new Holmes County sheriff, and it was becoming more apparent to Robert each day that such influence could be valuable.

John was a major player in the events in Miami. He exuded charm and charisma to such a degree some looked upon him as a rising star in the Democrat Party. And there were those who thought he had potential for the state house. As they considered him, they urged him to create the marketable appearance of a strong family man. As interest in his future increased, so did the number of queries about his marital status. He avoided lying by putting forth the notion he valued his privacy too much to speak of his own personal plans.

He did, however, mention his talented younger sister, Evelyn.

Although she was far too young to engage in the society scene and politics at this time, all who listened marveled as John regaled them with tales of her prose and poetry. They hung on every detail of her being.

. . . . .

After staging the successful galas in West Palm Beach and Miami, Robert and Judy traveled to Tallahassee where they sojourned at their mansion there. It was time to execute their plan for entertaining a select group of politicians and their wives and Judy spared no expense. It began with drinks and then a seven course dinner was followed by dancing to the sweet melodies of an orchestra. While Judy entertained the wives, Robert lit Cuban cigars for the menfolk as he made sure Ward money crossed the palms of the right guests. On one level, Robert sensed the loss of a soon-to-be bygone era, and he was saddened to realize it would never return.

Often, he contemplated how the effects of the Great Depression had blurred class lines within the Southern aristocratic echelons and had produced a rising social order of the new rich. His conclusion was always the same: The Depression had brought about what generations of people before had been unable to do. It fractured the economic and social structure of the South causing the rise of a plurality of classes in the rich. One class was composed of those with old money while the other consisted of those with new money.

Elitism and a measure of cynicism colored his thoughts on the changes that were occurring. Unlike the Old Guard around him, few in the newly developing social class valued a person's family background, breeding, degree of refinement, or place of education. Rather, the only consideration for inclusion in the new rich class was having considerable wealth. Within these new social circles, money was king and trumped anything else. "These are interesting times we live in," Robert thought.

.....

Robert spent the 1935 Thanksgiving holidays in Miami with John and Judy. Together they planned the details of the annual Christmas extravaganza they would host in Tallahassee in the coming weeks. This year it would be especially important because of the opportunity it afforded them to have some of their guests reaffirm their critical political support. In the event of their worst fears of the district attorney's filing charges against John becoming a reality, they would need this leverage to have charges dropped.

.....

Robert and Judy agreed they had accomplished their objective in Tallahassee. Their supporters in Holmes County brought pressure to slow the process of convening a grand jury. This delay bought them valuable time to develop a worst case strategy to deal with the sheriff and district attorney there.

It was a waiting game, and one they could play in High Springs as easily as in Tallahassee. However, they still felt they could not risk John's return just yet. In the event charges were filed, Jack Gunderson's threat of turning over John's location to the Holmes County authorities was still too great to risk; he would be arrested immediately if found.

Thus, in early December 1935, Judy and Robert returned home to High Bluff without John, who went back to Miami on his own. Although Robert was concerned as to whether he could trust John to stay the course and eschew his gambling, drinking, and generally wayward attitude, given his exceptional performance in South Florida and Tallahassee, he decided to take a chance on trusting him.

They were glad to be back home on the farm. Robert needed to handle business matters in High Springs; and although she had no concerns over Evelyn's well-being, Judy was eager to see about Jean. Her mother's indifference to her did not bother Evelyn in the least as she was perfectly content to spend time with her sister-in-law, Olivia, and her nieces at the cottage.

·····

Within a few days of Robert's return, Walt Turner came around to discuss the Southern Railroad spur in High Springs and to commence payment for its use. On the night Olivia was on Death's doorstep during Jean's birth, Robert had extended the privilege of free carriage on his spur in return for Walt's rushing Annie and Beth to be by Olivia's side.

Since then, Walt had come to understand and appreciate how Robert had looked after Olivia during her time in the Quarters after Walt had unceremoniously dumped her there. With Annie's gentle cajoling, he had come to realize the error of his ways and he felt a sizable sum of guilt that he had bargained a deal out of Olivia's misery. As such, now was the time to square all accounts.

After listening to Walt's heartfelt apology and request to pay his way "as any many should," Robert thanked him and reminded him of the sincerity of his offer in exchange for allowing Annie and Beth to see Jean and comfort Olivia in her desperate time of need. The men agreed that the deal had unwittingly served the purpose of reuniting the Turner family. There was no prize worthy of losing that. In the future, Walt's businesses would be billed at the preferred rate.

With that settled, Walt mentioned several Works Progress Administration, or WPA, contracts that had been awarded in Geneva and Houston counties in October. He knew the winning bidders and they faced the loss of their contracts due to insufficient funds for startup capital.

As Walt spoke, Robert recognized an opportunity to make loans at interest rates conducive to profitable returns. And, as part of a loan package, it would be possible to strike a deal for part ownership in each man's company. In the midst of it all, he had missed Walt's comment concerning John. Walt noticed and felt he needed to mention it again.

"I don't be 'a meaning to pry, Robert, but what is going on with John? When I was in Bonifay yesterday, I heard talk the Holmes County grand jury has handed down an indictment of him. Any day now, a warrant will be issued for his arrest. Can this be true?"

Robert shook his head, indicating he knew nothing about the indictment. Walt took his leave, and Robert headed home to acquaint Judy with this current development. She was not there and according to Flora, she and Evelyn were in High Springs, carrying Jean to the cottage.

. . . . .

Robert found Judy and Evelyn visiting with Kate and Jean but Olivia was not with them. "Where is Olivia?" Before Judy could respond, Robert hurriedly told her of John's indictment. "You need to go to Bonifay with all due haste and learn of the details."

Judy nodded in agreement. She had not deluded herself that John would not be indicted; Jack Gunderson had delivered the goods sufficient for even a first year district attorney to connect the dots implicating John's involvement in the bribery scheme. It was only a matter of time before the shoe dropped. Yesterday was that day. They had a plan in place, now it was just a matter of executing it effectively.

On a brighter note, Robert told her of Walt's inside information on the WPA contracts and that the opportunity to make some loans at high interest rates would prevent him from leaving before the deals were done. He waited for her enthusiastic response, but she made none. He found her lack of interest unnatural; she was always interested in their accruing more money. Something was wrong.

"Mrs. Smith suffered a stroke earlier; Olivia is with her and does not want to leave her side."

Robert was shocked and concerned. Mrs. Henry Smith, a widow who had given Olivia, John, and the girls a place to stay in her housekeeper's quarters had meant a great deal to them.

At the time, Judy had embarked on a one-woman crusade to destroy Olivia, her unborn baby, or both. Mrs. Smith's offer to allow Olivia to move in with her had saved Olivia's life. It got her out of the Quarters at High Bluff and out from under Judy's thumb. Robert, more than anyone else, was grateful. He had been virtually powerless to rein in Judy without destroying his own family.

Now, Robert suggested Judy gather whatever Kate and Jean needed for the next few days. "I'll go and tell Olivia you and Evelyn will take the girls to High Bluff."

Judy and Evelyn did as he asked, and Robert walked over to Mrs. Smith's where he found Olivia sitting with her. He motioned for her to come into the hallway and offered to have Flora look after the girls at High Bluff for a few days. Olivia gratefully accepted.

"Mister Ward, she is not going to make it through the night. Even now she is having difficulty breathing, and just lies there, seldom opening her eyes. I pray that God will take her quickly although I don't know how I shall deal with losing her."

Robert tried to comfort her. "She needs your strength to help her complete her last journey. When you return to her bedside, she must not see your tears. She must see a farewell smile on the face of the daughter she never had."

Before Olivia returned to Mrs. Smith's bedside, Robert told her of

John's impending indictment. "Judy is going to Bonifay tomorrow and as soon as I conclude my business, I'll join John in Miami. Before I leave, I'll update you on any new information."

"What will happen now that John has been indicted? I know some may think it odd, but I care about him, and I know how much he stands to lose. Please tell him that regardless of the outcome, he has my unfailing support. If he is released and needs to return to High Springs, let him know he will always have a place here with his daughters."

Robert was floored. After all his wayward son had put Olivia through, including outright denying he had seduced her, and the rejection of her girls, Olivia still wanted what was best for John and was willing to shelter him from shame and harm. She was truly an amazing woman and her actions validated the assessment he had made of her character on that November night when she sat shivering in his study.

He told her Judy would go to Bonifay and wait for John's transfer there from Miami. Then she would attend his arraignment to find out if the judge would set bail. Only then would they know what their next move would be.

Olivia remembered her warnings to John at the time Robert made his proposal for him to work for Ward Enterprises. She recalled how flippantly his father dismissed her query as to the nature of the work John would be required to undertake. She considered what was in store for him and bemoaned John's unwillingness to consider the red flags she had recognized.

If he made bail, Robert suggested it would be unwise to bring John back to High Springs. "He must continue to operate the Flamingo Club until his trial gets underway. We simply cannot lose ground there." Robert turned to leave, telling Olivia to send Martha Cox to alert him if Mrs. Smith's condition worsened.

CHAPTER 20

The red Georgia clay seemed to float by as Walt hurried to Savannah in response to Amelia's urgent telegram advising him he should drop everything and present to her immediately. "What could it be this time?" he asked himself for the umpteenth time. "I swear that girl is going to be the death of her mother and me."

.....

Robert arrived in Miami where Judy's message was delivered to him by messenger as he departed The Whistler. It was clear: a warrant for John's arrest was forthcoming. Although he knew she would work every angle to stop it, it was obvious she could not. Their best bet was to find a way to delay the matter being placed on the court docket.

They had to proceed carefully at this juncture. Knowing that any whiff in the air of mob activity would draw intense scrutiny from law enforcement, he and Judy decided they had best keep their communications brief and code them in such a way that their plans would not tip off anyone following their movements. After shredding her cable, Robert wired her back.

"Stay and watch."

Judy understood the cryptic message perfectly; she was to remain in place and look for an opportunity to counter any actions taken by the sheriff or district attorney. She would meet with her man in Bonifay to get his report on the status there and then, if necessary, she would take what actions she could to ensure they got a favorable jury selection.

Meanwhile, several questions plagued Robert. Should they work to delay the trial to allow them additional time to manipulate the process, or should they exert pressure to have the trial scheduled quickly in hopes they had done enough to insure an acquittal? There was no clear-cut answer at this time. He decided to wait to hear Judy's assessment after meeting with her man in Bonifay.

Robert left the telegraph office and went straight to the Flamingo Club where he hurried up the stairs to the penthouse suite. There he found John sitting among a bevy of beer bottles. He had just learned of his impending arrest. After a brief exchange, Robert concluded John regarded his conviction a foregone conclusion and appeared to have lost all hope of maintaining his freedom. Robert's confidant told him of John's drinking and gambling, and the scene before him convinced Robert he could do nothing more to salvage a fool.

Robert lit into John and he spared no words as he denounced him and his behavior. He was determined to make John understand how his actions gave the DA more information to use against him at trial. His mere acting as if guilty would become a self-fulfilling prophesy.

He got a cold rag for John's forehead and as they sat together on the bed, he told him they needed to prepare for what would likely be an extended incarceration. They could not afford to have John's absence leave a void in the club thereby opening the door for anyone else to attempt another takeover.

.....

Olivia was heartbroken. On December 15th, Mrs. Smith passed away in the night. Olivia knew she could never repay Mrs. Smith for the innumerable acts of kindness toward Olivia and the girls which had made their lives much easier. For her part, Olivia had done what she could to keep Mrs. Smith company while sharing the joy she experienced with her girls to help offset the loneliness Mrs. Smith felt after the loss of her dear husband, Henry. Olivia would miss her friendship.

After a short wake and funeral, Mack Hardy, Mrs. Smith's attorney, contacted Olivia to acquaint her with the terms of Mrs. Smith's last will and testament. He confirmed she had willed everything to Olivia except a small sum specifically earmarked for repairs and upgrades to her house, some cash in her bank account, and a small amount to help with Kate's education. He told her Mrs. Smith had included a sketch of her vision of her remodeled home.

Upon questioning Mack, she discovered there were no provisions for Martha Cox. Without any resources and with no place to go, Olivia knew Martha would be worried sick. As soon as she returned home, she sought out Martha to assure her she had a home as long as she wanted to remain in her rooms there.

"Martha, I am not unmindful you have need for employment. While I am not prepared to divulge details just yet, I have a plan for our future. Because of Mrs. Smith's generosity, I am considering definite changes in my life. Once I get things sorted out with Mrs. Smith's estate, I plan on becoming a teacher and at that time I'll need someone to care for Kate and Jean. You can be that person, if you desire, so cease your worrying; we are both going to be just fine."

When Mrs. Smith had taken ill, Judy Ward made arrangements for the care of Kate and Jean which allowed Olivia to remain with her until she passed. Nearly every day, Judy had either Isaac or Joe go to High Springs and let Olivia know how the girls were faring. After the funeral, Olivia sought to immediately bring Kate and Jean home, but, Flora insisted they remain with her to allow Olivia time to handle Mrs. Smith's business. There was no way Flora could know what her offer meant to Olivia. Flora's care of the girls would provide the invaluable time she needed.

Meanwhile, Beth kept Olivia abreast of the increased deterioration of their mother's state of mind, and it was imperative Olivia find time to assess what might be the cause of her mother's increasing lassitude, her melancholy.

When Beth picked up Olivia and carried her to High Point, Olivia recognized immediately that something had to be done to reverse her mother's behavior. What she learned from Beth and Gussie was that Mama refused to leave her bed. Although Dr. James had visited her, he was unable to attribute her behavior to any aspect of her brain tumor. As he said, "Annie Turner has decided to withdraw from those around her." She was consciously severing communications with her daughters.

Dr. James had no suggestion as to any medical resolution for Annie. Rather, he opined that she needed to be forced to dress and interact with members of her family as often as possible, preferably, daily. He said that something was bothering her that she was unwilling to acknowledge or share with Walt or anyone else. Until that festering aspect of her life was identified and addressed, he could do nothing for her.

Beth took Olivia back to High Springs where she set about handling her pressing business. Her anxiety about her mother's condition would not abate, and she pondered how best to help her recover her interest in life which she appeared to have squashed. Hearing Dr. James' diagnosis convinced Olivia that her Mama needed constant companionship. But who could fill that void?

Beth was not an option. Although she would have forsaken almost anything to ensure her mother's care and happiness, she needed to report to her job at the cannery every day. The boys were all busy tending their farms and families and could not be expected to find the time. Ruth in Pennsylvania and Jerry in Louisiana were both too far away, and Ann was living with Amelia and Pearl in Savannah and could not return for the foreseeable future. And, despite his desire to spend every waking moment with his beloved Annie, Papa was away more and more with his involvement with his WPA contracts, the increased demand on lumber at the mill, and delivering his trotters and Angus bulls. Thus, it would fall to Olivia to find some way to break through her mother's barrier.

Over the past year, Papa had Annie's sitting room converted into a tiny bedroom so Florabell could be near Annie to attend to her throughout the night. The Turner children became concerned as they observed his worry and his corresponding loss of vitality. Beth sobbed as she told Olivia how Papa behaved now that he had ceased sleeping beside Mama. Despite going through the motions of running his business, he appeared to have lost his passion for the farm, the mill, and his horses and bulls. He was a lost cause and she could not reconcile how to help him overcome his own depression.

Walt was aware of his need to get on with his life, but try as he might, he was unable to accept the probability of a life without his Annie. No one could understand his anguish. When he was alone in the barn or in his study, his thoughts nearly drowned him with grief.

"I have cared for my Annie for months and slept by her side for all our married life. Now, my slightest movement in bed disturbs her and she is unable to return to sleep."

He could not dismiss the constant worry that plagued him. His Annie was leaving him and he could not imagine life on this earth without her. He thought, "If only God would take me with her."

· · · · ·

Beth came around Olivia's on Sunday after church and Olivia could tell she was worn out physically.

"Let me pack a bag and return with you to High Point. I can stay for the next couple of weeks and help with Mama and Gussie. Flora is taking care of Kate and Jean."

Beth agreed, and after Olivia gathered a few things, they left. As they neared High Point, Olivia suggested she wait until Beth checked on Mama before she went in to see her. Both understood it was a challenge for Mama to follow more than one conversation at a time. By visiting separately, they could lessen her stress.

While Beth visited with Mama, Olivia went to the kitchen and discovered a frustrated Gussie. The kitchen was a mess and nothing was in its place. There were dirty dishes stacked on the counter waiting to be taken out to the back porch to be washed and the staples delivered from Adkins' Mercantile were haphazardly piled near the door. Everything was disorganized and Olivia quickly recognized Gussie was worn out, just like Beth.

Although Gussie had proven to be invaluable to the Turners over the years, Annie's lingering illness had taken its toll on her and she had found herself in an inescapable morass of emotions for the last several weeks. The truth was she loved Annie dearly and she was struggling to cope with her illness and its finality. Fortunately, Olivia understood as much and stepped in to right the ship.

"Gussie, we can get this kitchen in order if we stop to organize the tasks. Although you have always gone above and beyond, running this house is a job for more than one person and we should have insisted on getting you some help long before now."

While Beth visited with Mama in her suite, Olivia sat down at the kitchen table and outlined the things that needed to be done to restore order to the household. In just a few minutes, she produced a detailed list and went over it with Gussie. Then she told her to get three more women from the quarters to help her.

"Lawdy, Miss Olivia, this here lists you done made out will hep me assign some of these here tasks out to those girls."

"Gussie, you have the right idea. Assign these tasks out to the girls and then you check in on them from time to time to make sure they are doing them. They can catch up the cooking, canning, washing, cleaning, and ironing while you focus on getting the house ready for Christmas."

.....

Upstairs in her room, Annie started to doze off so Beth left her to find Olivia, telling her to hurry up to see her while she was still awake.

"Be mindful of Mama's anxiety over Papa's continued absence. Most of her conversation centers on learning exactly when Papa will return. It is confusing to her not to see him and hear his voice regularly. Frankly it worries me thinking of how long he has been away. It is unlike Papa to miss even a day being with Mama."

Beth and Olivia were unable to understand why their father continued his stay in Georgia for so long. They could not fathom what was happening with Ann that required him to remain there when Beth had written him several times explaining her mother's deteriorating condition.

The deep love their parents shared was not lost on Beth or Olivia. They knew Papa would not miss a day with Mama were it not critical that he settle whatever issue their grandmother had with Ann. Papa had written several brief notes to Mama and Beth had read each one. She shared with Olivia their contents and said she had no clue what was taking him so long. But she had her suspicions.

"Is it possible Grandmother Amelia has decided to turn Ann out? We both know she is a handful. Surely Ann understands she will have to return to High Point if her behavior has caused our grandmother to abandon her."

"Beth, if Ann has acted the fool and cannot stay in Georgia any longer, she'll have no choice but to come back here. Papa and Mama exhausted all other options before sending her there and Grandmother would not have taken her in had Papa not agreed to pay her the outrageous sum she demanded."

"I had no idea Papa had to pay our own grandmother to look after Ann. I hope she has not worn out her welcome there. I am afraid of what will become of her if she does not right her wayward course."

"I am too, Beth. More than you can possibly imagine. I cannot help but feel Ann's fate is out of our hands. I can only pray for God's intervention, to fill her heart with joy and cause her to welcome His love as well as ours, her family."

CHAPTER 21

Walt listened impatiently as Amelia delivered a detailed account of the happenings since his last visit. He felt like he was listening to the same song and verse on the Victrola since earlier in the day when Pearl had rendered her own version of events. On its face, it appeared Ann was thriving in Savannah. She had many young men vying for her hand in courtship and she was the belle of the ball.

It was nearly Christmas and he longed to finish up his business here by getting to the bottom of why Amelia had sent such an urgent summons. But, despite his repeated attempts, he was unable to end their lengthy discourses. What he had learned was that Ann continued to manipulate others. According to Pearl, Ann had succeeded in wrapping Amelia around her little finger. Walt knew the feeling, for he too had succumbed to her wily charms on many an occasion. Pearl continued with her rant and all Walt could think of was wrapping this up quickly and returning to his beloved Annie.

"When in God's name would these women get around to telling him the purpose of his being here?" he thought. "Maybe it is time to take the bull by the horns."

He interrupted whatever it was Amelia was waxing on about and confronted her. "Amelia, you said it was urgent I come here. I have been here more than a week and you have yet to tell me a single reason. Why, in the name of Jehovah, have you brought me here?"

Amelia was affronted by Walt's apparent impatience. Certainly he wanted to hear the full story in order to understand the potential tragedy that was unfolding before them and how she and Pearl intended to squelch it. Amelia spoke in generalities which did not bring Walt any closer to the crux of the matter. Nearly at wits end, he cut to the chase.

"Pearl, if allowed, your mother will stretch this out for hours. Can you tell me in plain English what this supposed tragedy is? Until I know, I am unable to intervene and at this pace we will still be discussing it on my deathbed."

Pearl looked at her mother and then back at Walt. "Well, if you must know, Ann is determined to repeat the same mistake Annie made when she fell in love with you. She is determined to marry a 'nobody.' " Walt shook his head in mild disbelief. He had heard this story before and loathed hearing it repeated again. Still, if that's what it took to move things along, he was game.

She continued, "You see, Ann attended a ball honoring the engagement of the host couple's son who is affiliated with a prestigious law firm in Atlanta. There she met and took a liking to a young man named William Bryant who is a friend he knew from law school. Although William was a top graduate of his class, he now works in the Fulton County District Attorney's office in Atlanta." She paused for effect and gasped. "Imagine our mortification in hearing a person in such a lowly position should be invited to the ball."

He listened as Pearl continued her assignation of the young man.

"Walt, you understand what his situation means, don't you? It mattered not that he was at the top of his graduating class; without the right family connections, he had no offers from any of the prestigious law firms in Atlanta and now works in a glorified clerical position. Thus, he has nothing to offer our Ann."

Amelia let out a heavy sigh and fanned herself before she added her two-cents. "Honestly, Walt, I see her situation the same as

Annie's when she met you. Her father warned her more than once not to become hitched to a grade stallion like yourself, but the stubborn girl would have no one else but you. It is now up to you to prevent Ann from making the same horrible mistake. Think of her life being married to a struggling lawyer who comes from a working-class background and with no resources to provide for her in the manner to which she has become accustomed. I shudder to think of the outcome."

Amelia looked to Walt for his reaction. He maintained his stoic silence and Amelia continued. "Her reaction is ludicrous. When I remind her of the young man's lack of resources, she laughs while saying *you* will support her where he cannot. You asked why I summoned you here urgently? She is making plans to wed him within three months. You must intervene before she ruins her chances with another, more suitable, young man."

Walt listened as Amelia went on. She had always been kind to him, even while Michael had worked to convince Annie he was not suitable for her. He did not sense Amelia was deliberately being cruel in her comparison of him and William Bryant. Rather, he knew she used him as an example in trying to save Ann from a miserable life of her own doing.

"Does Ann love this young man? I mean truly? Is it possible Ann has met someone for whom she would forsake wealth and social standing to be his wife? Do you know if the young man loves her?"

Pearl grasped Walt's hand as she spoke. "Mama suggests she knows Ann's heart, but she doesn't. Daddy might have considered you a grade stallion, but for Annie there was only one horse in the barn and it was you. Over the years, one thing I have learned is that my sister loved you then, and now, more than anything else. Since the day you loaded her and her belongings on that wagon and took her from us, she has never regretted her decision and has been content in the life you have built together. She had the courage to choose you over other well-heeled suitors. Ann is not her mother! She has a selfish streak and, unlike Annie, she will come to resent her choice."

Walt wanted to hug Pearl. "In other words, it's your opinion Ann's feelings are not of a depth sufficient to sustain her marriage to this young man. Is this what you are saying?"

Pearl nodded, relieved that Walt understood. Although it was difficult to betray her niece's plans, she owed this to Annie.

CHAPTER 22

Walt knew what action he must take but, before he confronted Ann, he intended to learn more about William Bryant and how determined he was to have Ann as his wife. Had the young man fallen hard for Ann's charms or was he susceptible to being swayed from her? With the upcoming Christmas galas to which Ann and William were invited, Walt knew he would have the opportunity to observe William firsthand and form his own conclusions.

There was, however, a more immediate problem. Since he was unaware of his need to attend the formal galas, Walt did not have suitable attire for the events. Although he was known to be frugal, Walt could not resist the opportunity to show Amelia and those in her social circles how far he had come up in the world. He had first appeared in these parts as a lowly horse trader. Now he came as a wealthy Southern gentleman.

"To hell with it, he thought. It may be extravagant to invest in clothing I already have, but some of these people attending these shindigs are the ones who once looked upon me as the grade stallion Annie married. Well, by damn, let's see how they react when we meet again and I'm outfitted in duds from the best haberdashery in Savannah."

.....

The next day, standing erect as the tailor measured his inseam for trousers, Walt thought about what he had to do. He was concerned with William, but at the same time Walt wondered if Ann had misjudged him. Did she understand he was no longer susceptible to her wiles? That time had passed when she displayed her detestable attitude on the day Jean was born. While her sister's and niece's lives hung in the balance, Ann had had the audacity to wish them dead. That was the straw to break the proverbial camel's back with him and was what spurred him to agree to send Ann off to live here with Amelia.

Now, he seemed to be caught up in her wake again and it angered him as he thought of how he would approach her. "It will not be difficult to express to her how it infuriates me to be summoned here to deal with her petty problems when I have such a need and yearning to be at home with Annie."

. . . . .

The time was upon them for the first social event of the holiday season and Walt looked dapper in his new clothes. At the first gala, he watched as Ann mesmerized those in attendance with her grace and beauty. Walt watched and reminded himself to share with Annie how their youngest daughter had blossomed into a reigning queen. He smiled as he thought of the joy and pride Annie would experience when she learned all of her efforts in refining Ann had not been wasted.

Satisfied with Ann's acceptance within the elite social circle, Walt turned his attention to William. As he watched, Walt could see how William was accepted by all in attendance and he came to the conclusion that the young man understood his worth and relied on no one to define it for him. "Certainly," he thought. "Ann would be fortunate to be married to such a man."

After three consecutive evenings of parties, Walt was confident he had gathered the information he needed. Although William was not employed in a glamorous position, Walt was convinced he was a hard worker who would climb the corporate ladder in his own time. So much about William reminded him of himself. Just like him, William regarded no man to be superior to him simply because of birth and family standing. Walt could tell William knew what he wanted and had definite plans to achieve his goals.

"This young man would take a backseat to no one and would be a worthy person to have as a son-in-law," he thought. But, when it came to marrying Ann, Walt clearly saw there was a hitch to William's achieving his goals.

Considering his own history, Walt recognized an undeniable fact: he would not be the successful man he was today were it not for Annie's encouragement, and most important, her patience. Ann possessed neither of these traits, and as soon as their honeymoon ended, the reality of her life without the wherewithal to maintain her accustomed social life would end her patience. Without a doubt Walt knew William Bryant would be miserable married to his daughter. Therefore, if she would not forego marriage to William, he would take another tack.

. . . . .

A light snow fell from the grey skies during the night and on Sunday morning, just before Christmas 1935, and the McGee home was aflutter with activity. All would attend church services and afterward, Amelia, along with Pearl and Ann, would host a luncheon. William Bryant wasn't invited but planned to pick up Ann afterward for an afternoon outing before returning to Atlanta.

Walt thought about how he would approach Ann to tell her he would not support William's courtship. "She'll suffer a brief moment of unhappiness, not because she will not have William as her husband, but because she'll not have her society wedding." He knew Ann would not be heartbroken; to be so inclined, she had to have a heart, and that she did not have.

Walt was waiting for Ann when she arrived in the foyer ready for church. "I know you'll be busy helping Amelia with the luncheon; however, when you are free, meet me in your grandfather's study. I want to talk to you"

Ann peered at her father with a questioning look. "Papa, have I done something wrong?"

Walt assured her she had not. "I plan to leave early tomorrow morning, and I thought this afternoon would be a good time for us to have a talk about your association with William."

"But Papa," she pouted. "William is calling on me after lunch and we want to take a carriage ride before he returns to Atlanta."

Walt responded in a manner she could not ignore. "Ann, you are to spend no more than an hour with him and then send him on his way. I'll be in the study waiting for you."

Ann moved to go past him and then turned with a flounce of her head and challenged him. "Papa, you do realize I am 26 years old. I am no longer under your thumb or subject to your whims. I'll spend whatever time I choose with William. Then, if you insist, I'll join you. Now, if you'll let me pass it is time we left for church."

Her rebuttal was an unexpected one and Walt soaked it in while thinking, "So, Ann reminds me she is a grown woman and is no longer under my thumb. I wonder what her attitude will be once she understands being independent means forgoing my financial support. I wonder how she plans to finance her independence."

As Ann and Pearl walked ahead to the car to leave for church, Walt and Amelia paused on the walkway. He advised her he was leaving the following morning and Amelia asked if he would handle the matter they discussed before leaving.

"I'll take care of the matter when Ann and I meet later today."

CHAPTER 23

William understood the intent of Amelia McGee's excluding him from the guest list for the luncheon. He simply wasn't welcome. But considering he was the houseguest of friends who were invited, he wanted to avoid any awkward situation created by her breach of good manners; and so he determined to ensure his arrival to coincide with the time the luncheon guests would have all departed.

He watched from across the park until he determined it was safe. Then he walked to the McGee house and prepared to pop the question he had been debating for the past few weeks.

Pearl answered the door and asked him to wait in the parlor while she advised Ann of his arrival. As he passed the study, he noticed Ann's father, Walt. Thinking how fortuitous it was to find him there, he pivoted and approached him with his hand extended. Walt stood and retuned the handshake. "So far, so good," William thought. Now it was time to state his business. He intended to ask her father's permission to marry Ann before he popped the question.

"Excuse me, sir, I don't mean to intrude, but may I have a word with you before Ann comes down? I'm sure you know you can depend on waiting for at least a half hour before she will appear."

"You're not disturbing me," Walt answered cordially. "In fact, I was sitting here remembering the times I sat in this room with Ann's grandfather, Michael, and enjoyed his company. To this very day I miss him. Some would think it strange, considering how strongly he objected to my request for Annie's hand." Walt paused as he reflected on the moment before he continued.

"You would not know how he insisted that a grade stallion like me had no business considering his thoroughbred daughter for his mate. In spite of his objections to our courtship, he considered me his friend, as I did him. We shared many a cigar and Brandy and indulged in swapping some Scottish tales in this room. Even after all these years since his passing, I think of him. The two of us being Scots, we were pretty well matched in our stubbornness and determination to prevail in an argument. You won't believe it but we nearly came to blows inside the barn you passed as you turned into the farm."

William listened, without interrupting and certainly hoped Walt wasn't considering duking it out over his daughter.

"Michael used all of his power of persuasion to prevent Annie from marrying me. But in the end, she convinced him of her love for me, and he agreed. It was a happy time for me but perhaps a sad one for Annie because Michael and Amelia would not agree to provide for her the wedding she must have dreamed about all of her life."

"How did your wife, Annie, react to her father's withdrawal of financial support? Were you put out by his pressure on her?"

Walt continued as his voice cracked. "We were both hurt, but Annie was especially so to think her father had failed to recognize that her love for me could not be thwarted. We discussed his behavior, and I helped Annie understand this was her father's way of impressing upon her how little I had to offer. Michael would never understand it, but the feelings in her heart were a greater treasure than the trappings of the lifestyle she had grown up with. There was nothing more precious to her than becoming my wife. So it was that Annie and I were married in a simple ceremony in the parlor of this house. I can't tell you the happiness that woman has brought to me, and I can only wish you may find such happiness."

William stood near the desk and did not follow as Walt paced about the room pensively. He asked if Walt had been thinking of his wife before William had interrupted him.

"Yes, I was thinking about her when you came in. Every day I think of her, wondering how her day has been. You may not know how ill my Annie is. Thus, every day I remain here is a day I am unable to share with her. After talking to Ann this evening, I'll be setting out for home tomorrow."

Over the past few weeks of Walt's visit, William's interactions with him had been brief. However, he would never have suspected how gentle a man Walt was, or that he was capable of the deep love for his wife he had disclosed. He had but one thought. "I hope Ann and I may experience the love her mother and father appear to have shared."

The sound of Ann's heels clicking on the smooth boards of the circular stairway echoed throughout the foyer and into the study. William moved toward the doorway to alert her to his whereabouts, but before he went to meet her, he turned to Walt.

"Thank you, sir. I hope to be able to speak with you again before I leave for Atlanta this afternoon. Would you have the time to spare?" Walt acquiesced, knowing the purpose of William's request.

·····

Ann appeared at the base of the stairs causing William to gasp at her beauty. She wore a blue velvet dress with long pointed sleeves and a stand-up collar which highlighted the curls framing her face. William thought how tiny she was. Even wearing high heels, she did not come up to his shoulder. Without a thought he bent and placed a tender kiss on her cheek. She looked at him in surprise. He had never before taken such liberty with her.

"Ann, forgive me if I was too forward. Watching you float down the stairs much like I imagine a fairy and I was overcome with my desire to kiss the woman I plan to marry. Do you really object?" He stood watching the emotions play across her face. Surprise was one of them, but coy satisfaction seemed the more prominent one.

"Did you say you plan to marry me? Don't you think you should ask a person first before you pounce upon them with a small sample of your adoration?"

William considered her response. Was she issuing a challenge by suggesting his kiss was not forceful enough? He was surprised and thought, "Well, I'll be damned, but she is a saucy one." He regained his composure and asked if she were belittling his kiss.

Ann stood looking up at him and before she could respond, he continued, "Do you want to reconsider your description or do I need to do a better job of it? Think carefully and know I am primed to act. And, while you are considering your answer, determine how you'll respond to this one. Ann Turner...," William paused to gather his courage. "Will you be my wife?"

As Ann replayed his words in her mind, she realized she stood at a crossroads in her life. She appreciated the consequences her decision would bring and as she weighed them, she was assailed with questions from within:

"Why did she prefer William, who had so little to offer, over others who were well-positioned and had family backing to ensure their place in society? Why was it she was attracted to William's determination which was much like Papa's when he ignored the odds and pushed his way through to achieve his goals?"

She did not have answers to her questions, but that did not stymie her desire to become William's wife. After all, their biggest issue for the immediate future would be money and she knew she could always count on Papa's continued financial support to allow their continued forays in the right social circles. Confident in her decision, Ann responded, "Yes, William. I will marry you."

William clutched her hands and pulled her tight against his chest. "Earlier, I gave you a small kiss, but now you are about to get a big one." He bent down and placed his lips upon hers. Then, for the first time since he had known her, he forced his tongue inside her mouth to experience the delights of this woman who was soon to become his wife.

Ann could not get her breath as her body tensed and her neck flushed from the fierce feelings his kiss generated. Then, looking up at him she meekly uttered, "Golly, gee, I am afraid to move with my knees trembling so. If this is how your big kisses are going to affect me, I think we had better plan on a short engagement."

Ann's response was everything he had hoped for and he beamed with pride at the effect his kiss had had on her. But knowing Walt was waiting for them in the study, William sobered quickly and ushered her in that direction on his arm. As they walked, he whispered, "I asked to speak to him to request permission to marry you, but now it seems I have put the cart before the horse. Do you think he will be angry?"

She smiled at William's hesitancy. This behavior was so uncharacteristic of him. Usually, he was one inclined to forge ahead, letting nothing impede his progress. Now he was doting on her as her father always had.

"Are you afraid to face Papa alone? Never mind, I know you are not; however, we'll go in together because there are matters we need to discuss with him. We need to be assured of his financial support for us before we can proceed with our plans."

CHAPTER 24

Arm in arm, the couple entered the study where Walt waited. He was not surprised they were together, although he had hoped to speak to William alone. The adoring looks passing between them did not escape him, and he wondered if he had misjudged his daughter. For William's sake, he hoped so.

"Young man, you indicated you wanted to speak to me. What can I do for you?"

William shifted nervously while considering how to respond now that he had committed the faux pas of asking Ann for her hand before receiving her father's permission. He placed Ann's arm by her side and left her behind as he approach Walt who was standing near the fireplace. Sheepishly, he began.

"Sir, I had every intention of asking your permission to have Ann's hand in marriage. But…, it seems I have not been disciplined enough to wait to make such a request. Why the mere sight of your beautiful Ann descending the stairs caused me to lose my good manners…, and some might say good sense, and spurred me to blurt out my question without thinking. I know it is hard to understand, sir, but in that moment, I knew I must have her as my wife."

Walt noticed William turning red from his forehead to his neck and he understood how awkward it was for him. For a moment, he was taken back to the first time be saw Annie mounted on her horse and had felt the same emotions. He could hardly blame the boy. He suggested they sit down. They all exchanged glances but dead silence ensued. After a few awkward moments, Ann spoke first.

163

"Papa, I want to marry William, but it seems the cat has got his tongue and he can't talk."

William quickly interjected. "Mr. Turner, I humbly ask your permission to wed your daughter."

"Young man, before I give you my permission, you must assure me you are prepared to provide a good life for Ann. Where will you both live, and what are your plans to provide for her? Have you thought about the cost of Ann's upkeep? Let me hear your answers."

"I reside in a furnished two-bedroom, walk-up apartment near the municipal building in downtown Atlanta where I live rent free in exchange for maintaining the other apartments and attending to the building's central furnace." He had not considered Ann's upkeep so he needed some clarification on Walt's comment. "Sir, I don't exactly understand what you mean by 'maintaining' her."

Walt hid a grin. As he suspected, William had not considered anything more than the bare essentials of marriage. Ann, however, required more.

"By maintaining her I refer to how you plan to provide her wardrobe and the accessories she requires for her social obligations throughout the year. More specifically, how do you plan to pay for her ball gowns, slippers, clutches, jewelry and furs?"

Silence ensued and Walt could tell William was baffled. Still, there were other issues William needed to consider.

"Will you have a cook, laundry girl, and maid? I ask this because Ann, at her age she has never cooked a meal, shopped for groceries, or washed and ironed a load of clothes. You are asking my permission to marry someone who is either incapable of or is too lazy to do these chores. Are you truly asking my permission to marry so inept a person?

Ann was flabbergasted. "Papa, you make me sound so terrible. Of course William's civil service job does not pay enough to cover all these things. You know we can't live where he currently resides. It is surrounded by government buildings and is inhabited by immigrants and transients; we could never entertain anyone in such base surroundings. Why, I can't even imagine any of my friends visiting that part of Atlanta, much less living there. You'll provide for me as you do now. Won't you?" Ann looked at her father expectantly.

Before her father could respond, William interceded. "Mr. Turner, I have not had any conversation with Ann to suggest I would expect or accept any financial support from you. I am the son of a working-class mother and father who reared me in a God-fearing home. My mother worked as a school teacher to earn money for my college and law school tuition and my father owns an automobile repair shop from whence he has provided for his family without any help from anyone. You need to understand sir, as does Ann, I count myself equal to any other man and rely upon my intellect and personal drive to succeed."

As he continued, William's eyes turned to Ann. "It may be a few years before I achieve all I plan to accomplish, but I am confident with Ann content and by my side I'll achieve my goals. My only requisite is that we must forego some frivolous things we cannot afford such as having a cook and maid, attending parties, and entertaining. I am confident Ann will learn to manage these tasks."

Having said his peace, William turned and looked to Ann for her to confirm her commitment to him and the life he could provide. He needed to hear she was prepared to sacrifice to have his love and devotion. He wanted her to speak from her heart and state unequivocally that becoming his wife was everything she desired for her future. He waited but Ann remained silent with her eyes cast downward.

"Surely Papa will set William straight any moment now," she

thought.

Walt broke the silence. "I understand your commitment, William, but I am unsure of Ann's. Before either of you say more, I need to share with you both what I had planned to tell her earlier."

Turning to face Ann, Walt continued. "This morning you told me you are and adult and no longer under my thumb. I understood this to mean you no longer require my support. Although your declaration of independence caught me off balance, I agree with you. The time has come for you to make your own way. Over the past two years, your grandmother has agreed to have you live with her and Pearl in exchange for a substantial monthly payment. Tomorrow, I'll tell her I have made my last payment on your behalf. While I have no crystal ball to foretell your grandmother's reaction, I will wager that when she learns of my decision, she will no longer agree to have you stay here. Without my payments, they barely eke out a living. So, depending upon what she says, you need to decide where you will live. You may stay here in Savannah and get a job to pay your own way or you may return home with your mother and me. A place at High Point is always an option for you provided you agree to abide by my rules."

Ann was nearly speechless. "Papa..., you... can't mean what you say. You know I have no way to survive without your support."

In his heart, Walt felt vindicated as it gave him an opening to bring home all the mean and hateful things she had said and done to Olivia over the years.

"Ann, you have only to look at your sister, Olivia, to find an example of how an independent woman supports herself. You are better equipped than she was at the time she found herself alone and abandoned by all of us. You have a college education and are qualified to make something of yourself as a nurse or as a teacher as is your sister, Ruth. With your charm and the contacts you have made, you shouldn't have any difficulty obtaining a position here in Savannah. While the pay will not be enough to sustain your frivolous lifestyle, it is enough to allow you to live better than Olivia who lived in a shack in the Ward's Quarters. Consider what I have said as you determine if you want to go it alone here in Savannah or at High Point, or become William's wife on his terms. Either way, my financial support for you has ended."

MCMURTRY

CHAPTER 25

Walt put his hand on William's shoulder and squeezed it. "Young man, with all you now know, does your proposal still stand? Ann's maintenance is a heavy burden to carry and one you may decline to assume. There is no dishonor in withdrawing your proposal. What say ye?"

William did not waiver as he smiled at Ann and declared his love for her while reaffirming his commitment to have her as his wife. Seeing how completely William laid open his heart to Ann, Walt knew too well she did not deserve a man like him. In his estimation, Ann did not have the capacity to love anyone but herself and it saddened him to know she would eventually break this fine young man's heart. He would suffer immeasurably because of his loyalty to her.

Ann reached for William's hand as she addressed him. Papa had given her only one choice despite his suggestions to the contrary.

"William, Papa has made certain you know all of my faults and shortcomings, but if you still want me as your wife, then let us decide on the date now so we can get you on your way to Atlanta."

"Of course I want you to be my wife and you must never doubt that. I know you want a big wedding and you certainly deserve one, but given what your father has just told us regarding his financial support, please consider my situation and let's settle for a small one right after the New Year with just our families as guests. If the truth be known, neither of us can afford anything more than that at this time. And, considering your mother's ill health, I do not feel it would be prudent for us to impose on her to plan and organize a big affair. Does this sound reasonable to you?"

Before she could answer, Walt interrupted. "I agree with William's sensible approach to your wedding. You can have an intimate ceremony at High Point. Your grandmother and Aunt Pearl can stage a reception for you here in Savannah upon your return from your honeymoon. Ann, your mother will be delighted. She never had the privilege of planning a wedding for any of her daughters because both Ruth and Olivia had civil ceremonies and Beth remains unmarried. I want you both to know your mother and I intend to write William a check for whatever such a wedding would cost. This will be mine and Annie's wedding present to you both."

William could not thank Walt enough as he beamed at Ann who was still taking in what had just transpired.

In the past year, Amelia had planned weddings for daughters of two ladies in her social circle so Walt knew he could rely on her to help him establish a budget. As he set out to find her, Walt had two concerns on his mind. First, he wanted to spare no haste in returning home to be with his Annie. Second, he needed to figure out how to come up with whatever sum Amelia advised him would be needed to cover a large wedding and reception.

"You two lovebirds revel in your moment of happiness. I'll seek out your grandmother and Aunt Pearl to let them know of your impending nuptials. I'm *sure* they will share in your excitement."

The last statement was a lie and Walt knew it. Amelia's objection to William's courtship of Ann was so strong she had summoned Walt to break it up. But despite his brutally honest assessments to the contrary, the pair had made their choice and Walt realized wild horses could not keep them apart.

Amelia and Pearl were waiting in the kitchen for Walt to

conclude his talk with William and Ann. As he entered, Amelia could tell by his smug expression he had accomplished what he had set about to do.

"Walt, you were in the study with Ann and William for some time. Were you able to send him on his way without too much drama? As I told Pearl, he is a nice young man, and it is a pity he doesn't come from an acceptable background. Tell us. What did he have to say for himself?"

"This is not going to go over well," he thought. "But here goes, anyway. Walt held chairs for Amelia and Pearl and pulled up another for himself and sat.

"What was I doing in the study with William and Ann for so long? I was listening to an intelligent young man who is too good for my unworthy daughter. That is what I have been doing." He considered how to shift the conversation to the cost of a wedding but he could not continue as Amelia stood up with her arms akimbo and demanded that he clarify his remarks.

"Have you both forgotten why Ann has been living with you for the past several years? True, you have kept her to a straight and narrow pathway. She is respected and sought after by many suitors, but nothing has changed in her. She still remains the spoiled brat I brought to you. She wants to have her cake and to eat it, too."

Amelia and Pearl stared at Walt but did not understand his assertions. Pearl challenged him. "Did you or did you not make Ann understand she cannot consider William as a husband?"

At that point, Ann and William entered the room arm in arm and greeted them. "Papa, did you tell grandmother and Aunt Pearl of our wedding plans?"

She dropped William's arm and turned to Amelia, throwing her arms around her and hugging her. "Before William leaves, I wanted you both to hear our news. We will be married at High Point on the third week in January. It will be a short time to plan a wedding and reception. Do you think you can manage?"

She slowed down to accept what she expected to be congratulations to William and a wish for her happiness, but neither was forthcoming. Rather, an expression of incredulity flashed across Amelia and Pearl's faces. For a moment, it appeared neither was able to speak. Walt broke the silence.

"Ann, you and William came in before I had an opportunity to share the good news with your grandmother and aunt. I'll fill them in while you see William off. I know he has a big day in court tomorrow and needs to be on his way." Walt hurriedly shook William's hand and guided him towards the door as he wished him a safe journey.

As soon as they were out of hearing range, Walt shared his proposed plans for Ann's wedding and the part he would ask them to play in giving a reception.

"Amelia, don't harbor any regrets with the outcome of this afternoon's discussions. Ann really had no choice considering the options I gave her. Am I wrong in suggesting to her you would be unwilling to have her continue living with you and Pearl without benefit of my financial support?"

Her answer was clear. "Why, Walt, you understand our financial situation. There is no way we could stretch our meager funds to support Ann without your generous contribution each month. So, no. I am not prepared to have her stay here without your continued support. That is my answer. But, what do you mean she has no better option than to marry a man such as William?"

Walt repeated the options he had given Ann and he could tell that neither failed to understand Ann's situation. She could not go back to High Springs with the baggage she left there, and she certainly did not plan to get a job and support herself. Resigned to the outcome Walt had outlined, Amelia agreed to honor her granddaughter.

"Pearl and I will get busy planning a reception that will be regarded as the outstanding social event of our town. You did indicate that we could plan the event with a generous budget, didn't you?"

"Yes," Walt responded. "And to minimize any inconvenience for you and Pearl, and William's parents, Annie and I will foot the bill for your travel by train to and from the wedding. Also, there will be plenty of room for you all at High Point so you won't have to stay in the hotel."

"Gracious me, Pearl, we can't waste any time. Before we can turn around we'll be opening our home for Ann and William's reception. There will be some sad young men who had high hopes of making Ann their bride. Oh, well, let's hope she is prepared to lie in the bed she has chosen."

Admitting defeat with her snarky volley, Amelia resigned herself to planning the most elegant party she could muster. "We will have champagne and wine," she thought. "Nothing makes a poor decision more palatable than champagne; and for this one, we will need lots."

Shortly, Ann returned to let them know William was on his way back to Atlanta and he could not be happier. "Papa, you said you were leaving in the morning. Should I return with you to help Mama with my wedding plans?"

Walt thought carefully, and realizing Ann was best managed by Amelia from afar, he responded, "No, Dear, there is much for you to do here helping your grandmother plan your reception. It is best you wait and come via train the week before the wedding with your aunt and grandmother."

CHAPTER 26

Although he and Annie were far from destitute, the downturn in the economy had adversely impacted Walt's businesses, and he needed to keep a focused eye on their bottom line. He and Annie would put on a small, intimate wedding for the couple at High Point; and in lieu of the high society wedding they would have had in Savannah, Walt had made a commitment to William to write him a check in an amount of the cost of such an affair. That would be their wedding gift from Annie and him. He had also pledged he would pay Amelia the cost of the reception separately. He prided himself on being a man of his word, and he was determined not to go back on either of those promises.

Before he returned to Alabama, Walt sat with Amelia to work out an estimate. Within a few minutes, she handed him a paper with the figures he needed. Altogether, the wedding would likely cost two thousand dollars and the reception around four hundred dollars more.

He schooled his features not to register his alarm in front of Amelia. "How am I to come up with these sums in such a short time?" he asked himself. Then he remembered several pieces of jewelry he had given Annie which she had never worn. Provided she was willing to part with these, they would account for a sizable chunk of the anticipated debt. Upon his return, he would carry them to Montgomery where he could get the best price for each. He would make up the difference by selling one of his prized Angus bulls.

Early the next morning, Walt and Amelia ironed out the reception details and a schedule for her travel to High Point with Ann and Pearl. Satisfied that nearly every facet was covered, Walt prepared to leave. As they walked to his truck, she plagued him with her concern that Ann would not have a proper wedding dress. Walt assured her Olivia would design and make Ann's dress and bake her wedding cake. He left Amelia with enough cash to cover initial costs of the reception and he promised to have the balance available when she arrived for the wedding.

·····

With the exception of stopping for gas, Walt drove straight through from Savannah. It was late in the evening when he arrived at High Point and, from the looks of the darkened house, he assumed everyone was in bed and was careful not to awaken anyone as he entered. From the darkness, Olivia addressed him.

"Papa, I heard the truck as you drove up the hill. I know you've had a long drive and must be tired and hungry. What can I fix for you before you go to bed?"

Walt thanked her and asked only for a glass of milk which she poured for him and deposited on the kitchen table. As he took a long draw from the glass, he asked about Annie. Olivia shared with him what had happened at High Point these past weeks, and how her mother remained the same health-wise, but was now listless and not interested in what was going on around her.

"Papa, it is difficult to coax her out of bed. I hope your return will breathe some new life into her. She adores you so."

Walt drained the last of the milk and wiped his chin on his sleeve as Olivia returned from the cupboard with a stack of envelopes which she handed to him. "These are checks that have come in your absence."

Although he was bone tired, the sight of envelopes he knew

contained payments for substantial lumber deliveries brought a sigh of relief and a smile to his face.

"Aye, the Lord has answered our prayers. These could not have come at a better time. Now, tell me more about your mother. Do you think she is up to hearing news of Ann's upcoming wedding?"

Olivia hesitated as she searched for the right words to prepare Papa before she answered.

"Papa, you will find out in the morning when you see her, so I feel I need to warn you now that she remains in bed most days and has no appetite. The medicine Dr. James has prescribed appears to control her pain, but it is my opinion a major cause of Mama's decline is your absence. She has longed for your return and it seems you are her only joy and her best medicine."

"Are you certain what you say is true? Have you been here all the time since I left? Are your girls here with you also?

Olivia started to answer and then stopped, realizing what she thought she heard Papa say. "Ann is getting married? When and to whom?"

Due to the lateness of the hour, Papa gave her short answers to abate her curiosity while promising to fill her in on the details in the morning when he told Annie and Beth. He said he would tell the boys when he got around to it during the next week.

Although Ann had been away nearly two years, Olivia was nonetheless surprised that she had become engaged to be married without so much as a peep from Ann or Amelia. Remembering his unanswered question, Olivia confirmed that she had remained at High Point with her mother, and Flora had been taking care of Kate and Jean at High Bluff.

Walt listened and admired Olivia's forgiving nature. He had

wronged her so grievously as a young girl, yet here she was caring for her mother. In addition, from what he could see, she had spent considerable time over the past few weeks helping Gussie run High Point. Walt said as much and thanked her for ensuring the household was in order, thus eliminating any unnecessary stress for her mother.

"You are welcome, Papa," Olivia said in a serious tone. "Now that you are home, I plan to pick up the girls from Flora and return with them to High Springs. Since you mentioned it, there is a matter I would like to discuss with you before I leave."

Olivia pulled up a chair across from him at the table and Walt looked at her while wondering what was causing her such consternation. He did not have to wait long.

"Papa, Gussie is incapable of handling all the chores you have given her. When I arrived here to help out, I found so many things were left undone and I have now arranged for the help she needs. As a result, everything is working smoothly now. From now on, with Beth's help, I think I can watch over the women I brought in to do the washing, ironing and cleaning. Gussie can concentrate on the cooking which has always been her strong suit. You will not have to worry about this; that is, if you find the arrangement satisfactory to you."

A smile crossed Walt's face. "Olivia, what would we all do without you? Nothing has been the same here since I acted in such unjustified anger and sent you away from your home so many years ago. It has been a long time coming, but now I ask your forgiveness."

Olivia recognized Papa's sincere apology but she dismissed it, having long ago forgiven him for reacting so harshly to her deplorable situation. If nothing else, being cast out of her home had brought her closer to God as she drew comfort and guidance from His word. If Christ could forgive a world of sinners, she certainly could forgive her father.

Walt continued to talk until he got all he wanted to say off his chest. Then, he responded to her question. "Whatever you have worked out I have no doubt it is the best way for us to handle things. Tell Gussie I approve and that I want her to continue as you have arranged things. However, I'll appreciate it if you can look into how things are going from time to time. Beth, bless her heart, is willing but just not able to manage as you do. Now, I am tired, and need to get to bed, but before I do I need to tell you a little more about Ann."

While Olivia did not wish her sister any ill will, she really did not care to hear about whatever Ann had done this time to cause Papa to leave Mama for weeks. Papa succinctly explained Ann's blossoming in the social scene in Savannah and her courtship and engagement to William over Amelia's objections.

Then he pointed to the date on the calendar on the wall and asked Olivia if she would handle the details of the wedding and make Ann's wedding dress and cake. Olivia's response was straight forward, "Do I have a choice?"

They agreed she did not. But that was a discussion for another day.

CHAPTER 27

The next morning, Olivia awoke early and met Gussie in the kitchen to see about breakfast. Papa had a lot to share with the family today and she wanted to ensure they all got off on the right foot. Soon, Papa emerged from his room and sat down with Olivia at the table.

"I didn't get a chance to ask about John last night. When have you heard from him? I suppose he and his parents are in Tallahassee for their annual Christmas and New Year's Eve parties. A little over a month ago when I was in Bonifay I heard John was to be indicted on charges of bribing government officials. I relayed this information to Robert, and he indicated Judy would go to Bonifay."

"Just as you thought, they left High Springs the day after you left for Georgia. Judy went to Bonifay to learn firsthand what was happening, and Robert was on his way to Miami. Yesterday, Flora told me the Wards intended to be in Tallahassee during the holidays and John was supposed to be with them. That is all I know."

Walt asked if John's sister would be with them in Tallahassee.

"I plan to take Evelyn home with me to celebrate Christmas. I am determined she will not be alone as she has been most years. She'll come with us to High Point on Christmas Day 1935. Papa, can you imagine she will celebrate her twelfth birthday on January 2nd without any of her family? It breaks my heart."

Walt turned and put his arms around Olivia, hugging her as he declared, "Lord, but you were born with a tender heart. There is no doubt you will find a way to make her birthday a special occasion, and it appears to me Evelyn would rather be with you and the girls than with her parents. So, don't fret and make an issue of it. About Christmas, though, do you think the Wards arranged for any presents for her before they left?"

Olivia assured him they had. With that, Olivia went to Beth's room to rouse her and tell her about Ann getting married. Her thoughts were of the tasks facing her. "I must begin planning for Ann's wedding dress and cake, but first I have to take care of the business with Mack Hardy.

Walt had risen early to ask Annie's permission to sell a few pieces of her jewelry. Thus far he had not burdened her with their financial situation. With the added expenses of Ann's forthcoming wedding and his need to make good on his promise to William and her as to their wedding gift, he had no alternative. He would have to offer her some explanation for his need. He had no anxiety concerning her agreement because he knew she would insist that he sell whatever pieces he needed. Rather, he dreaded having her learn of how they had come to this point; he dreaded telling her of Amelia's demands that he continued to meet.

Annie's response was as he expected. "Walt, here are some nice pieces, all of which should bring a fair price. Take them for we both know it will not be long before I'll have no further need of them."

By the time Beth and Olivia came in to check on their mother, Walt was telling Annie of his plan to take the pieces to Montgomery where he would get the best price for each.

Papa hugged each of his daughters and kissed them on their cheeks before leaving. Then, Olivia handed Mama the sketch of Ann's wedding dress she had completed after hearing of the upcoming event. Mama was pleased with it and asked about the material she intended to use.

"I think Ann will look beautiful as a winter bride dressed in white satin velvet with an exquisite veil made of Venetian lace. I am afraid, though, I'll not be able to get the material and lace in High Springs."

Walt suggested Olivia write out specific descriptions of the material lace; he would look for the items while he was in Montgomery. After Olivia gave him her list, he sat beside Annie and told them about the situation with Ann in Georgia.

He assured them Ann's bad behavior was not the cause of Amelia's frantic summons. He laughed as he explained the irony of Ann's decision to marry what Pearl and Amelia referred to as a grade stallion. Walt and Annie chuckled as they considered the parallel of hers and Ann's choice of husbands.

She was concerned that William Bryant, as Walt had described him, was not someone Ann would be content to have as a husband for very long. However, when Walt continued telling of William's character and his deep love for their Ann, she felt relieved.

When Papa finished telling about Ann and her upcoming wedding, Beth pointed out there were several hours before she had to leave for work. "Olivia and I will move to the kitchen and go over some plans for the wedding."

Before joining Beth, Olivia relieved Mama's anxiety about the Christmas meal and plans to decorate the house. She outlined all Gussie and her helpers intended to accomplish and how she and Beth would handle serving their noon meal so those in the Quarters could enjoy their celebration.

"Remember, I leave with Beth this morning and will not return until she comes for the girls along with Evelyn and me early on Christmas morning." Olivia asked Papa if he approved of her arrangements.

"Annie, this daughter of yours has a heart so big that, if she could, she'd feed everyone in the Quarters. Of course, I approve. I am just grateful we have this bounty to share. Far too many will not have much to celebrate. As I do every year, when I settle with my share croppers, I'll have gifts ready to hand out to each family in the Quarters."

.....

Hearing Papa talk about settling with his sharecroppers reminded Olivia of her responsibilities at High Bluff.

"I'll go to High Bluff and confirm that Flora has everything prepared for their Christmas festivities. On Christmas morning, it is customary to have Frank and Flora distribute gifts from Robert Ward to those living in the Quarters. After that, I'll spend time with the girls and Evelyn. Then, I'll keep my appointment with Mack Hardy."

Walt asked about her business with Mack Hardy and Olivia explained she wanted to make sure he followed her instructions for the handling of the distribution of funds Mrs. Smith had willed her, and the money she had bequeathed to Kate for her education.

"Papa, I don't trust Mack Hardy as far as I can throw him. It is necessary to have him understand I'm capable of managing my affairs without further assistance from him. Do I sound too hardnosed?"

Walt laughed and Annie and Beth giggled. "Annie, I think we reared one smart daughter. Olivia, you are not too cynical and you are smart enough to work rings around that wind bag. Stick to your guns and don't allow him to swindle your money as he has others. If only I could be a fly on the wall and see Mack's face when he discovers my kitty cat has claws."

Beth suggested she and Olivia leave Papa and Mama alone to 'visit.' Hearing Beth's suggestion, Walt whistled with a wolfish expression and turned to Annie, "I said we had some smart daughters. They know when they are not wanted!" Then he smothered a laugh and turned to Florabell and asked her to leave and not return until he called her. As she walked away, he told her to tell Gussie to bring his supper to Annie's room when it was ready. With Florabell gone, he turned to the girls.

"When you come in tonight don't disturb your Mama and me. As I told Florabell, I intend to have my supper Annie alone."

Beth and Olivia smiled at each other, and Beth, unable to hold back her thoughts, whispered in Olivia's ear. "Can you believe Papa behaving like an old goat? Thank the Lord Mama is past having more babies."

Olivia giggled, "You know, a body would think Papa was taking Mama to bed when you know he says they just like to eat alone in peace and quiet.

Beth just couldn't let it alone. "Oh yeah, and pigs fly!"

They went to the kitchen and told Gussie to serve Papa's supper in Mama's room that evening. Gussie slapped her hand on her hip remarking "Y'all won't do." She chuckled as she thought: "Mister Walt and Missus Annie is in that room by theyselves while their two daughters is in the kitchen speculating on what's be gonna happen up there. Lawdy mercy you girls need to find you some polite company to mix with."

Olivia laughed and turned to Beth. "She's right you know. You certainly do!"

.....

Olivia arrived at Mack Hardy's office and she was ushered into his conference room where he delivered the warranty deed to Mrs. Smith's house and land, along with the proof of recording. She was anxious to conclude her business before he attempted to convince her she needed to have him handle her affairs. Before she could get past his door, he stopped her. He asked if she knew anything about Robert Ward's unusual request to have him transfer money from the local bank to one in Dothan.

He went on to comment about how tied up in knots Jack Gunderson was with Robert's transfers, and that he was curious if she had any idea about Robert's reason or why he was asking for records of the transfer of bank stock.

Olivia assured him she knew nothing about Mr. Ward's business other than her observation that he never acted without good reason and was cautious to avoid unnecessary risks. Mack did not attempt to retain her any further; he was too busy considering what risks Robert Ward might be attempting to avoid.

As Olivia left, he attempted to get a grasp on what had happened. Before encountering her, he had never dealt with any woman he could not bring around to his way of thinking when it came to managing money left to them in a will.

In reality, he made more money from management of these women's funds than he ever had in his law practice. But try as he might there was no way to circumvent Olivia Ward's clearly articulated decisions. He had no alternative but to do as she asked and in so doing watch a healthy legal fee evaporate before his eyes.

"What did I do differently with this woman? Nothing." Olivia Ward was simply a woman with an iron will who knew her own mind and would not be coerced to act contrary to her plan.

Olivia crossed the street and walked the two blocks to Mr. Adkins' Mercantile. As she rounded the corner she recalled a conversation she had overheard between John and his father the morning before they left for Miami.

Robert had told John that it might take a little time, but Jack Gunderson would pay heavily for his actions. He just had to make sure Paul would not be harmed. Olivia wondered if Robert's recent actions with the bank transfers were related to his payback of Jack Gunderson.

When Olivia reached the mercantile, Mr. Adkins asked if she could furnish three fancy cakes by the next day and five additional ones by Friday. With his brisk sales of her braided rugs and aprons, he needed as many additional ones as she could send him when Ben picked up the cakes later that afternoon.

Olivia was delighted to have these additional orders; she would have enough store credit to allow her to purchase supplies Kate needed before she returned to school. As best she could estimate, there would be enough left over to purchase a hair brush for each girl for a surprise Christmas present.

She made it home in record time and baked and iced the cakes. She gathered her supply of rugs and aprons and had them ready for Ben to pick up when he came for the cakes. Once she completed these chores, she sat and reviewed the sketches of repairs and renovations Mrs. Smith had attached to her will. After her preliminary pricing of these repairs, she concluded there were enough funds in the earmarked account to accomplish the work.

·····

Later that night, Florabell was in a tizzy when she greeted Beth in the hallway to the main house at High Point.

"You ain't gonna never guess what Missus Annie done done! She done sat up in a chair with Mister Walt. Lord, but she was a happy woman. Ifn anyone didn't know no better they'd think all the medicine she done needed was for that man to come home and spend time with her doing I don't know what. I'm here to tell you whatever he done did worked some powerful magic on her."

CHAPTER 28

There were vast differences in how the Wards and Turners prepared for Christmas celebrations. In the main house at High Bluff, there was nothing going on to suggest a holiday was approaching. There was no tree, no smell of apple cider laced with cinnamon, nor any decorations. If it hadn't been for Flora quietly humming Silent Night as she dusted, there would have been no holiday season at all.

However, at High Point, there was a flurry of activity. Everyone was busy preparing for Christmas Day, which was three weeks away, and the wedding of Ann and William on the Sunday after Christmas.

Although Ruth and her family could not come, Walt and Annie expected their other children and their families, other than Ann who would spend Christmas day with William's parents, to gather at High Point. Jerry planned to arrive on Christmas Eve, but without his wife who was tending to her sick mother, and would stay until after Ann's wedding.

·····

On one of Olivia's visits to High Point, she discovered Papa was at home. This was rare, considering how far afield he now traveled to market his Angus bulls and his trotter horses. He came in to the kitchen, and Olivia observed a change in his behavior.

On the few times she had been with him since his return from his visit with Ann in Georgia, he had appeared anxious; to her he seemed worried. Something had changed.

"Papa, Gussie and I have everything under control for our family gathering, and the tasks yet to be completed in preparation of Ann's wedding are manageable. I hope your knowing all is taken care of will alleviate some of your worries."

Walt smiled broadly and explained she should not be concerned since he felt the burden of the world had been lifted from his shoulders in recent days. He indicated he would remain home until after Ann's wedding. "Right now, I need to check with Gabriel at the stables."

What Walt did not share with his daughter was the reason for his lack of worry and why he did not find it necessary to leave High Point during the holidays to attempt to make another sale.

As he walked from the main house to the stables, Walt thought about the many challenges each member of the Turner family had met and overcome during the past year. They, like most in their community, endured the lingering Depression. Even so, he knew for a fact each of his children had reasons to be grateful for the bounty of the harvest of their last crops and the fact that each family member did not lack for shelter or food.

Walt considered himself to be most grateful. For the first time in weeks he was able to breathe a sigh of relief because he had the funds he needed. He had sold two pieces of Annie's jewelry and received sufficient funds to cover the amount promised William and Ann as well as what Amelia expected to cover the cost of the reception.

.....

Once Olivia was satisfied Gussie and her helpers could manage the preparations for Christmas Day, she left them and joined Beth and their mother who sat watching Walt and Gabriel work several of the trotters.

After assuring her mother that Gussie had everything under control she prepared to leave.

"Mama, I've been so busy with orders for Mr. Adkins that I had to delay tackling Ann's wedding dress. As soon as I return home tonight, I will get started right away. I'll have no trouble cutting and sewing the dress, but it will require a lot of my time covering the small buttons I shall need for the back opening and sleeves."

Beth spoke up and offered to cover the buttons. It was, she said, "The least she could do to help." Both Annie and Olivia looked at Beth as though she had sprouted horns, or perhaps a halo. Olivia found it difficult to keep from laughing at the thought of her tomboy sister tackling the tedious task of covering one button, much less three dozen. Annie was not as successful as Olivia had been in containing her merriment. She could not help herself; she began to laugh.

Olivia quickly accepted Beth's offer with the stipulation that Beth could return the buttons if she found the task too taxing, but she needed to decide quickly whether she felt she could complete covering them within the next two weeks.

Beth picked up on Olivia's backhanded questioning of her commitment to the task and she thought, "Ya'll go ahead and snicker all you dare, but you just wait and see. You best not underestimate what I can do if I decide to; these buttons won't be coming back without their covers!"

. . . . .

As arranged, Joe arrived at the cottage with Evelyn. Olivia had made arrangements with Flora for her to spend the night with her and the girls. Olivia was grateful Evelyn would be with them. She was always helpful in caring for the girls which left Olivia free to begin work on Ann's dress. She would have just enough time but only as long as Beth came through with her task of covering the buttons. Olivia doubted Beth was up to the task but what she had not factored into the equation with Beth was her sister's stubborn determination when it came to proving her mother and sister wrong.

Beth worked on the buttons in the early morning hours before going to work, and every evening when she returned to High Point, and after she had checked on Mama and eaten supper. Some nights she worked until after midnight until her eyes were too tired to do more. Finally, the last button was covered. She decided, "I shall wait a while before I tell Mama or Olivia I have finished. It will do them good to stew about it for a little while longer."

About a week later Beth decided it was time to tell her mother she had completed her task so she took her basket of buttons to show her. When Annie examined a few of them, she remarked on their fine quality and how Beth's commitment surprised her. She had to ask, "What made you undertake this tedious job? I know how you deplore this type of work."

Beth assured her mother that she sure enough didn't like covering the buttons.

"As a matter of fact, I would rather do most anything other than covering these dad-blasted buttons. But I worked on Ann's wedding gown because I love her. As I covered each button, I silently prayed she won't spoil this chance for happiness."

Annie was overcome. It reminded her how, too often, she and Walt had failed to appreciate their deep-thinking daughter.

"Mama, I don't think Ann is capable of finding happiness. When she lived here, she pursued something beyond her grasp and never took time to enjoy what she had. So, as I labored to cover these devilish buttons and please Olivia with my handiwork, I prayed she has changed and has learned how to be happy with her life."

CHAPTER 29

The following morning, Annie received an unexpected visitor. Judy Ward arrived at High Point where she was met on the porch by Gussie.

"It's a good time to visit with Missus Annie since she had a good night." Gussie showed her to the parlor to wait until Florabell had Annie all fixed up before letting Missus Ward visit her.

Judy could tell how pleased Annie was to see her. Annie suggested Florabell go and have her breakfast; she desired private time with Judy.

As soon as Florabell had left the room, Annie asked about John. She was blunt and was both curious and concerned about him. "You do know our family is indebted to him. It was John who convinced Ann of the folly of her affection for him."

Judy confessed she had not a clue what Annie was talking about.

"Annie, I was unaware John had been of help to you and Walt, but hearing you say so pleases me very much, for you must know you are a dear person to me. And, while I am passing out compliments I might as well pass out another one."

Judy went on. "I have always known your pedigree is impeccable, but I did not value what the bloodlines of a thoroughbred actually meant relative to subsequent progenies. I do now." Judy paused to see if Annie was paying attention to her.

"Just a few weeks ago, I kept both girls while Olivia was taking care of you, and it amazed me to observe their behavior. It surprised me how they carried themselves and how they communicated so well with adults. Our granddaughters have been trained by Olivia to acquire the manners of a genteel woman just as you had trained her."

True to her nature, Annie graciously accepted Judy's praise with merely a smile and an utterance.

"Judy, contrary to my father's grim warnings, I have proved a thoroughbred and a grade stallion can defy odds and produce fine specimen from the two blood lines. Thank you for confirming my belief. "

Judy realized she had overstayed the time considered to be a permissible visit with Annie, and she prepared to take her leave. But Annie detained her.

"You know, Judy, Ann will be home this weekend with the young man, William Bryant, whom she plans to marry. From what Walt tells me he is much more than Ann deserves, but he lacks the requisite background and family connections we always assumed Ann would require in a husband. He is a brilliant young man with great potential as an attorney, but with present low expectations. My mother and sister insist Ann is repeating the tragedy of my marriage to Walt. In other words, she, too, is going to marry a grade stallion."

Annie continued, "I am unconcerned about his lack of family standing, but I am concerned with whether our extremely self-centered, selfish daughter loves him as I do Walt. If she does, she will have happiness. However, if she does not, then her life with William will become a living nightmare. I cannot cease thinking William cannot be happy with Ann. Try as I might, my foreboding feeling of a doomed marriage will not leave me."

Judy noticed tears appearing in Annie's eyes, and she clasped her hands and expressed her hope that all Annie's anxieties would prove unfounded. "I have overstayed my time with you. Is there anything I can do to help out with the wedding? Let me know if you think later of anything Robert or I can do for you more than help Olivia with the girls to give her unfettered time with you."

"Judy, there is something you may discuss with Robert and send a message by Olivia of your answer. William has little money for a honeymoon so Walt intends to ask you and Robert if he and Ann might use your Key West beach home. I know it is an imposition but Walt thought this was a way to spare William embarrassment over his lack of funds."

It did not take Judy a minute to answer. "Why Annie, of course they may. Robert and I would be thrilled to have a part in aiding Ann and William by having them enjoy our home. I'll send a note to the couple who live in our guest cottage and have them ready the main house to receive Ann and her husband."

Judy prepared to leave just as Olivia, Kate, and Jean arrived. She suggested she take the girls with her to run a few errands and pick up Evelyn from school so they could all come with her for a treat at Jerrell's.

Kate walked ahead and Judy took Jean's hand and headed for the front door. "Olivia, I understand I'm in for a surprise when I see the changes you've wrought in my daughter. Flora tells me my shy child has been turned into a delightful young woman. And, as Flora reports, Evelyn no longer slumps her shoulders because you have worked a miracle with her. You have my gratitude."

Olivia stood silent as the shock of the moment washed over her.

CHAPTER 30

While Olivia was busy getting Ann's dress finished and organizing the small reception to be held at High Point following Ann's wedding, she worked with Isaac and Joe on plans to begin renovating Mrs. Smith's house. Mrs. Smith had left sketches and suggestions, all of which were to be subject to Olivia's approval, which she quickly gave.

With the crops harvested, Joe and Isaac now had time to begin working on the renovations. They reviewed the sketches and determined that if they began right after New Year's they could complete the work and have Olivia and the girls moved into the house by the middle of March. There was one problem. At the next meeting with Olivia, Isaac brought up their concerns and asked how Miss Olivia planned to handle it.

"Miss Olivia, you know how it is with us colored folks. It don't matter none that the people at Gates' Feed and Seed or Mister Adkins' Mercantile knows us. They won't let us pick up the materials we'll need without cash money to pay on the mark or some arrangement made to cover the purchases on credit. I expect some will add up to a right big sum by my way of figuring." Isaac looked from Joe to Olivia, waiting for what he said to register with her.

Olivia understood Isaac's concern. As he said, there was no way he and Joe would be allowed to purchase materials on their promise that she intended to pay for the purchases.

"You are absolutely right, and I thank you for alerting me to a matter I need to handle. I'll go to the places where you'll probably get your supplies and arrange a credit line."

Because local merchants would not extend credit to coloreds, but would to women. Olivia made it clear to both Joe and Isaac that she would make certain they had no difficulties.

"Trust me when I tell you no one will question either of you or your authority to purchase whatever is since the bill for materials to be sent to me."

It was Isaac, the more questioning of the two, who suggested that either he or Joe go with her when she established the accounts so there would be no issue later. Olivia agreed it was a good idea and they agreed upon a time the three of them would make the visits to the various businesses.

After they left, Olivia outlined what she needed to accomplish before their move. She thought of the girls having their separate rooms and the extra space for her and considered how she could acquire enough flour sacks to make new curtains for each room. Mrs. Smith was responsible for this blessing, and Olivia would never forget what her generosity had meant to her and her girls.

. . . . .

Pulling Jean in the wagon, Olivia and Kate made their way through the crisp December air toward the bank. There, Olivia needed to open the accounts to enable Mack Hardy to transfer funds as she had directed. Then, she and the girls were to meet Beth at Jerrell's.

She was just finishing up when Paul Gunderson entered the teller's cage in front of her. As he greeted her and the girls, he motioned for her to follow him back to his office. As they walked, Olivia cautioned both girls to be quiet and on their best behavior.

"Olivia, I'm concerned because I have heard nothing from John or Mister Ward and I dare not attempt to find out anything from others because of the strained relationship between my Dad and me. Can you tell me if John is alright? I've driven by your cottage several times but have never found you at home. I just wanted to let you know if you need anything you can call on me and Sandra."

She did not doubt Paul's sincerity, and she wouldn't hesitate to share with him news of John, but she had none.

"Paul, you know as much as I do. John mentioned before he left for Florida that he probably owed his freedom to you. He wrote a note and asked me to deliver it to you at the bank the next day. Did you get it?"

He nodded, "I did as he requested and withdrew my recommendation to the Mason's membership committee."

Olivia thanked him again and before she marshaled the girls out of his office, she decided to tell him about Ann's upcoming wedding.

"You are aware how Ann's behavior almost destroyed her reputation. For the past several years she has lived with our grandmother in Savannah and earned her acceptance into grandmother's social circle. Now she is to wed a young attorney in Atlanta whom Papa says has his feet firmly planted. They will be married at High Point the third weekend in January but I'd appreciate it if you would not mention it to anyone. Papa intends it to be a wedding without fanfare. I thought you might appreciate hearing Ann has turned her life around."

Paul thanked her for sharing Ann's good news. "If there is an opportunity, would you please convey my heartfelt wishes for her happiness? You know, Olivia, had Ann exercised some restraint, our futures might have turned out differently."

Olivia said she would write him a note to tell him of any news. "I'll leave it with a teller if you are not available. Will this be alright?"

"Yes, but do not give your note to anyone but the man at the first cage; anyone else will give it to my dad. Please give your mother my regards. She is truly a lovely woman."

Olivia left the bank, pulling the girls in the wagon. As they headed across the square to Jerrell's to meet Beth. There, they loaded the girls in the back seat and placed the wagon in the trunk, then headed toward Olivia's cottage.

During the drive to Olivia's she and Beth discussed their last-minute plans for handling the Christmas Day meal. At High Point, it was customary to allow the colored help to have the day free of work. Therefore, Beth and Olivia had to figure out how to handle the serving of the meal Gussie and the women would prepare the night before.

"Beth, could you stop at Thomas' and James' homes this evening and ask Jane and Emily if they are prepared to help out like they have in the past? If we can count on them, then serving the drinks and desserts will be taken care of; the two of us will handle dishing up the meat and vegetables, and baking the biscuits."

Once their plans were firm, Beth left to visit her sisters-in-law and arrange for their help. Olivia still had to make plans for the arrival of her grandmother and aunt as well as William's parents, Mr. and Mrs. Bryant. The four of them planned to arrive in Dothan the afternoon before the wedding and would leave the day afterwards.

Olivia was grateful Ann and William would arrive on the day after Christmas. She was counting on Ann to make the Bryant's feel welcome at High Point, and for Beth and her four brothers to become acquainted with William. Such were Olivia's plans. What she could not have known was Ann's disposition toward William's parents. As she suspected though, she was about to confirm that Ann had not changed from the selfish person she was when she left High Springs to live in Georgia.

CHAPTER 31

The Turner clan enjoyed their time together on Christmas Day. Throughout the day, each of them spoke of Ann's and William's pending arrival the next day. Olivia's brothers were eager to learn what kind of person was willing to accept their brat of a sister for a wife. Walt heard their remarks and if he had a mind to, he could have enlightened them about the man about to become his son-in-law. But he decided to let them interact with William and learn to pity him as he did.

Walt thought, "If there is any way under God's sky I can find to put a stop to William making the biggest mistake of his life, I shall do so. I plan to try once again to acquaint him with Ann's true nature and persuade him to call off the wedding and take his parents and leave. This I'll do to attempt to save a very good man from what I know will be hell on earth living with my rotten to the core daughter."

. . . . .

On the afternoon after Christmas Day, Walt met Ann and William at the train station in Dothan and carried them to High Point. Within an hour of their arrival, Ann's brothers came to meet William and take him under their wing. They were on a mission and it was to discover how William was smart enough to have passed his bar examinations, but was too dumb to figure out Ann.

When Ann arrived, she went directly to her old room and closed herself in until Beth walked in without knocking. Beth wasn't in the mood to deal with Ann and so she firmly stated, not suggested, that it

MCMURTRY

was time for Ann to visit their mother. Ann reluctantly accompanied Beth to their mother's bedroom where her one-word responses to her mother's questions ended any attempt Annie had to communicate with her youngest daughter. What Annie found was that Walt was correct in his assessment of Ann. Her spots had not changed; they had merely been well-disguised to those who did not truly know her.

· · · · ·

If either Walt or Annie had any doubt about their assessment of Ann, it evaporated the next afternoon with the arrival of Ann's grandmother and aunt, and Mr. and Mrs. Bryant.

Walt had approached William with the proposition that he call off the wedding but his plea had fallen on deaf ears. But when William's parents arrived and he witnessed Ann's disgusting behavior toward them, Walt thought surely it would be sufficient reason for him to end his engagement. When William did not call Ann out on her disrespectful treatment of his parents, Walt gave up. It was a lost cause and his energies were better spent elsewhere.

· · · · ·

Ann and William's wedding took place as scheduled. Through it all, Annie and Walt did all in their power to make the Bryants feel welcomed at High Point. But they were unable to undo the affront they endured from the person soon to be their son's wife.

Although neither Amelia nor Pearl favored the union of William and Ann, they put aside their personal feelings and put forth their joint efforts to engage with the Bryant's and ensure they were introduces to Ann's siblings and their wives. Both Walt and Annie noted their strategy and were grateful to them.

Walt and Annie made their way to Ann's bedroom where she was changing into her traveling clothes to depart for the train station.

The Wards had offered Ann and William use of their beach home in the Florida Keys for their honeymoon. As Walt and Annie entered, Ann abruptly told them she had no time to spend with them before she left.

Surprisingly, it was Annie who responded to Ann's attempt to dismiss them. "We have no intention to spend time with you. But we do intend to make you aware of the great embarrassment you have caused us due to your unforgivable behavior toward your husband's parents. Never have we been so ashamed of our lack of hospitality at High Point." Annie seemed to want to say more but Walt interrupted her.

"We have done everything we could to help you overcome your past mistakes and learn from them. But nothing has changed with you, and we acknowledge this. I have given William the money I promised the two of you, and Amelia has received the funds she needs for your reception upon your return from the Keys. You should understand that your mother and I have no interest in your returning to High Point at any point in the future. Although we have abided your unruly behavior for years, your deplorable behavior these past few days has made it easy for us to cut our ties to you. I think it is impossible, but we both hope you'll find the impetus to change your ways and make a go of your marriage to a fine young man."

Ann was floored and she slammed the door behind them as they retreated to the hallway.

Downstairs, Annie exercised her most gracious manners as she joined the Bryant's and spoke of their return journey the following morning. They thanked her for her hospitality and excused themselves to pack their trunks. It was conspicuous that nothing was said by either Annie and Walt or William's parents of any future encounters they might enjoy.

. . . . .

When William's parents retired to their bedroom, Annie and Walt followed suit, leaving Beth and Olivia to handle restoring High Point to order.

While the two girls worked with Gussie and her cadre of helpers from the Quarters, Florabell looked in on Kate and Jean and reported back to Olivia that they were asleep in Beth's room. As they prepared baskets for the travelers' trips, Beth and Olivia were careful not to discuss their concerns about Ann and William; Gussie and several of the colored women from the Quarters remained nearby.

After the leftover food was stored, and the dishes and silverware were washed and prepared for the next morning, Gussie and her helpers retired. Finally, Beth and Olivia had some time alone and they sat together to enjoy the first food they had eaten throughout the evening.

"Olivia, I told Mama when I was working on the buttons for Ann's dress I felt it impossible for Ann to be happy. I watched her tonight, and not once did I see any expression on her face to suggest any abiding love she had for William. Is it only me or did you see something different in her behavior?"

Olivia's observation was the same as Beth's.

"You know, I think Papa prepared Mama to expect this very behavior on the part of Ann as to her regard for William. But what Papa did not prepare either him or Mama to witness was Ann's insufferable behavior toward Mr. and Mrs. Bryant. You know Mama is known far and wide for her gentle ways and her hospitality. It must have hurt her greatly to have guests at High Point disrespected."

"It may be harsh of me, but I have no desire to have Ann come back to High Point. All she does is spread her discontent to a point it impacts every one of us. I have suffered enough of her mean ways and I feel confident everyone else has too!"

•••••

The following morning, Walt took Amelia and Pearl and Mr. and Mrs. Bryant to the train station in Dothan where they embarked on their separate journeys home. He bid Mr. and Mrs. Bryant what he felt would be his final farewell to them and suggested Amelia and Pearl consider a future visit with Annie.

While Amelia stood on the station platform, Walt pulled her aside.

"Amelia, I need you to understand what I am about to tell you. I have given you the funds you said you required to host a reception in Savanah for Ann and William. You must plan wisely for the use of those funds because there will be no more money made available to you. I have reached my limits with Ann."

Amelia stared at him for a moment and her lip quivered. Then she silently turned from him and boarded the train.

CHAPTER 32

After Walt left, Olivia asked Beth to drive Kate, Jean and her to High Springs, stopping by High Bluff to pick up Evelyn to stay with them for the coming week.

On January 2, 1936, Evelyn turned twelve, and as in the past, her parents had made no arrangements to celebrate her birthday. Evelyn had grown out of her undisciplined ways and had been transformed into a delightful young girl. Still, there were things that bothered Olivia.

In past years, Evelyn was content to have Flora present her a gift Robert and Judy had left for her. Evelyn never seemed to be any worse for the wear and in fact, she appeared to be quite content sharing her special day with Flora, Frank, and the boys every year.

But as Olivia considered the past, she questioned whether at this age Evelyn would continue to be content with such a celebration. As much as she thought about it, Olivia was unable to understand Judy's sense of propriety.

Since Jean's birth, the woman had spent weeks planning and hundreds of dollars to ensure her birthday parties were the talk of the town. It was so unfair to Evelyn who never complained in the least. That didn't deter Olivia, though; she could not reconcile Judy's rationale and she said, and thought as much.

"Why in the name of Sam Hill had she done so little for her own daughter? Come hell or high-water, Evelyn Ward will not turn twelve without a big party for her birthday."

A few minutes later, Olivia joined Evelyn on the floor beside Kate and Jean. "Rabbit, we are going to celebrate your birthday in a big way this year. But first, you have to tell me what would most please you for this special day."

Evelyn thought for a moment before she responded. "I don't know Cotton. No one has ever considered my birthday a memorable one." Her voice was sterile and without emotion but she continued, "As far back as I can recall, none of my family has ever been with me on my birthday. I guess they might have been there when I was a baby, but I don't much remember."

Evelyn's stoic acceptance of being ignored brought Olivia to tears. Not one birthday had ever gone unmarked for all of the Turner children before Papa had banished her from High Point. Her experience in a loving family made it unthinkable to have her special Rabbit denied a family celebration all these years. Olivia thought, "The past is the past; we'll change things for the future starting now."

After Olivia and Evelyn considered several possibilities, they concluded that, with school out for the holidays and not scheduled to restart until the Monday after the New Year, it would be difficult to assemble a group of Evelyn's classmates. Olivia could not figure out how to make the day special for Evelyn.

It was Evelyn who suggested the thing that would please her most. "Please let me have my special day at your cottage with Kate and Jean. I would like this more than anything else."

What Evelyn shared with Olivia next almost broke her heart, so hurtful were Evelyn's words. She addressed her as she had in the Quarters.

"Cotton, before you came to live in the Quarters at High Bluff, I was very lonely and had no one to talk to or care about me except maybe John when he was home and had time for me. The happiest days of my life have been those spent with you in your shack in the Quarters, at Mrs. Smith's, and in your cottage."

Evelyn paused before she continued. "Why couldn't I just have a party and spend my day with those who bring me such joy and happiness? Could we do this?"

Olivia was humbled hearing Evelyn tell how she wanted to spend the day. "Of course, we can be together right here, you and me, and Jean and Kate. Shall I make a birthday cake for you and top it with all twelve candles so we can challenge you to blow all of them out at one time?"

Evelyn laughed at the absurdity of Olivia's jest as she thought, "Finally, I'll have a birthday celebration."

They spent the night making decorations and planning where to place each one. Kate and Jean huddled together trying to decide what they could make Evelyn as their gift. They finally decided, with some help from their mother, to make a booklet with one page for each year of Kate and Jean's life.

Olivia related to them many instances where Evelyn had played with each one of them and the funny incidents of each, such as the time Kate found a frog and attempted to give it to Evelyn. They laughed together thinking how they would make a page describing Evelyn as their mother's 'rabbit.'

What they finally decided to do was to choose one story and write an account of the incident in book form. Then Olivia fashioned a cloth cover painted with water colors to resemble the cottage with a woman and two little girls digging in the flower bed, with a rabbit sitting on the edge of the bed.

On her birthday, the four of them enjoyed it as much as they had hoped. They were seated ready to enjoy Evelyn blowing out the candles and serving her cake when Kate heard a knock at their door.

Olivia answered and found the delivery man from Mr. Adkins' Mercantile. He had volunteered to ride his bike to deliver a telegram for Evelyn.

Olivia was unable to express her gratitude for his thoughtfulness when he stated in a low voice so Evelyn would not hear. "I couldn't let her birthday greeting wait for the next day's delivery."

Once Olivia shut the door and returned to the kitchen, she put on a serious face. "Now I wonder who would send a telegram to Evelyn Ward. What could be so important to merit sending an expensive telegraph message? Evelyn, do you want to put it away to read later or is it something you might want to read right now?"

There were squeals all around and Olivia didn't know who was more excited, Jean or Kate who both urged Evelyn to open it right away. Evelyn opened the envelope removing the telegram gently between her thumb and forefinger.

"Olivia, it is from my brother. Oh my, he remembered my birthday. Listen to what he said."

"Happy 12th Birthday" signed your loving brother, John."

Evelyn put down the telegram, covered her face with her hands and wept. Olivia put her arms around her, and Kate and Jean each took hold of an arm. Kate continued telling her she loved her, not to cry, and Jean would say over and again she loved her, too.

Finally, Evelyn's sobs subsided and, she wiped her eyes and smiled the biggest smile possible, exclaiming, "My big brother remembered my birthday even if my mother and father did not. I am special to him, aren't I Olivia?"

At that moment, Olivia, herself, could have hugged John.

CHAPTER 33

On the second Monday in January 1936, Robert was in a quandary. Wanting to ensure the warrant would not be served on John in High Springs, he had sent him back to Miami. Both the serving of the warrant and his impending arrest were inevitable; therefore, their next course of action was to allow it to go forward and then to work on securing bail for him.

Robert and Judy concluded their holiday in Tallahassee and drove toward High Springs. As they passed through Bonifay, Robert pulled over at a roadside diner to allow Judy to make a telephone call to her man in Holmes County. She learned he was making progress.

Within a few weeks, he expected to have gathered sufficient information to broker a deal with the sheriff to approach the District Attorney to convince him to take no action on the Grand Jury's indictment. He cautioned Judy to exercise patience because a false move at this juncture could nullify his efforts.

As they left Bonifay, Robert observed how Judy's contact prefaced most of his comments with a lot of 'ifs.' It seemed there was nothing concrete in any of the reports. The problem was they had no alternative. They had to plan for every contingency and hope for the best. Additionally, there were several pressing issues Judy and Robert would need to handle upon their return, and they used the time to discuss how to handle each.

Robert intended to visit with Paul as quickly as possible to help him save his reputation and position at the bank. Next, he planned to visit Mack Hardy and confirm that he had carried out his instructions

211

for the transfer of funds to a Dothan bank. He intended to have Mack give him a referral for a reputable law firm in Dothan or Montgomery that was known to handle corporate matters related to fraud and embezzlement.

Judy intended to check on Annie. She knew Evelyn had started back to school, but she did not know what arrangements Olivia had made for Kate and Jean's care. She would leave it to Robert to discuss with Olivia how the situation with John stood. She knew he would determine how Olivia was managing.

She also realized Olivia could not take care of her responsibilities at High Point while simultaneously managing to bake cakes and braid her rugs. If this were the case, Judy suspected Olivia had little to barter with Mr. Adkins. In the past, she would not have cared if Olivia starved; she couldn't fully understand why her feelings had changed.

No matter how poorly John behaved, Olivia never complained or blamed him. Instead, she worked hard to support herself and John's children, and did a marvelous job of rearing the two girls. Judy could not help but admire her character and her tenacity to make lemonade out of a bag full of lemons which seemed to be a constant commodity in her life. Therefore, she intended to have Robert find out what she needed so they could help.

·····

When they arrived home, they found Evelyn was with Olivia and the girls. Flora told them Evelyn had been invited to some sort of party or dance or something that the middle school was sponsoring. Isaac or Joe was to pick Olivia up from High Point and take her and the girls along with Evelyn back to High Springs to work on a dress for Evelyn. As far as she knew, the dress would be finished this evening, and Evelyn would come back to High Bluff the next afternoon.

"Missus Ward, you'll be mighty proud of Evelyn, seeing as how Miss Olivia cut her hair and plucked out a bowl of them eyebrows. Why, Evelyn sho 'nuf has the biggest brown eyes, now that you actually sees them. Ain't no wonder somebody done axed her to go to the dance the way she looks now. She twelve now and ain't never been asked to any of them school parties 'til now. I be so happy fer her and she be too."

Flora worried about Judy's reaction to Evelyn's makeover, but thankfully she had none except to say it was nice of Olivia to look after her. Then she said, "All this talk about Evelyn is well and good but what I want to hear is how Jean is doing. Has she grown? Is she going with Olivia to High Point every day?"

She told how Jean went with her mother most days but if it happened to be on one of Annie's bad days, she stayed with her. "Jus as Mister Robert said do, Isaac or Joe always goes by to check on Miss Olivia and they brings Kate and Jean back here ifn they needs to stay with me."

"Flora, I thank you for taking good care of everything, especially Jean. It's late so go on home and be back early in the morning because I plan to leave before eight."

CHAPTER 34

While Flora was filling Judy in on the whereabouts of Evelyn, Robert walked down to the Quarters to see Frank and learn how the farming operations were going. As he expected, Frank and the boys had everything under control. There were a few questions Frank needed to have him answer about land to lay fallow and the cash crops he was to plant.

Frank wanted to hear from Robert what he knew about the impending war overseas people talked about in High Springs. "Every times we is at the mercantile or the feed store we hears tell of the war coming here. Some of the colored folks from other farms has done told us we is gonna be taken off the farms to help fight. The question some of us be asking is where is we gonna get the labor to harvest these here crops ifn our men done been taken to be soldiers. This is all I knows, Mister Robert, but, I ain't sure ifn this here is the gospel or someone's fancy. Does you know?"

How was he to answer Frank? He was able to form his own opinion based upon what he read of the latest actions of Adolph Hitler in Europe and of Roosevelt to cut off the supply to Japan of iron and other materials necessary for building their war machine. He understood the implications. The United States sat in the middle of one big messy sandwich of war in both Europe and the Pacific. How could he explain to Frank what failed diplomatic actions could mean as to war?

Speculation abounded in all quarters concerning the United States joining former Allies in France and Britain to fight Germany's expansion under Adolph Hitler. At the parties he and Judy hosted or attended, talk prevailed about the time table for the United States' entry into the war. He had listened and learned one thing. All the talk was mere speculation. Roosevelt was too shrewd a politician to enter the war unless there was some provocation significant enough for the American public to support his decision.

"Frank, I'll tell you the gospel truth. Not one person spreading such rumors knows what he is talking about. I think there is a good possibility our country may be forced to aid our European allies at some point, but at what point I do not know. I can tell you it appears to me that it is inevitable we will be at war, but when I don't know."

Robert observed Frank's reaction and knew he accepted his explanation. "At this point I am going to plan our farming operations as though war is imminent; the matter of labor is something I'll have to tackle, but in the meantime, we are going to expand production beyond any we have attempted in the past. So, plan to increase our acreage by double what we did last year. I still want you to lay fallow the twenty acres out by the old school building, and then add another fifteen bordered on the north by the fruit orchard."

Frank's uncertainty was vanquished. He was satisfied with the way Mr. Ward explained things. He knew for a fact Mr. Ward didn't talk out of both sides of his mouth. He said what he did not know as quickly as he said what he did know. As far as Frank was concerned, this was the kind of man he and his sons respected and found it a pleasure to work for.

"Thank you, Mister Ward, for putting my mind at ease. My sons I will look after your farm now and don't you worry none."

"I won't Frank. Thank you."

"And by the way, Mister Robert, us three has knocked a few heads to make them understand Mister John is doing right well for hisself, no matter what they be saying. We got the message across right good."

Robert expressed his appreciation for the loyalty of Frank and his family to the Wards and asked if the Christmas presents he had arranged had met with everyone's approval.

"Honest, Mister Ward, ain't no other colored peoples has given to them a box of staples what be enough for most of the year and then some. And, not one other colored family on any other farm has a ten-dollar open credit in their name at Mr. Adkins. Yes sir, your gift was well received by us all, and I can tell you how much every one of us 'preciates what you done did for us."

Robert thanked Frank again and with that he walked back up the rutted path, meeting Flora along the way. "This is a beautiful January night with the moon full and mild temperature. I know you are anxious to get home but I need to ask, is everything in good shape or is there something we need to attend to in the morning?"

"As I told Missus Judy, there ain't no spoke on this here wagon out of place. What with Missus Olivia coming by and checking on everything, there warn't nothing needed fixing that she did not see to afore she would leave. No sir, she done took it upon herself to step in and look about things whilst y'all be gone. Course you know I done fell for her from the moment she came to us. She is one of a kind is Missus Olivia."

Robert agreed and they each went on their way.

. . . . .

Robert and Judy woke with the first light of morning and shared what they planned to accomplish that day. Foremost on Robert's mind was dealing with Jack Gunderson and Judy could not help but laugh outright as she heard him outline his plan for him. She almost felt sorry for him, knowing the junk-yard dog was about to bite Jack when he least expected it. What amused her most was how Robert planned to make certain Jack knew who pulled the strings, even though he would be powerless to prove it, and even more foolish to suggest it.

"Judy, I have to see Paul today and warn him to keep his distance from his father, and to especially stay away from any unusual transactions. After all he has done for John, I cannot let him take the fall with his father. Paul is as much unlike his father in character as night is from day."

She embraced her husband and looked him in the eye as she told him how very much she loved him and even how much more she respected him. She would have expected nothing less from him with respect to how he proposed to handle Paul... and Jack.

CHAPTER 35

Judy got out of bed and dressed. As she slipped on her skirt, she told Robert she was on her way to see about Jean. She did not share with him what Flora had told her about Evelyn being asked to one of her school's parties. She would leave that as Evelyn's surprise for her father. Her thoughts turned to John. She hoped he would survive the situation in Holmes County and could one day soon be home. She hoped, too, he would come to realize what a blessing he had in Olivia and his two daughters.

. . . . .

It was nearly noon when Paul looked up to find Robert Ward standing in his doorway. "Good day Mister Ward, is there anything I can do for you?"

Robert walked in and asked if Paul was available for lunch off premises. He went on to say that there were some things he needed to discuss with him, and he would prefer to do so away from his office. Paul, thinking he had news of John to share with him, hastened to lock his desk and accompany him.

Instead of walking across the street to Dallon's Diner, Robert motioned for Paul to get into his car. "Paul, I need to talk to you in private for it is imperative that no one overhear our conversation."

Paul got in beside Robert and immediately inquired if something had happened to John. Robert updated him on the state of things with John and expressed his gratitude for Paul's timely warning.

"As you probably know, John and I left the next morning and got to Miami in time to forestall several mobsters from Chicago who intended to take over some of our operations. Fortunately, we were able to demonstrate to local authorities that there was no intended connection between the mob and our clubs. If not for your warning, they likely would be closed now."

After telling Paul about John and what had happened in Miami, Robert explained why he had asked Paul to join him. "Tomorrow night the bank's board of directors will hold a meeting to remove your father as president."

Paul's stared at Robert with an expression of disbelief. "Sir, will the board terminate him or simply demote him? I fear neither my father, nor mother, is strong enough to withstand that level of backlash in High Springs.

Robert considered how much he could tell Paul of the board's intended action and their strategy to lessen the embarrassment to him. "There is little I can share with you about the action the board intends to take. That is not my prerogative or my purpose at this time. I tell you this only because I am determined you will not suffer any repercussion because of your father's misdeeds."

He turned to face Paul. "You must distance yourself from your father's activities. It is imperative that you not involve yourself in any transaction he might make before the board's meeting. The issue before the board is your father's actions to override the decision of the senior loan officer and one or more of the bank's underwriters."

Robert waited for the information he shared to register with Paul as to its critical nature. Then he explained what Paul must do if any one of the directors asked what he knew about instances when Jack had overridden the decision of his loan officers and made bad loans.

"You must declare emphatically that you have no knowledge of your father's actions when he either makes a loan or denies a loan.

Do you understand what I am asking of you and the importance of your following my advice? I hope you do!"

Robert prepared to start the car and return Paul to the bank. He gave him what he considered his final instruction.

"From the moment you step foot inside the bank this afternoon, let your actions demonstrate your distance from your father's activities."

Paul mind was swimming with questions but only one mattered. "Can you at least tell me if he is going to jail?"

"It is the decision of the board not to bring charges against Jack because such charges could undermine the confidence of its depositors. It is bad enough that his actions have undermined the viability of the bank. As a vice-president of the bank, you have an obligation as an officer to protect the bank's solvency and the funds of the depositors. To act in any way contrary to fulfilling this obligation is unethical. By your father's actions he has betrayed the trust of the board of directors, as well as that of the depositors. Now, as to your question of how his unethical behavior was discovered, it was I who discovered what he has done, along with his attempt to cover up the consequences of his actions. I ask that you not judge me too harshly before you hear me out as to the facts."

Paul remained silent and Robert could only imagine what was running through his mind. He thought it was probably something to the effect of, "A man for whom I risked so much to help is the person responsible for the pending action which will destroy my father's reputation."

"Paul., a day or so before I left for Miami, I learned of the emergency situation at the bank. Your father's high-risk loans of substantial amounts were in default and no recovery was possible because there was no collateral backing them. Without recovery of depositor's money used for the loans, it was questionable whether the bank could survive if his actions became known. The directors realized such knowledge in the public domain would result in a run on the bank."

Paul understood how defaulted, uncollateralized loans, if in large numbers, could damage a bank. However, it was inconceivable his father, who had lectured him since childhood to conduct his life with honor and integrity, would have acted so unethically. Surely Mr. Ward did not have facts to support his implications. Or did he?

"While I was negotiating a loan for a farmer, whose loan had been turned down by your bank's senior loan officer, he remarked that my interest rates were higher than the bank's, but in the long run not so, considering the fee he would have needed to pay in order to get your father to override the decision of his senior loan officer. This was not a one-time thing. He gave me the names of other farmers who were forced into the same scheme. He said it is pretty much common knowledge in Geneva County: if the bank turns you down for a loan, go see Jack Gunderson."

Paul grimaced with embarrassment as he wondered how he had never become aware of his father's illicit dealings. He also lamented the fact that after his father was removed he would be left behind to deal with the aftermath. With the last name 'Gunderson,' Paul worried he would always be deemed guilty by association. Robert continued.

"After I was in Miami, I had Mack Hardy send me information on minutes of the bank's loan committee and I found discussion of default of large loans with notations where each had been denied by one or more loan officers. In each case, your father had overridden their recommendations. Mack sent me information he obtained from an unnamed bank employee and this information exposed how your father covered his actions until the borrowers defaulted."

It was unnecessary for Robert to say more. Paul asked if the board planned to terminate him as well; he asked Robert if there were anything he could do to convince board members he was not a part of his father's scheme.

"Yes, Paul, and that is why we are here together. I have met with each director and have convinced each one that you knew nothing of your father's behavior. Collectively they agree you will be retained in your position as vice-president and will be groomed to become president one day."

"What will happen to my father? What can I do to save my mother from the embarrassment she will suffer? As for me, I fear some in the bank and on the board will subscribe to the notion that the apple does not fall far from the tree. Do you really believe they will find me trustworthy? And, once the facts come out, what will our depositors think of me?"

"You need not worry about that. Your father will be offered the position of manager of a new holding company created to market insurance policies. The board members plan to put forward the notion that he voluntarily decided to accept this new challenge. You and your mother will not suffer embarrassment; your standing will be secure."

Paul shook Robert's hand, remarking how fortunate it was he did not hold grudges. Robert considered the remark and thought how little Paul understood him. His actions had been deliberately designed to achieve his payback for Jack's numerous underhanded attempts to harm John.

"You need to get back to the bank. I have shared information with you that only my wife and Mack Hardy know. It has been my intent all along to prepare you for what was to come. When all is said and done though, the outcome depends on how you demonstrate your independence from your father. At tomorrow night's meeting I'll resign from the board because I don't plan to restore the funds I withdrew. Within a few months, I plan to sell my bank stock."

Paul exited the car to return to the bank, thinking along the way, "Mr. Ward, I don't know how to thank you for intervening on my behalf. I do know I shall act with integrity, never giving you cause to regret having backed me."

Everything transpired just as Robert Ward said it would. Jack Gunderson stepped down as president of the bank and assumed a position with the newly formed High Springs Insurance Company. True to his word, Robert's plan insulated Paul, allowing him to retain the respect of the directors and those with whom he worked.

CHAPTER 36

For several weeks before Ann's wedding, Olivia had spent most of her time at High Point supervising Gussie and her helpers as they prepared to receive the wedding guests and to put on the small affair Walt and Annie were planning following the ceremony. Now that the wedding was over and all the guests had departed, she had time to take care of some personal business she had neglected.

She visited Robert at his office just off the main square in High Springs to discuss how best to handle the matter of her cottage. It had been customary for Robert to stop by to see the girls several times during the week but he had not done so for the past two weeks, so she decided to take Jean and Kate to find him.

"If you can spare a little time, I need your advice."

Robert closed the door assuring her he always had time for her.

Before she discussed with him what she should do about the cottage, she asked about John. "My constant fear is he may not be strong enough to overcome the temptations of living and working in a nightclub and casino. Is there anyone there to whom he is accountable?"

Robert candidly shared with her the reports he had received about John's behavior in Florida, and he ended his discussion expressing his belief that John understood the importance of not giving law enforcement any ammunition to use against him. He was, by all accounts, walking a straight and narrow path.

"I'm sorry, Olivia. I've turned your visit into a session about

John, but I know you are here for some other reason. Tell me how I may help you."

"That's just fine, Mister Ward. I am pleased to hear John understands the gravity of his situation and is acting accordingly. All I have ever wanted was for him to respect our girls and to gain the maturity to become a positive influence in their lives. Now, as to my business, I hope to move into Mrs. Smith's house once the renovations there are completed in mid-March. Once the cottage is vacant, I've been thinking of either renting it or selling it outright and I wanted your advice. You see, I've had an ongoing battle with Mack Hardy. He is determined to involve himself in my business decisions and I am equally determined he will not. I am not about to let him have carte blanche to run up excessive legal fees!"

Robert noted Olivia's no-nonsense approach to dealing with Mack and listened as she continued putting her concerns before him.

"First, he harassed me about letting him handle the sale of Mrs. Smith's house. Then, when I made it clear I was not selling the house, he insisted I should and should let him handle the sale of the cottage at a ridiculously low price. I have concluded he must think I am ignorant. When I explained I would take no action until I discussed the matter with you, he seemed perturbed and became even more so when I made it clear I am capable of handling my affairs without his assistance."

Robert burst out laughing. "You never cease to amaze me. I bet old Mack is fit to be tied. He has pulled this stunt with many widows. Bully for you in shutting him down. Perhaps I can offer a few suggestions. Considering your business ventures along with this rental property, have you developed any plan on how you are going to proceed to make a living for you and the girls?"

Olivia outlined several plans, all of which seemed viable to him. But he was most intrigued by her plan to expand her sewing business.

"When I have saved up enough, I am going to purchase another sewing machine and hire Martha Cox to help me with cutting and sewing. She was Mrs. Smith's housekeeper and is an excellent seamstress. If I can do this, I am certain I shall increase my dressmaking by more than twofold and it will give the girls and me some breathing room in our budget. I hate to complain but things have been a bit tight this year."

As Robert listened, he felt deep shame, realizing his son had ignored the needs of his family. He said nothing but promised himself that he would see to it his granddaughters had whatever they needed. When she concluded, he suggested she consider renting the cottage.

Olivia agreed. Then she laughed as she told him how Mack had tripped himself up when he argued she should sell the cottage rather than rent it. He slipped and admitted *he* wanted to purchase it. She said she thanked him kindly but she would have none of it.

"Do you know he tried to tell me there was no demand for rental property while in the next breath telling me how High Springs was fast becoming a bedroom community for people who worked in Dothan and who found it cheaper to live in High Springs? He admitted there would be a shortage of housing?"

Robert chuckled and told her he happened to know Mack was looking at the cottage for his son and his family. "Olivia, count on it, they will be your first tenants. Now that is settled. Is there anything more we need to discuss?"

"No, just that I don't want you to think that I will settle for being a seamstress for the rest of my life. It is merely a means to an end until I am hired as a teacher. I wanted to become a nurse, but that is no longer a viable option. I have my temporary teaching certificate, although I have been unable to use because the principal thinks I do not meet the moral standard of the local school board. I am not discouraged though; I have faith there will come a time when some principal will agree my qualifications are more important than the opinions of a few narrow-minded people in High Springs."

"You have developed sound plans, Olivia. One piece of advice I offer is to hold on to your property. We learned after The Great War that our Armed Forces need more than the thirty or so cantonments and training camps established to garrison and train our men. Now, there are rumors that several investors are looking at a large tract of land not far from High Springs in Dale County as an Army training camp. Should this develop, our community will be greatly impacted, and property values will soar. And, the most important thing is, workers who move here will need affordable housing."

Olivia saw the wisdom in Robert's logic and assured him she was grateful for his sharing it. Robert looked at his watch and to his surprise, they had been talking for nearly two hours. He quietly looked around for Kate and Jean and found them asleep under his desk. So, he suggested he and Olivia reward them for their good behavior with lunch at Dallon's Diner. Olivia agreed and they set off in search of a hearty meal.

CHAPTER 37

In the first week of February, John prepared to return to Miami. He had ridden the train from Miami to Tallahassee the week before to look in on the juke joint in Esto, and had then driven up to High Point for the weekend. He hoped to see his mother and, if possible, Paul before he had to return to Miami the following week. Evelyn had just turned twelve and he hoped to spend some time with her. Time was flying and he felt like the important people in his life, his mother and sister were passing him by.

While he was at home, Flora brought him a peach basket with some of his belongings he had not packed when he was kicked out of the main house and forced to live with Olivia in the Quarters a few years ago. Inside the basket were his high school letter sweater, a few work shirts, and a pair of dress shoes that were two sizes too small now.

On top of the heap lay his baseball glove. He set the basket down and pounded his fist into the mitt. Surprisingly it was still as supple as the last time he had used it. He tossed it back on top, bid Flora farewell and carried the basket under his arm out to the farm truck where he unceremoniously dumped it into the bed. Shortly, he was on his way to High Springs to meet with Paul.

As he waited outside Dallon's Diner for Paul, one of the local boys, Gus Wynn, wandered by. "What's aces?" he asked the boy. "Nothing much, Mister John. How's yore pa? I ain't seen him at my daddy's shop in a while. He doing okay?"

Gus had certainly grown since John had last seen him. Now, at

16 years he was nearly six-feet-tall and around 170 pounds, by John's estimation.

"Yeah, he's doing good. He and I been spending time down in Florida on business. I'm just home for the week to see my kid sister and mama. You sure enough have filled out since I saw you last. You playing football this year?"

"Naw, I broke my leg last year playing football so Pa says I can't play. I can only play baseball now. He played semi-pro and he says if I work hard I can maybe play semi-pro too one day."

"You think you're gonna be good enough to play pro ball one day?"

"I don't rightly know Mister John. There's a tryout for the Washington Senators next week in Florida but I ain't got no way to get there and I ain't got no glove. The boy I was borrowing one from moved away and daddy says we ain't got the money to drive to Dothan to buy a new 'un."

"Well hell, Gus. Today's your lucky day. You a righty?"

"Yes sir, I am. I bat both ways but I throw with my right arm."

John reached over into the back of the truck and pulled out his 1926 Wilson baseball mitt and held it out for Gus to admire. Gus slid the mitt on his hand and flexed the cowhide webbing open and shut. His smile beamed his satisfaction. Reaching into his trouser pocket, John pulled out five one-dollar bills and handed them to the boy.

"Boy, you take this glove and money and you find a way to get yourself to Florida for that tryout. If you're half as good as your Pa was, I'll be hearing your name on the radio one day."

Gus interrupted as if he was hesitant to accept the gifts.

"No. You take 'em. I lost my chance to play football at the

University of Alabama and the University of Tennessee because of some dumb bad luck and I can't sit by and see you miss your dream because you don't have a glove or a few smackers to get you there. Good luck, Gus!"

With that, Gus wandered off to marvel at his good fortune. Meanwhile, John was off to find Paul.

MCMURTRY

CHAPTER 38

In the third week of March 1936, Isaac and Joe moved Olivia into Mrs. Smith's house. As Olivia had predicted, with the new space and the second sewing machine, she nearly doubled her design and dressmaking business with new requests for outfits from people in other towns.

Her cake orders from Dothan and Enterprise stores continued to increase to the point she hired Rachel to help her. She used funds Mrs. Smith had left her to purchase and install a third oven. Things were coming up aces for her and she could not have been more pleased.

No matter how busy she was though, Olivia did not fail to visit her mother as often as she could and at least once or twice a week. On one visit Mama shared a letter from Pearl telling about Ann and William's reception. Because of her precarious health and the distance, Annie and Walt had not attended. She read directly from the letter and went into great detail to describe the affair. The first two pages suggested the reception was the most successful affair ever held within their social circle.

It was not all good news, though. On the third page, Pearl wrote of Ann's return to her horrible behavior. Ann allegedly moved from guest to guest bemoaning the deplorable conditions William expected her to tolerate in Atlanta. Pearl concluded her epistle stating that most agreed Ann was discontented with her marriage.

These revelations alarmed Olivia, fearing Pearl's observation had upset Mama. They had not and she was surprised to hear Mama's reaction.

"Your father and I understand Ann married William because her only other option was to return to High Point. We have never considered Ann's marriage to be a permanent situation for her. She is, if nothing more, a survivor. Thus, if she is discontented with her marriage, she will leave him. That would be consistent with her nature. What concerns me is the misery she will cause poor William while she remains with him. If he isn't careful, she will be the death of him."

•••••

Business at Mr. Adkins' Mercantile was so brisk he sold out of his supply of rugs almost as soon as he placed his latest order on the shelves. With her uptick in dress orders and cakes for the surrounding areas, Olivia had found it difficult to keep pace with the demand for her rugs. She often found herself falling asleep in her chair or at the table while drowning in a pile of materials and needles.

On her most recent visit, Beth noticed the feverish way Olivia worked in the evenings and at night, and she decided she could help. She had seen how to make a braided rug from start to finish, so for a little over two months Beth stopped by each evening after work and on some Saturdays to prepare the strips and sort them for Olivia. Soon, she too was braiding rugs. Olivia was grateful for the help. From standing up for her in church to standing her ground against Papa's wrath, Beth had always come through for Olivia and she would be forever grateful for her sister's unconditional love.

•••••

As Robert had predicted, Mack Hardy approached Olivia about renting the cottage for his son. He appeared at her house with a rental agreement in hand and asked her to sign it so they could move in right away. However, Olivia insisted she study its wording before signing. Mack agreed, saying he would return the next evening to pick it up.

As she studied the document, her head swam. It read like Greek, was ambiguous, and at times contradicted itself. "I'll not sign this rental agreement until I discuss it with Mister Ward." She thought. "I can't trust Mack Hardy as far as I can throw him."

When Robert stopped by that evening he looked over the document and discovered Mack's deliberate inclusion of terms unfavorable to Olivia. Especially disturbing was a clause providing his son with a long-term renewal provision to prohibit Olivia raising the monthly lease payment. When he left, Robert took the document with him and told Olivia he would ask an attorney friend of his in Geneva to rework it into one she could sign.

Olivia was grateful Mister Ward continued to be a benefactor to her and the girls although she suspected it had to be bittersweet for him considering the circumstances in which she had come to him along with John's tenuous relationship with them all.

. . . . .

The 1930 Ford stake-bed truck laden with scrap metal pulled over on the side of the road near the ball fields. The sweet smell of freshly cut grass tickled Gus's nose as he hopped down from the passenger's side of the cab.

"I ain't got much mister, but I shore do 'preciate the ride," he said as he held out his hand with two quarters for the driver.

"Naw. Ain't no call fer that, young man. You keep it and pay me when you sign you one of them big league contracts and pitch for the Yankees. You ain't getting off easy fer two bits," the driver chuckled as spittle oozed between the gaps in his tobacco-stained teeth. "If you don't make it today, come find me at the junk yard here in town and I'll drive you a piece of the way back to yer home."

"Aw 'ight. You got yorself a deal mister. Thanky!"

Early "Gus" Wynn tucked his 'new' glove under his arm and trotted across the dirt parking lot of the small baseball field where the Washington Senators were holding tryouts. After meeting the coach, he dutifully took his spot in line and began to throw with a partner. Unlike the other boys who were dressed in baggy baseball pants, wool jerseys, and black leather shoes with metal spikes; he wore a white t-shirt, blue dungarees, and black Converse All-Star "Chuck Taylor" high-top shoes. To say he looked out of place was an understatement.

What wasn't understated was his ability on the baseball diamond and it didn't take long for Early to set himself apart from the other players. When the club's pitching coach heard the crack of the horsehide ball slap the catcher's mitt and echo throughout the park, he knew this boy was special. He quickly summoned head coach Clyde Milan. After a brief talk with Early, Milan offered him one hundred dollars cash and a minor league contract. He explained further that it would pay him the same amount every month provided he reported back to training camp the next week.

By Early's estimation, the money he held before him was the most he had ever seen at one time. And, they were going to give him that much again every month? It didn't take any effort to convince him. Although he would probably have to skip the rest of the school year, it was worth it. He was going to be a professional ball player.

Tired and hungry, he made his way to the Greyhound bus station to buy a ticket home. But first, he went looking for the junk man who had given him the lift. He figured he owed the old man a grilled cheese sandwich at the diner and, probably, a whole lot more.

CHAPTER 39

The nearly five and a half years since Olivia had been thrust into a shack in the Quarters at High Bluff had flown by. She pondered all that had happened to her in those years as she recalled her fateful trip to Camilla, Georgia where she and John were married, giving birth to Kate on the Ward's kitchen floor, and the physical and mental abuse heaped on her by Judy before Jean was born. But the most hurtful thing she had endured, by far, was being unable to worship in the church she had attended for 25 years.

As she recounted each episode, the hardships she had faced and overcome were inconsequential when she acknowledged what she had gained from them. The blessing of having Kate and Jean was far greater than anything she had endured. Finally now, she could look ahead with optimism to the future because her plan to support her daughters and herself had come to fruition.

"Don't count your chickens before they hatch," Papa had often said whenever life around him appeared too satisfactory. Life was good and she offered up a prayer to God, asking Him to show her His will. She prayed for strength and faith to continue to stay the course and keep to the path He had for her. She would indeed not count her chickens.

. . . . .

After three months of laying low, the inevitable had arrived. A doormen at the Flamingo Club approached John tentatively on the floor of the main ballroom. With him walked the sheriff who was not alone as he arrived with several deputies in tow. They produced the warrant for John's arrest and he went with them willingly. As a courtesy to Robert Ward, the deputies led John out through a side door so as not to hurt the club's business or publicly embarrass John or his father. Perhaps the Christmas card list had paid off in some small way? In any event, the Ward family was entering a period of uncertainty. Only time would tell how they would fare.

·····

The end of March 1936 had mostly been cold and rainy; but on the last Tuesday morning in the month there was little sunshine. Olivia completed her baking for the day and settled Jean and Kate in the sewing room while she worked on an outfit for a customer. Martha Cox was busily using the new sewing machine, intent upon completing the final stitching of an outfit before she stopped to assist Olivia with the design of one.

Olivia laid out the pattern she had sketched and had begun cutting the material when she heard a knock. She was surprised to see Robert Ward.

"What a pleasant surprise. What brings you here at this time of the day? Wait, don't answer yet. Please come inside and allow me to fix you something to drink to warm you up. But first, I'll get the girls. They will be thrilled to see you."

Uncharacteristically solemn, Robert stopped her in her tracks as he gently grasped her upper arm. He said he preferred the girls not be present to hear what he had come to tell her. Olivia instantly assumed the worst but tried to remain calm.

"I guess I am here to tell you that Judy and I have come to an epiphany recently. We have failed both of our children mightily. You see, after John was born, Judy and I were satisfied with one child and did not care to have another. Evelyn's arrival in our home was a surprise which frankly, we were unprepared to accommodate. We had John, who was 'perfect' in our eyes and therefore we made no effort to involve Evelyn in any aspect of our lives. Rather, we were content to permit Flora, Frank, their sons, and the other colored people in the Quarters to become Evelyn's family and to make up her world. That is until you came to us. You have come to mean a great deal to our daughter, so much so that we both recognize Evelyn has grown to prefer being with you and her nieces rather than at High Bluff whether or not Judy and I are there."

Olivia waited, sensing Robert had more to say. He went on to share his new-found feelings about his daughter.

"In our physical and emotional absence from her, you filled a gaping void. You groomed Evelyn into a beautiful and charming person. Judy and I always regarded her as a sweet but unremarkable individual and I cannot tell you how appreciative we both are of your undying love and concern for her."

Olivia blushed slightly. Robert took notice but he continued. "There is no way I am able to explain how I felt when I returned from Tallahassee and Evelyn walked down the stairs to greet me before her school dance. In that moment I realized I had missed her developing into a gracious and beautiful young person. I can't get that time back, but Judy and I are both committed to doing whatever we need to do to ensure we provide the support Evelyn needs to be happy and successful in life."

She followed Robert's train of thought. He was right. He and Judy had not realized how Evelyn had matured and he certainly had not realized she had planned her future to the point of deciding to become a physician one day.

"I am ashamed to admit that it was only through John's sharing of Evelyn's letters to him that we have discovered her academic achievements so far. You, see, I never looked at even one of her report cards. I just always accepted the notion that she, like most girls today, would grow up to become a nurse or a secretary. John, however, has told us she intends to become a doctor. Although we were surprised at her ambition, Judy and I are compelled to accept that Evelyn can be whatever she wants to be and that we must support her."

Olivia agreed saying, "Evelyn has a sharp mind, and I have no doubt she can achieve any goal she sets for herself. I am honored to have played a small part in her development. She is truly a sister to me."

Robert could not agree more. Olivia was grateful for Robert and Judy's new-found interest in their daughter. She thought, "It's a pity it has taken him nearly twelve years to discover the jewel he has in her."

He thanked the good Lord for Olivia and turned his thoughts to John. "Olivia, I have disturbing news. Yesterday he was arrested in Miami and is being transported back to Holmes County where he will be held without bail. I don't expect him to be arraigned before sometime Thursday."

Olivia hung on Robert's every word as he went on to explain how he and Judy were making sparse use of the telegraph, knowing nothing coming over the wires in High Springs would remain confidential.

"Judy received a wire from her contact in Florida stating, *W in place.'* We had worked out a code in advance and we knew this meant the warrant had been issued. Yesterday I received a coded wire from our club's assistant manager stating, *Ducks are flying north for summer, E.T.A. Thursday.'* We knew this was code for news that John was being transported to jail and the date when he was expected to be arraigned."

What Olivia most feared for her daughters was their father being jailed and going through a public trial. She knew this would feed the gossip mill in High Springs and bring more shame upon them. Desperately she asked, "Is there anything I can do?"

"No, at this point there is nothing anyone can do to help John. I am leaving tomorrow morning early on 'The Whistler' from Dothan and will arrive in Miami later in the evening where I will attend to business for both clubs and oversee the transition of responsibility there to the new manager. In the meantime, Judy is on her way to Bonifay to be briefed by an informant there. He will outline any avenues to forestall the case against John and perhaps influence the district attorney there to dismiss the case. While it seems contradictory to what I've just told you about her mother and my epiphany about Evelyn, we will be leaving her in Flora and Frank's care once again. I'd appreciate it if you would continue to act as her guardian angel. I promise we will take more interest in her once the trouble with John blows over."

Olivia nodded her head in understanding. "I'll look after her for all of her life. I promise…."

"Thank you," Robert interrupted.

"You're welcome. And… one more thing…," Olivia swallowed hard. "Will you let John know his wife and children will welcome back home if he ever wants to return to High Springs."

Robert recognized Olivia's effort to give John every opportunity to avoid missing out on his daughters' lives as he and Judy had with Evelyn. He tipped his hat in agreement and quickly left to join Judy to make preparations for their separate trips.

CHAPTER 40

From the time Olivia was ten years-old, her father had relied upon her to oversee the running of the Turner household. Moreover, when he was away from High Point for extended periods she was expected to provide guidance to those responsible for the Turner farming operations. It was Olivia's decisions Walt had relied upon, rather than those of his sons.

The following day around noon, Isaac arrived at Olivia's door with a note from Robert he had penned before boarding 'The Whistler.' He went on to say that given her experience at High Point and being unsure of the length of time he and Judy would be away dealing with John's situation, he asked her to check on things at High Bluff. Specifically, he requested she check Frank's planting plans for the fields and generally oversee things once or twice a week until he and Judy returned.

With business booming for her she had no time to undertake such responsibility, but as she considered all Robert Ward had done in his self-appointed role as her benefactor, she could not refuse him. Therefore, she agreed. Olivia took a pad and pen and scribbled a brief note to Robert. She then instructed Isaac to deliver it to the telegraph office at the High Springs depot where they would transmit its contents to Mister Ward en route to Miami.

. . . . .

In was the first week of April 1936 when Beth arrived at Olivia's to share news of Papa's return and Mama's 'miraculous' recovery. Olivia was amused to hear Beth repeat Papa's message.

"When you stop by Olivia's this afternoon tell her Mama is not receiving visitors for the next few days. Tell her we have personal business, and it'll take us a couple of days so we need to be left alone; we don't need visitors."

It was difficult, what with her belly laughs, for Beth to finish her message. Olivia joined her and they shared the same opinion: Papa was the only medicine Mama needed to have a resurgence of strength and vitality. It amazed them to consider how their tough father was so gentle and possessive of his Annie. Olivia thought, "If only they could bottle whatever it was their father gave her!"

Beth had other good news. She was promoted to the position of senior secretary to David Anderson at the cannery. As such, she was privy to confidential matters. Some talk she overheard recently troubled her. Olivia listened as Beth told her about Mr. Anderson's telephone conversation with someone in Washington.

"From what I could hear they were discussing the potential for building an Army training camp in Dale County. Mr. Anderson was asked how much food his cannery could produce. For Christ's sake, Olivia, they were talking about armed soldiers being stationed near our town. You'll have to admit it is enough to scare a body."

"Beth, these are troubling times for all of us. I don't fully understand the goings on around the world. We must rely on Papa to give us direction."

"I know," Beth lamented. "Mr. Anderson told me of the goings on in Germany last month. From what the papers in New York and Atlanta are saying, the leader of Germany moved some troops into an area he wasn't supposed to and everyone is getting really nervous. No other countries did anything to stop it and many people here in the United States wonder if he will keep going until he takes over all of Europe, and maybe even the United States."

Hearing her sister's comments, Olivia realized the extent of Beth's anxiety and she was surprised. She had not realized how seriously Beth had followed news of the war in Europe and how deep was her concern for the fate of the people there.

Olivia said she had asked her father-in-law the same questions and his answers helped her understand why Germany had lost The Great War and why they were bitter at the United States and the European countries after the Treaty of Versailles which had essentially stripped them of their ability to have an army.

"Both Papa and Mr. Ward have always said they suspected the Germans would find a way to get back at those who had defeated them, and it looks like they are starting now. Because the war left the militaries of the European countries in shambles, they are now powerless to do anything, even if they wanted to. After a long war with millions killed, no one has an appetite for starting it all over again."

Olivia attempted to lessen Beth's concerns as she spoke of how she was at present planning to prepare for war if it did come.

"Beth, both Papa and Mister Ward have seen this coming for over a year. Understand, we have no control over what happens over there just as we cannot control things here in the grand scheme of things. Even so, in our community we are better off than many in other parts of America who suffer greatly from the Depression. Listening to both Papa and Mr. Ward, it appears there may be a resurgence of adverse economic conditions. We can do something about this possibility. What we can do is what Papa has urged us to do: save for a rainy day and preserve as much food as we can for hard times whether they are from the economy or from some far-off war. There is no question we shall all be required to make personal sacrifices, and our way of life will change."

Beth listened to Olivia's comments about what they could expect in time of war. However, it was difficult for her to accept Olivia's pragmatic assessment of the situation abroad and its consequences. Her thoughts had wandered, but Olivia's serious tone drew her attention back to what she was saying.

"Don't laugh when I tell you the plans I have made. I have given careful thought to what I'll need to ensure the survival of Kate, Jean, and me. Food is a necessity. Too many farmers will not have funds to put in their crops and those who do will not have labor sufficient to produce and harvest large crops."

Olivia related what she had learned from Frank and his sons about what word was traveling the grapevine throughout the county. "There is already concern about a draft which will take away many men who would usually be available to make the crops. According to what Frank hears, men in the Quarters on other farmsteads throughout Alabama and some of Georgia are required to register in each county. I have considered what a draft would mean relative to our ability to plant and harvest sufficient food for our needs, aside from our marketing. I am determined to offset its impact."

As Olivia continued telling about actions suggested by Mr. Ward, she shared her plan.

"I plan to have Isaac and Joe work to double the size of my current garden plot. Not long ago I read an article in one of Mr. Gates' farm journals describing how to increase the length of time roots will last in a root cellar; I am having them make changes to my cellar as the article suggested, and with these changes it will be possible to store twice as much for a considerably longer time."

Beth's concern lessened, knowing Papa, like Olivia, would prepare for their survival. It was, as Olivia suggested, a matter of the survival of the fittest and those who prepared!

Olivia waited until the girls had eaten their afternoon snack and went to their rooms to play before telling Beth about John's arrest. She asked her to share the news with Mama and Papa.

"Judy is in Bonifay determining what arrangements she can make to free him on bail. Robert is in Miami and West Palm Beach checking on the operations of those two clubs. Then, he will then join Judy in Bonifay to see John."

Beth didn't know how to respond to this news. There were some times when she thought John was an awful person and other times when she felt pity for him. At this time, her feeling was that of pity.

MCMURTRY

CHAPTER 41

When Robert arrived in Miami on Wednesday, a limousine from the Flamingo Club picked him up at the train station and whisked him to the property where he found everything in good shape. After looking over the Club's operation, he was confident of the ability of the interim manager to operate it efficiently and also provide oversight to the West Palm Beach Dolphin Club. The best news, however, was there appeared to be no indications of mob activity in either of the clubs. Ingrid Schonen had been right; the New York boys had been just what the doctor ordered.

A few days later, Robert returned to Dothan on 'The Whistler' then drove down to Bonifay by car to meet Judy. Their first order of business was to meet with John in jail. After making the necessary arrangements with Able Baker, John's attorney; they met in a solitary holding room with him.

Inside, they observed he was not handling his incarceration well. John was a free spirit by nature and having to follow the jail's coming days. John was nervous and his hands twitched. "Perhaps," thought Robert, "He is withdrawing from alcohol."

At the end of their visit, Judy could not hold back her tears as she watched her son being led back to his holding cell in shackles. As he retreated to his cell, the drab white shirt and pants with "PRISONER' stenciled on the back presented a sorry silhouette of her son.

They left the jail and traveled to a seedy motel nearby to meet with Samuel Bloodworth, the private investigator Judy had retained.

The first question Judy posed to him regarded the progress he had made in identifying witnesses to collaborate his findings. His response was not encouraging. As on their last visit, Bloodworth predicated every remark on the supposition of 'if this or that' could be confirmed. It was evident they were no further ahead in getting John released.

Although Bloodworth had developed more specific information, it was worthless considering there was nothing to substantiate his 'findings' which were little more than suspicions. Reluctantly Robert and Judy accepted that he was not close to gathering sufficient proof to cause the District Attorney to drop the Grand Jury's indictment of John. To top it off, they also knew the governor would not intervene because he could not risk becoming involved in the affairs of Holmes County without bulletproof evidence to support his actions. So, without any prospect of the governor's help, they were forced to consider other options.

·····

The following morning, they met with Able Baker again and shared with him information they had gained from Samuel Bloodworth. Baker was a highly regarded attorney in North Florida and both trusted him implicitly with John's case. He knew of Samuel Bloodworth's work and gave him a glowing recommendation.

"If 'Bloodhound Bloodworth' can't find out anything, it's because the DA and sheriff are keeping a tight lid on everything here. The new sheriff ran on a platform of cleaning up corruption and he's hell bent on keeping his promises. Everyone at the courthouse is wound up tighter than Dick's hatband. Nothing is getting in or out."

Baker went on to discuss with them John's arraignment which was set for later that afternoon. Sheriff Myron 'Handcuffs' Handley had been bragging about getting a conviction of a big fish racketeer like John Ward. He suggested Handley was motivated not by the merits of the case but by how he intended to use John's conviction as a signal to other racketeers that they no longer were above the law in Holmes County.

"I predict he will use all his power to see that John is convicted. He has too much at stake politically to allow him to slip through his fingers."

The arraignment was an important next step for the Wards. Not only would they hear the formal charges against him but they would learn of the Judge's terms for bail. Able Baker cautioned them against acting too quickly though.

"If you post his bail today, Handley will feel the political pressure to push for an early trial and conviction. He would not want the public's interest to wane, which it would, once John was out of jail and out of Holmes County. Therefore, it is my advice to leave him right where he sits. If I know Bloodworth, this will give him time needed to…, ahem…, shall we say 'find' the witnesses he needs to get the charges dropped. It will be a rough road for your son to ride sir, but it's the best for all considered."

Robert understood the merits of Baker's recommendation and he told Judy as much. She agreed with Baker's advice but were torn whether or not to heed it. They decided they would attend John's arraignment and later, when they were allowed to visit him, share his attorney's recommendations. John would have to decide his own fate.

At the arraignment, the judge reiterated the charges against John of unlawfully attempting to influence a county election and set John's bail at $10,000. Following the bail hearing, John was taken to a dimly lit room with bars across the windows. It was barren except for a table and four wooden chairs. John, handcuffed, was escorted into the room and seated at the table where Robert, Judy and Mr. Baker were waiting for him. He looked haggard and defeated and it broke Judy's heart to witness her son in this condition. She had to fight to keep tears from falling. Seeing Judy was in no condition to address John, Robert took the lead.

"Son, I know this is difficult for you but your mother and I are proud of how you are carrying yourself. Stay strong. We are sparing no expense to exonerate you and clear your name. You must be patient; we will fix this. On another note, our last visit was too short to tell you but Olivia and the girls anxiously await your return. She asked me to tell you that regardless of any feelings the two of you have for each other, you will always have a room where you are welcome under her roof." As he spoke, Robert watched his son's eyes sparkle and a brief smile wash across his face.

"Dad, after all Olivia and I have been through, and none of it pleasant for her, I am grateful she is generous enough to open her home to me. Please let her know how much her gesture means to me. Now, get to the bad news."

There was no need to delay longer. The allotted time for their visit would be up soon. Robert asked to Abel Baker to share his advice. John listened with a sinking heart. He understood his chance to avoid prison hinged on Mr. Bloodworth's having enough time to develop facts incriminating another party which would prove sufficient to persuade the sheriff to encourage the DA to drop charges.

Once the attorney finished laying out his recommendation, John responded. "I really don't have a choice, do I? It seems my best chance of being exonerated is to remain here in jail."

There was silence around the table as Abel and Robert looked into the brims of their hats in their hands and Judy sobbed quietly. Robert sighed, and just as he was about to speak, the jailer signaled their time was up. Robert and Judy bid their son farewell knowing his time in jail would seem an eternity.

Before John was escorted out, he paused to ask about Evelyn.

His jailer, being a father himself, allowed a minute for Judy to tell John she asked about him daily and she was maturing into a smart and beautiful girl. She likened her transformation to a swan.

John wanted to ask about Paul, but he knew his time was up; the jailer said it was time to go. Robert offered Judy his arm and Mr. Baker trailed behind them. As Baker passed the jailer, he cupped his hand in the jailer's while slipping him a few dollars for the extra time. The jailer continued walking without so much as an acknowledgement.

Outside, Baker reiterated his plan and promised to visit John regularly. "The best part," he said, "Is that I've now got a man inside who can look after John and get messages to him. Add one more name to your Christmas card list."

.....

After driving around for an hour or so to clear their heads, Robert and Judy found a nearby diner and had an early supper. As they ate their burgers and fries, they realized two things: it was critical that Bloodworth was thorough in his efforts to manufacture exculpatory evidence for Baker to use to create reasonable doubt in the District Attorney's mine, and it was time for Robert to pay a visit to some old friends in Tallahassee.

In addition to approaching the Governor directly, Robert also intended to arrange for a trusted ally to acquaint the Governor with what was happening to John down in Holmes County and ensure the Governor understood there would be steep political consequences if he failed to influence the sheriff. If he didn't play ball, the Governor would have to remove the sheriff for cause.

When they finished eating, Judy and Robert began their separate journeys, with Judy traveling on to High Springs and Robert to Tallahassee. Robert arrived at the Governor's mansion at nearly nine o'clock that evening. When he stopped at the gate, the highway patrolman on duty advised Robert he was not on the list for visitors for the evening. Robert responded gruffly, "Give him my name and tell him I'm here to talk about Cedar Key. He will want to see me; I'm positive of it."

· · · · ·

Having arrived at High Bluff late the night before, Judy arose later than she had planned. She hurriedly dressed and set about her mission to feed the High Springs' gossip mill with information to explain what she expected to be extended absences for both John and Robert. It was important she succeed in establishing a plausible explanation for their whereabouts. She shopped at the mercantile, ate lunch at Dallon's Diner, and visited Gates' Feed and Seed store. At each of her stops she spread 'believable' gossip and achieved her objective.

· · · · ·

Days became weeks with John remaining in the Holmes County jail. At least once a week Abel Baker visited him, and although he had nothing to share concerning John's release, he made sure to shake hands with the jailer before he left.

Although they were meant to allay John's fears, these visits only served to increase John's anxiety about his future. After several weeks, he forced himself to consider life as a convicted felon; much of his waking hours were spent attempting to reconcile himself to serving a lengthy sentence behind bars. His thoughts often drifted to his daughters and his absence in their lives. It was an odd occurrence especially considering how he had cast aside his opportunities to accept their love.

Nights were the worst time for John. As he languished in his cell, he kept thinking about his naivety in handling the political contributions he had funneled to support the unsuccessful candidate for Holmes County sheriff. The more he thought, the more he realized the numerous mistakes he had made. The one that proved to be most damaging to him and the one responsible for his current predicament was that he had not followed his father's specific instructions. He had been sloppy and allowed a paper trail that could be traced back to him.

The minutes seemed like hours and as they drudged by, John considered his future and concluded that he could not return to Miami. He simply was not strong enough to resist the temptations he faced daily in the club's party-like environment. But, what could he do to support himself? Paul always had good advice for him. Perhaps would have ideas for him once he returned. Or, maybe he could just pack up and head west like so many others seemed to be doing these days. If he posted a sign in the window at Ward Enterprises stating "GTT," everyone would know he had "Gone To Texas."

CHAPTER 42

Olivia checked her plants in her garden plot and was overjoyed at finding green plants were thriving and sticking above ground. It was the third week of April 1936 and it appeared nearly every seed had germinated and was set to produce the harvest she had hoped for and least expected.

Although there was still coolness in the air, the bright sun warmed her skin and she stood for a moment, eyes skyward while enjoying the early morning. Her mind wandered a bit and she thought of how proud she was of Evelyn's progress in school. And, for all of her good grades, she was also becoming more adept socially. Olivia's make-over for her had completely changed the perception of her with her teachers, classmates, and anyone else she encountered. The best thing was she had begun to come out of her shell with anyone not named Olivia, John, Flora, or ... Rufus.

Olivia cherished the moments she had with Evelyn. "In a few years," she thought. "Evelyn will discover boys, date, go to college, marry, and start a family." It had once seemed so far away and ludicrous to consider it but then Olivia realized nearly six years had passed since the little pipsqueak had spied on her from the porch at High Bluff on the night Olivia went to live there. Every day they inched closer to the day when their time together would never be the same.

She remembered those days in the Quarters when Evelyn, as a young child, hauled countless buckets to water the plants. Now Olivia had running water from a well powered by an electric motor and Evelyn did not have to use the hand pump any longer. She also remembered the first time Evelyn had addressed her as 'Cotton.' Once just a pet name, Evelyn had resorted to calling Olivia by the name every time she addressed her.

Evelyn was truly an enigma. Because of her family, it was possible for her to have most anything she desired. However, she required little, other than to enjoy her nieces and her sister-in-law's company and to be happy with them. Olivia thought how Evelyn was content to live a simple life without the clutter and the trappings of her school friends' social circles.

What she didn't know was that Evelyn had purposefully patterned her life after Olivia's or how she valued how Olivia made a home out of nothing but filled it with love for her children. But perhaps the most influential thing she had observed about 'Cotton' was the strength she had to withstand the often harsh treatment she suffered at the hands of some cruel people in High Springs. Through it all, Olivia had never displayed any bitterness and that, above all else, was perhaps the most important thing Evelyn noticed and was determined to emulate.

.....

Judy made a rare stop by Olivia's new home where she revealed she had made two trips to Bonifay to see John. She hoped desperately for his release within a few months. Olivia listened intently and could tell Judy was worried about something more. So she encouraged Judy to open up if she thought it would help her cope with John's situation.

"You must be a mind reader, Olivia. You are right; there is something more, and it concerns you. You were very generous to offer John a place in your home after his release. I sincerely believe his knowing you believe in him has bolstered him through this terrible ordeal. On Robert's last visit, John confessed his fear he could not withstand the temptations he would face if he returned to Miami. Robert told him he had come to the same conclusion and had arranged for a different job for him once he was released."

"How does this concern me?" Olivia asked.

"When John left High Springs to take up residence in Miami, it appeared to Robert and I both that you two parted ways with no intention of ever sharing a home again. Is that correct?"

Olivia confirmed it was, "John made it clear he did not intend to return to High Springs, even for a visit and I inferred it was his intent to end our living together. Frankly, his decision was welcomed because I have no desire to live with a drunkard, especially an abusive one who barely tolerates his daughters."

Judy found it hard to hear Olivia's harsh assessment, and yet, she realized Olivia had every reason to be thankful for his absence.

"The message I sent John was a simple and sincere one. If he is released and needs to come home, I'll agree, provided he makes a genuine attempt to have a fatherly relationship with his daughters. In her last act of kindness to me, Mrs. Smith graciously provided me a home, and I have found ways to support us. Frankly, we don't need John. Certainly not the one we knew."

Judy winced. Although she understood John's actions had been hurtful to Olivia, she had mixed emotions, knowing Olivia had moved on without him.

"Mrs. Ward, if John desires to come back to High Springs and maintain his own living arrangements, there is always the cottage. It is deeded in both of our names and my father donated the lumber, but you and Mister Ward provided the money to build it, so I consider it to be partly John's. I have a tenant, Mack Hardy's son and his family, but there is a provision in the lease for ending it early. Should John decide to live there, he would be free to do so after an appropriate notice to them."

Judy couldn't fault her and said she and Robert would go over the options with John and pin him down on what he intended to do upon his return to High Springs. In the meantime, she had things to do and signaled Olivia their talk was over when she stood and began to gather her things. She started for the door but stopped short..

"I'll get Evelyn in a minute and we'll be on our way but first, please know how much both Robert and I appreciate what you are doing with Evelyn and the girls during this difficult time. I know you worry about what will happen with John. He is, after all, the father of your girls. We haven't told anyone else yet but I think you deserve to know that after he is released from jail in Bonifay, John will commence training to become a railroad engineer with the Southern Railway. Robert used his connections there to ensure John will have something that will get him out of the club atmosphere for good and that the demands of the training will be enough to keep him away from gambling and drinking. Although we know nothing is a sure thing, we won't give up hope or stop trying to help him."

CHAPTER 43

Walt entered the main house at High Point and went straight to Annie's room where he found Beth chatting with her at her bedside. Slightly out of breath, he took a moment before he regaled them with news from his travels from the past week.

"On my way back from South Carolina, I stopped in to see Ann and William in Atlanta. I was flabbergasted! In fact, there is only one word to describe their apartment and that is 'filthy.' To top it off, I could not believe my eyes when I saw Ann. I was there at nearly noon and she was still in a wrapper."

He continued describing what he had observed, and spoke of the constant tension between Ann and William. "He came home for lunch and was pleasant, but I could tell he was embarrassed that he was unable to offer me more than a cheese sandwich, which he said was his usual meal."

He went on to describe how William and Ann exchanged nary a word while he was with them. At one point, William secretly motioned for him to join him outside.

"There is no way I can describe his situation. He told me of his inability to satisfy Ann's cravings for expensive gifts and her desire to travel. He said he had experienced with her everything I had warned him to expect and more. He is nearly as miserable with her as she is with him. And, based on a few things he hinted at, I don't know it to be fact but I do not believe they even engage in marital relations. That is odd for a young couple who were so recently married."

Beth noticed Papa's distress and the tears in his eyes. She thought, "Only once before have I ever seen Papa cry. It was the morning Sheriff Miller came to tell him of Jim's death in an automobile accident."

Walt hurriedly wiped away his tears before he continued. "Beth, Ann is a sot! William told me he has found her drunk and sometimes passed out when he returns home in the evenings. Just as I suspected, he explained to me that he cannot continue to live with her unless she is willing to change. We both agreed she will not."

Annie and Beth looked at Papa in disbelief. Of all Ann's antics over the years, drunkenness had not been one of them. Then, Papa shocked them both with his revelation: he had requested William to allow him to bring Ann back to High Point despite his realization that she was beyond any help William or any of them could provide.

"I have returned without her because William momentarily declined my offer, even after confessing he could not live with her, until he could launch one last attempt to salvage their marriage. When I left, he was waiting for Ann to sober up before he issued his ultimatum. She would change or he would send her back with me. He intends to give her until August to alter her behavior. I told him she hasn't toed the line since she was nine years old and he is naïve to believe any ultimatum will bring about change in her."

Beth asked what he thought would happen and Papa did not hesitate with his answer.

"William is naïve in his assumption that he can help her to change; he cannot. I told him as much and I told him I would return here to High Point to make the necessary arrangements for her. Then, if their situation has not changed in a timely manner, 1 will return to Atlanta in early August and bring her back here. I will not allow her to destroy a fine man like William."

Beth thought about Olivia's problems with John's impending return, but Olivia's problem did not compare to Papa and Mama's if Ann returned to High Point as a divorced woman. She would bring disgrace to her family and there was no escaping the fact she would make everyone here miserable. It was ironic that Papa was an honorable man and would dutifully suffer the disgrace of a divorced daughter rather than allow Ann to tie William to a marriage she entered into without any intention of making it work unless it suited her.

She helped Mama get ready for bed and then joined Papa in his study where she listened to him rehash the whole scenario three more times while coming to the same conclusion. He only thought he had been done with Ann.

.....

Robert returned from visiting John in jail in Bonifay and delivered to Olivia his son's decision on what he wanted her to do with their cottage. He said he saw no reason for them to incur the added expense of his living somewhere separate.

Olivia interpreted John's message to mean he would live with his daughters and her and he would abide by her conditions. Having the matter of the cottage settled, Olivia advised the tenants of its continued availability for another year.

Throughout May and June and the first two weeks of July, there were no changes in the District Attorney's prosecution of the case against John. He remained in jail, and Robert and Judy continued visiting him. In the third week of July, the case broke and Robert and Judy burst in at Olivia's to share their exciting news.

Finally, their steadfast efforts had paid off. The charges against John had been dropped. They would head to Florida and bring him home sometime on Sunday.

Robert sensed Olivia's anxiety at the news and hastened to assure her John would abide by her conditions.

"Olivia, I understand how difficult it is for you to accept the truth of what I say when I tell you John is a changed man. There is not a time I have visited with him that he has not expressed more than once how grateful he is for your willingness to permit him to return to High Spring and to this house with you and his daughters.

Although Olivia was relieved John was a free man, she was unable to accept Robert's comments with any credulity. Her feelings were mixed when thinking of John's return. She was full of angst and she often found herself wondering, "Considering how long he has been absent in their lives and the fact they seldom talk about him anymore, what will his return mean to Kate and Jean?" She wondered, too, how she would behave toward him. "What would it be like to share again a bedroom with him again?"

There was no doubt the living accommodations would be awkward but they had lived together before and somehow, she would find a way for them to get through it. Meanwhile, Olivia was grateful that John was being released without his having to going through a trial. Miraculously, it appeared that the gossip Judy had planted as a cover for Robert and John's lengthy absences had taken root and no one was wiser to the truth. Olivia was relieved that it had worked out like it had. Bonifay was only a little more than thirty miles away, and a high profile trial prosecuting John as a 'Miami racketeer" would have produced a myriad of cruel taunts aimed at herself and the girls. Fortunately, it appeared the girls would not have to go through life with their father labeled as a 'jail bird.'

Robert left quickly and with her sewing projects completed, Olivia planned to spend the weekend at High Point. During her visit, she would tell her Papa and Mama of John's release from jail and his planned return to High Springs in a few days. She hoped they would be joyous for his return but she could not be sure. One thing was for sure, she wasn't going to break the news to Kate and Jean until she saw the whites of his eyes. He had disappointed them far too many time to rely on anything concerning him with any degree of certainty. Either way, it would be difficult but she intended to encourage Kate and Jean both to accept their father's return. With Jean it was a matter of her having time with her father. However, with Kate it was a different matter. Unfortunately, Olivia was uncertain how to help Kate rekindle a care for John.

·····

It was Friday and Beth arrived around eight o'clock in the morning to pick Olivia and the girls up to go to High Point. Before Olivia could tell her about John's impending release, Beth told her about Papa's visit with Ann and her possible return. Olivia was not surprised but she was sad Ann had heaped more disgrace upon herself and Mama and Papa.

Once they arrived at High Point, the girls ran off with Gussie and Olivia to the opportunity to break her news about John to Beth. She still had not found a better way to break the news to the girls. She knew she had to do so; it was just a matter of when. She asked Beth for suggestions but she had none. While they chatted, Olivia decided she would just stick with her original plan and wait until John actually arrived home. Then she would let the girls react however they truly felt. That way their reaction would be genuine and they would not feel as though she had talked them into anything. It was a bit risky, but Olivia decided this was one time risk-taking was important.

After chatting with Beth, Olivia went upstairs to find Mama and Papa where she told them about John's impending return. Based on what he had heard from his contacts in Bonifay, Papa was surprised John had gotten off. Mama on the other hand was relieved. She still felt they owed John an immeasurable debt for his role in convincing Ann there was nothing left for her in High Springs and helping convince her to take up with Amelia and Pearl in Savannah.

Generally, her parents were concerned, but they acknowledged his being home provided another opportunity for him to develop a relationship with his girls and them with him. They hoped he would take advantage of it.

......

On Saturday, Olivia and the girls coaxed Beth out of the house and down to the stables. Together, she and Olivia put together a makeshift petting zoo from all of the barnyard animals on the farm. Kate was particularly enamored with a goat while Jean loved sitting on the back of a Shetland pony. In a moment of inattention, Olivia allowed the girls to cut behind a feeding trough and both girls emerged from the other side covered in mud and dung. To say they stunk to high heavens was an understatement.

Gussie had one of the girls from the Quarters draw up a washtub of hot water down by the burn barrels and Olivia and Beth took turns dunking the girls, clothes and all, in the warm, soapy water much to the girl's delight. The girls were so worn out they could barely keep their eyes open. In fact, Olivia and Beth carried them both to bed without any supper. As they traversed the stairs, Kate could be heard making her half-awake case for their keeping a baby goat in their sitting room.

.....

On Sunday morning, Beth dropped Olivia at her home before she and the girls headed across town for Sunday school and church. Olivia was anxious to straighten the house and prepare for John when he arrived. Then she completed her tasks and sat down with her Bible to spend time with the Lord.

Her heart was heavy with concerns for their future as a family. Her prayers were fervent as she asked for God's direction in accepting John in her life and those of Kate and Jean's. She prayed

John would not behave in such a way so as to hurt them.

Before she knew it, Beth arrived back with the girls and she agreed to stay and have lunch. She sensed Olivia's anxiety and made light conversation in an attempt to ease her mind. As a result, the conversation turned to Jean's upcoming 4th birthday. At its mere mention, Olivia's eyes lit up. As it turned out, that was just the thing to get Olivia's mind off of the situation with John.

As they outlined the possibilities for Jean to have a fun party, Olivia shared Beth what Judy had suggested. She had asked Olivia to allow her and Evelyn to plan Jean's celebration and hold it out in the country at High Bluff rather than in the city. Beth thought it was a good idea and said as much.

"Heck, Olivia. It seems to me we should just sit back, relax and let the good times roll at the Ward's. You can bet Flora will take charge and put out a spread for the occasion. You know her corn pone cakes are the best in the county. I will bet, though, Judy will ask you to bake Jean's cake. I'm all for it. Just tell me the time."

Olivia smiled to think how simply Beth lived her life. She really did just go with the flow, and every time Olivia was downtrodden about something, all she had to do was talk with Beth and her worries seemed to evaporate.

"It's settled then. We'll spend Jean's birthday at the Wards. Judy will be ecstatic."

As they changed the girls out of their clothes, Beth remarked that Olivia was fast becoming a first-class business woman with people beyond High Springs now clamoring for her services. She also mentioned that in order to ensure she could continue to grow, she would need reliable transportation. Olivia agreed and Beth gave her some interesting news. There was an older Model T Ford for sale out by the cannery.

"One of the men the Andersons let go needs the money for his mortgage. Although it is worth considerably more, you could buy it for a hundred dollars. I've got a little nest egg put away for what you always warn will be a rainy day, and I'll contribute my fifty dollars if you can raise the other. What do you say?"

Olivia promised she would consider Beth's suggestion but would ask Mr. Ward for his opinion. With that concession, Beth took her leave.

"A car of my own," she thought. "I guess I had never really considered that as an option."

CHAPTER 44

Around noon on Monday, Olivia received a call from Robert Ward. He and John had just arrived in High Springs on "The Ward Whistler" and they were going to stop in at Dallon's for lunch and then make their way to her house. He hoped this would provide her ample notice for John's arrival.

It was Olivia's own "Meet Jesus time." She rounded up the girls and sat them at the kitchen table as she explained she needed to talk to them. Although Jean was not quite four, she understood Mama had something really important to discuss with them. Kate's reaction was one of anticipation of some stigma she would be forced to suffer over.

Olivia made it as simple and she could and prepared to judge the girls' reaction.

"Today, your father will return to High Springs to live with us."

Neither girl registered any emotion. It had, after all, been nearly two years since they had seen him. Jean spoke first and remarked he was the man in the picture album Mama Ward showed her and talked about a lot. After thinking about it a little more, she asked why he didn't come to see them for a long time. Didn't he miss them? Fortunately, she didn't seem to expect an answer, which was just as well because Olivia could not have provided one.

Then Kate spoke up. She shared how Evelyn often spoke of her big brother and how often she reminded her he was hers and Jean's father. According to what Evelyn had told her, he was the only one in her family who paid any attention to her when she was a child, and for that matter, even now. She also recalled accompanying him on his rolling store routes. Sadly, these were the only pleasant memories Kate could resurrect. Her more pronounced memories of her father were he anger at her mother and his distasteful smell and frequent falls when he came home late at night making a lot of noise which woke her up.

There was more that Kate remembered but she didn't recount the stories in front of Jean, who was young and wouldn't understand their implications. But Kate did. She understood what it meant when her father yelled bad words at Mama and threw things at her. She also had come to understand what he meant when he spoke of her and Jean as 'those brats.' Although she didn't quite understand what a horse had to do with them, she heard him speak several times about his of his disgust at being 'saddled' with them. While Jean was not old enough, Kate had a clear understanding of his strong dislike for them and their mother.

Kate sat patiently listening to her mother tell her and Jean what she considered to be grim news; news she did not want to hear. She could not cause her mother more worry, so she struggled to refrain from asking the question that was on her mind, "Why is he coming back to live with us just when I've stopped having bad dreams about him?"

· · · · ·

It was just a little before two o'clock when Olivia heard what she thought was Robert's car. She went to open the door for John and discovered his parents were with him. The girls ran to their grandparents with glee; Jean to Judy and Kate to Robert, leaving John and Olivia face to face.

After an awkward silence, Olivia welcomed them all and suggested she fix coffee for them as she headed to the kitchen.

Robert called to her asking where he should put John's suitcase; she hesitated and then told him to put it in *their* bedroom.

Judy, sensing Olivia's hesitation, decided to linger and accept Olivia's offer of coffee although she wasn't in the mood for it. Once the coffee was ready, they gathered around the kitchen table and Robert spoke of his concerns.

"So far we've kept the people of High Springs ignorant of John's troubles. Now we must consider questions we'll probably have asked of us and the answers we are to give."

For an hour they discussed questions they were likely to encounter and plausible answers. Olivia was struggling with what to say and who to say it to. Judy noticed this and offered her advice.

"When you are unable to answer a question with absolute truth, you should just incorporate a modicum of truth into the answer. If you do so, most times your answer will be accepted. As to any question about John's absence for almost three years, we'll tell the truth: he had responsibilities that would not permit his absence from two construction projects and the subsequent successful opening of two clubs in South Florida."

Mentally, Olivia questioned how Judy defined the truth of a situation. It seemed to Olivia that Judy was inclined to depend upon a number of white lies to underpin her declaration of a 'truth.' Olivia had the audacity to ask Judy how it was she could mingle so many partial truths with her version of the truth of a situation. Judy's response was priceless.

"Honestly Olivia, you really just have to practice a little before it comes naturally to you. That is, until the mixture of truth and half-truths can become acceptable to others. With practice, you can create a certain reality for the one asking; they'll accept your explanation regardless of any facts they might know to the contrary. Besides, it really isn't a lie if you believe that's the way it really happened. Try it. You'll get the hang of it like I did."

Olivia could not believe her ears and buried her head in her hands on the table while Robert continued covering different scenarios. Never had she regretted being involved with this family than in this very minute. But, a funny thing happened. The longer they talked, the more relaxed everyone became, including John and her. After an hour or so, it was just like John had never left; or so it seemed.

Meanwhile, Judy prattled on. She reminded them not to offer too many details because doing so created the risk of exposing not only John but Ward Enterprises, Robert, and her to new investigations. John must have considered the same because he raised the question of how his time in Bonifay would be explained.

Robert reminded him there was no indication anyone in High Springs had an inkling of his jail time. However, to cover this situation, they would tell of John's prolonged training in Memphis where he was becoming a railroad engineer.

With that said, Robert shifted gears from the prospects of keeping John's absence a secret and what he was actually going to do now that he was a liability running their clubs. As he spoke, Robert made it clear that John had to spend the time necessary to master the materials on which he would be tested for his certification as a railroad engineer. He could maintain his position only if he met the all of the requirements for certification. The company would not compromise the safety of its passengers and its reputation with an unprepared engineer.

True, as John knew, to gain the opportunity for him to become an engineer, meant at least one high railroad official had waived some basic requirements. Robert emphasized John could not expect other accommodations; he had to earn his certification! Finally, Judy and

Robert prepared to leave, with Robert reminding John of their planned trip to Dothan the following morning.

John closed the door behind his parents and followed Olivia into the kitchen. The relative ease she had felt a short time before had evaporated and she had no idea how to act toward him, a man who left her almost two years ago. She winced and felt physically threatened when he stepped in front of her and took her by the hands.

"Olivia, at the time Jean was born I told you not to depend on any promises I might make because I could not be relied upon to keep them. Nothing has changed; I am the same flawed person I was then. Given the truth of this, there is something I want to say to you, and I hope you'll consider it for what it is worth. Sitting in my jail cell day after day gave me time to think about what I wanted if I gained my freedom. It was clear to me then as now I want to be a part of Kate and Jean's lives. But I don't know how to go about restoring a relationship with either of them, especially Kate."

He went on to say that his feelings for Olivia had not changed. While he respected her for all she had accomplished, he had not altered in rejecting the idea of any personal regard for her.

"Will you give me a chance to live here with our daughters and you? I need the girls to give me a reason to resist temptations I have faced and succumbed to for almost a decade."

He stammered as he told her he expected their marital relationship to be as it was when he agreed to move to Mrs. Smith's with her. "Of course, we'll need to talk about what Dr. James suggest as birth control." With that, John dropped her hands and awaited her response

"If you commit yourself to behave toward Kate and Jean as a father, then you may live here. I want nothing from you. I do admit there was a time just before and after Jean was born when I was foolish enough to think our relationship might develop into more, but you vanquished my silly notions. As to the prospect of our being intimate, it is not something I need, but I know you do, so I'll see Dr. James in a few days."

John appeared to want to say more but Olivia was not prepared to listen.

"Go to bed now. In the morning you may start your campaign to win back the affection of your daughters."

CHAPTER 45

The next morning Olivia awoke and found John in the girls' room fumbling to help Jean dress. He was about as adept at dressing children as he was changing diapers. Jean cooed as he struggled to slip on her dress. She was eager for his attention, but not Kate, who remained distant. Olivia fixed their breakfast and joined in their conversations as she attempted to create as normal an environment as possible. John said he had an errand to run but suggested she and the girls be ready to accompany him to Jerrell's upon his return in the afternoon.

. . . . .

During the first week of August 1936, Robert and John arrived in Dothan at the Southern Railroad dispatcher's office. There John met the chief engineer who was responsible for his training. The meeting was expected to last for several hours so Robert excused himself. He took the Southern Railroad pool car out to look at several commercial properties he was interested in buying on the south side of town. He said he would return by the time John was finished with his orientation.

Over the next few hours, the chief engineer laid out his expectations for John over the coming months. He would be required to be on time, refrain for using drugs or consuming alcohol, and pass all of his written and practical examinations. He told John most prospective engineers found the first part to be easy with the latter part making of breaking them. John chuckled when he thought to himself, "Well you will find I'm not most people. The examinations will be a breeze. The first part, I'm not so sure."

Once they were done, the dispatcher handed John a detailed schedule of his classroom and practical application schedule for the next 30 days. The classroom instruction would be at the rail yard and the chief engineer would accompany him on his run from Dothan to Mobile, New Orleans and Memphis, and then the return legs via Tupelo, Birmingham, and Montgomery. The dispatcher cautioned him to square himself away with his 'the missus' at home. He would be away... a lot... and such would be the case until John became certified for his solo runs.

John assured the dispatcher he was squared away at home and was more than up to the challenge for the work. He seemed genuinely grateful for the job, saying he would do whatever it took to keep it. As he and Robert boarded 'The Whistler' to head back to High Springs, he worried about how he was to get to and from Dothan.

"Dad, will it be possible for me to rely on one of the scheduled trains making runs to and from High Springs? With her increase in orders for cakes and rugs, Olivia can't spare the money to help me purchase a car because she needs to get additional supplies."

"I will arrange it with Frank for you to use one of the farm trucks," Robert said. "It can stay parked at the depot while you're gone and be there ready for you when you get back."

At one time, John would have reminded his father that he had once owned his own car, a beautiful sedan that he treated as a prized possession. He was heartbroken when Robert had taken it back and sold it to help cover the costs of supporting Olivia in the Quarters. Now, he demonstrated a modicum of maturity in accepting the use of the farm truck. It might not have been the flashiest vehicle he had ever driven but it sure beat the heck of out walking or waiting for a train and he was grateful for his father making it available to him..

. . . . .

Upon John's return home that afternoon, he kept his promise of treats at Jerrell's with the girls. As soon as he told Olivia they were leaving, she loaded the girls in their wagon. They waved goodbye and John pulled them along behind him telling them stories and making them laugh as he walked. Jean giggled with glee, but Kate sat silently at the back of the wagon as it rolled along. Even the casual observer would have recognized she had developed an iron will with regard to her father. No matter what John did, he didn't seem to be able to crack her tough outer shell. And he didn't know why.

. . . . .

That evening Olivia observed the spontaneous exchanges between John and Jean. Kate warmed up a little but was still standoffish. Olivia developed a sense of hope for the girls as she observed their interactions with John and he with them. She dared to be optimistic that perhaps their new living arrangements could work out amicably after all. After supper, she put them to bed and John came to where Olivia was bundling rugs and took a seat. It was apparent he had something to say.

"This old house doesn't seem the way I remembered it; the changes you've made are great. I am really impressed."

She explained that Mrs. Smith's provisions had made it possible to make repairs and renovations to the house. Then she shared her experience with Mack Hardy.

"He's nothing more than a scoundrel. He tried to take advantage of me by bullying me into allowing him to handle my affairs for an exorbitant fee. Thanks to your father I was able to confirm my suspicions about his paperwork and I didn't sign away my rights to him. Heaven forbid other women in this town, especially widows, figure out they don't need an attorney to manage their affairs. He would go broke missing out on all the fees he overcharges them.."

"Honest to God, Olivia, I imagine it took weeks for him to get over dealing with you. I bet he will give you a wide berth from now on."

She agreed and brought him up to speed on the cottage. Once he said he didn't want to live there, she rented it and it was under lease for the coming year. Since Robert and Judy had paid to remodel it, she considered it to belong to John. It was in his name and the rent money went into an account she has set up for him.

The only business she had with the cottage or the bank account was to write a check yearly to cover the taxes owed on it and Mrs. Smith's house. She reiterated that the property was his to do as he pleased. If he wanted her to do something different, he just needed to tell her and she would make other arrangements. In the event he wanted to sell it, the only thing she needed to do was fetch the nearly 200 jars of canned goods she stored in the outbuilding behind the cottage. Joe and Isaac were building her a new root cellar at Mrs. Smith's but it was not yet complete.

Yet again John found himself impressed with Olivia's business savvy. He asked that she proceed as she had planned. Besides, he would be away on his train route and it was probably best that she just continue to handle things as she had over the past two years. As they talked, Olivia shared her plans for future endeavors as well as the prospects of a war in Europe. Then she recounted most of the things she had accomplished with her cakes, rugs, and dresses over the past two years. Although it was not usually his demeanor, John listened intently now before commenting.

"I do not know of any other individual with the foresight to prepare as you have for an uncertain economy and the potential for another war! Thank you for managing the care of this family. I'll find some way to make my contributions."

As John spoke of his intentions, Olivia appreciated his sentiments. Perhaps his stint in jail had changed him in some measurable way but she knew too well she could not rely upon him to follow through and make them a reality. Therefore, she made no comment and instead decided to share with him her news.

"You may not remember but I obtained my temporary teaching certificate. I plan to look for a teaching job in a nearby town; the School Board members in High Springs will not permit me to teach here but there are some promising opportunities over in Slocum and Daleville."

He was at a loss for words. He knew Olivia was an excellent teacher by the work she had done with Isaac and Joe, as well as their daughters. He understood her situation and felt bad that she was 'branded' by the marital situation but he knew there was nothing he could do to change it. He could not go back in time, although there were countless nights he had prayed for the opportunity.

"There is one more thing," she said. "On your next visit to town, I'd like you to check in with Dr. James' receptionist and make an appointment for him to see me."

John agreed thinking to himself he would not have the battle he expected from Olivia. Her request was tantamount to her acquiescence to his desires to exercise his marital rights.

. . . . .

By early October 1936, John and Olivia adopted a well-oiled routine for themselves and their daughters. Few people questioned them about his years away from High Springs. Most were more interested in his work on the railroad and confined their questions to that subject. Even so, he was seldom at ease, fearing his past would become known and he would be exposed as a criminal, or worse, a failure. Predictably, his time spent with Paul was the only time he ever truly felt at ease. Paul had a capacity for forgiving John of his past transgressions and in the process, lived up to his title as 'best friend.'

During the day and most evenings, John devoted every spare minute of his free time to studying and preparing for his upcoming engineer exams. Still, he and Paul found some time to get away together for a soda at Jerrell's or a bite to eat at Dallon's. Paul had even offered to take John flying with him, but John vehemently rejected the notion.

"I'm keeping my feet on the ground, friend. If the good Lord had intended us to fly, he'd have given us wings."

One thing was certain, they would be lifelong friends and although they enjoyed their time together, they had a tacit agreement to forego including their wives. Both knew that ship had sailed long ago.

Paul and Sandra had hit their rocky patches over the past few years but were still together. He had experienced some difficult challenges professionally, especially with the removal of his father as president of the bank and all the attending questions in the community. And she was not content to sit at home while he 'played pilot' at the airfield.

Particularly aggravating was the fact that he refused to share any details of his business with Triangle Aviation or his mysterious trips, lasting a week or more, to Kansas. Had Sandra not known Paul better, she would have assumed he was having an affair..

When she and Paul met in college, she had envisioned marrying someone of importance; a real 'mover and shaker', not being relegated to being a housewife in High Springs, Alabama. Although she took day trips to Dothan and Enterprise, they were nothing to compare with trips she had taken as a girl with her mother to New

York, Chicago, Birmingham, and Atlanta.

As a result, Paul and Sandra's marriage was on its last leg. They had rarely been intimate and only communicated in muffled sentences. Likewise, Paul's relationship with his mother and father was strained. Although it had come as a surprise for both him and Sandra, it was his hope this situation would change now that they had learned they would be grandparents around the first of the year. Paul anxiously awaited the arrival of his son. He was so excited that he already had purchased a tiny University of Alabama sweater and a miniature flight helmet for the boy.

CHAPTER 46

Early on a Friday morning in mid-October 1936, John left on his inaugural four-day railroad line run from Dothan to New Orleans and back by way of Memphis, Birmingham, and Montgomery. He would not return until Monday evening.

Although it was still dark outside and the girls were still asleep when he rose and dressed, Olivia met him at the door with a Thermos bottle of hot coffee and a paper sack loaded with a warm biscuits with jelly, and sandwiches. Outside the house, Isaac exited the Ward's idling farm truck and hopped into another with Joe behind the wheel, and they waved at Olivia as they sped off.

As John stepped up into the cab of the truck, he gave a brief salute to Olivia before he pulled away. Olivia had mixed emotions. John had been good to the girls over the past few weeks but she felt guilty that a sigh of relief had escaped her as he disappeared into the distance.

.....

A week passed and Olivia and the girls settled into their routine without John around. Olivia, though, felt that a change of scenery would benefit the girls so she called Papa on the party line and he said he would stop by the next morning.

Around ten in the morning the following day, Papa kept his promise and stopped by to invite Olivia and the girls to High Point for Kate and Jean to have lunch with Annie and him and then ride the ponies later that afternoon. He said Beth would stop by later to pick them up and would carry them home afterward.

Olivia was surprised. "Papa I thought you would be in Atlanta this weekend to pick up Ann.

"There's been a change in plans. The last letter from William urged me to delay. So, I'm waiting to hear back from him. I'll fill you in on the details when I know them."

Beth was due to arrive any minute now but the news from Atlanta troubled Olivia. As she hurriedly dressed the girls, she had a sneaking suspicion Ann's marriage was not long for this world. She hoped against steep odds that she was wrong.

·····

Upon their arrival at High Point the fall air was crisp, and Beth, as she and Olivia had discussed, they had lunch with Papa and then drove the girls down to the paddocks to join Papa and Gabriel. Olivia watched as Gabriel and Papa helped each of the girls mount her pony and then paraded them slowly around the corral. Both girls squealed with delight at the experience.

When they finished their riding lessons, the girls and Gabriel piled into the back of Walt's truck and held on dearly as they prepared for the bumpy ride up the dirt road to the main house. Papa opened the door and held it for her as Olivia slid into the front seat. Olivia thought back to her last time there: the night he had unceremoniously dumped her out on her own at the Ward's house.

"Times have certainly changed," she thought.

A few minutes later they arrived at the main house and Gussie greeted them at the front door. She ushered Jean and Kate inside while telling them of the special treat consisting of candied apples she had waiting for them in the kitchen. They set off running in utter delight.

With the girls suitably occupied, Olivia and Beth went to their mother's room where they found Papa telling Mama about his discussions with Robert Ward.

Although he had initially accepted Robert's offer of free carriage on his rail spur in exchange for finding his way to welcoming Olivia and the girls back into the Turner Family, Walt had later come to see the unconditional love Robert had for Olivia, and the many things he had done for them to make the girls' lives more tolerable.

As such, he did not feel he could accept Robert's generous 'offer' any longer. He would pay for his carriage fees. Today, Walt had business with Robert regarding several freight charges for which he had not been billed.

Now, Papa was relating some of what he had learned from Robert about his experiences in The Great War while serving in the United States' Armed Forces in France.

As the two entered their mother's room they heard Walt tell her, "Robert was twenty-seven years old when he enlisted in 1916; much older than many of his Doughboy counterparts. When he shipped to France a year later as part of the American Expeditionary Force, he witnessed the horrors of war in the trenches and knew that those who were poisoned by mustard gases the enemy used had died horrible deaths.

"Between the gassing and the carnage left by the strategy on both sides of charging into direct machine gun fire, millions of survivors relived the war nightly, hearing the 'tat-tat-tat-tat' of British Vickers and German Maxims even now, twenty years later."

Annie remarked that she understood Robert had remained in Europe, and specifically France, following the Armistice, and had not come home for approximately two years. She was curious to know if Robert spoke about his time after the war. From what she could learn, he rarely, if ever, referred to this period of his life or of his activities in post-war Europe.

"I have heard that Robert managed to acquire some French artifacts he shipped back home, and subsequently sold. Some suggest that it was from the sale of these artifacts that he acquired much of his present-day wealth. Others discount such a notion, especially when they relate the successful business endeavors Judy undertook throughout Robert's time in the service. Personally, I give credence to the story of Judy's impact on their business because, knowing her, a person comes to understand she is a shrewd business woman who built wealth and acquired considerable farmland while Robert was away."

Annie continued explaining the perceptions of many concerning Judy. "Even today most people attribute much of the successes of the Ward Enterprises to Judy's active involvement in its business matters. One thing is for sure, most people who know her or of her refer to her as a real 'barracuda' in business matters."

Walt agreed with Annie's assessment and noted, "I asked Robert about his time in France, but he was reluctant to tell me much more about his wartime experience except to say he was in the Battle of the Ardennes Forest late in the war and he doubted hell could be worse. On the other hand, he shared some aspects of what the French people, as well as citizens of other European countries endured at the conclusion of The Great War. According to him, there was nearly complete devastation of the infrastructure, and the citizens' economic situations were much worse than anything we Americans have suffered during our lingering Depression."

Olivia listened intently as Papa repeated some of Robert's opinions concerning German Chancellor Adolph Hitler's rise to power in Germany.

"It is Robert's opinion that Hitler has succeeded because he capitalized on the severe sanctions imposed upon Germany under the Treaty of Versailles. He used Germany's inability to satisfy these sanctions to generate a strong movement of German Nationalism across the nation. 'Germany,' he proclaimed, 'would not become beholden to any nation.' Despite being prohibited by law from building a large standing Army, the Germans seemed to be finding ways around the Treaty. While most European countries and provinces were financially bankrupt and unable to rebuild their militaries which the war had decimated, Germany's inability to defend its borders provided the opportunity Hitler needed to expand his power."

Beth asked if Mr. Ward had expressed an opinion on whether the war would ever involve the United States.

"It seemed he had an opinion but did not express it. He did, though, explain his plans to buffer his businesses and farming operations from the economic impact of our involvement in war. His remarks suggested he had accepted our involvement as an inevitable aspect of our future."

Papa paused to gather his thoughts and share what he learned with them.

"There is one aspect of our conversation I found intriguing and one I do not plan to ignore. He suggested that any year now could be the last crop year we farmers would have adequate farm labor to harvest our crops." He explained the basis for this conclusion.

"Some of his highly-placed Washington friends had shared with him that President Roosevelt was considering instituting a draft of men to buffer the armed forces. Such a draft would be tantamount to stripping the homesteads of many of our people upon whom we now rely for labor to plant and harvest our crops. According to Robert, we have no replacements for these farm laborers if the draft becomes a reality. Based upon the projected time table for such a draft, by the time our crops would be ready for harvesting the draft would have had its effect. Thus, he plans a major crop expansion this year, and encouraged me to do the same to prepare for what may happen over the next few years."

Olivia listened but she could not fully concentrate on the significance of Robert's advice. She was too anxious to learn news of Ann.

"Papa when you stopped by earlier today you mentioned you had news of Ann and William. Are you prepared to share it with us at this time?"

He sighed and told of William's letter. "He writes he believes that Ann is approximately four months pregnant. However, according to his letter she insists she is not and is behaving in a way that is detrimental to the baby she is carrying."

Olivia could not believe her ears. Papa continued.

"According to William, Ann continues to refuse to see a doctor and will barely eat. He is at his wits end with her but will not consider sending her back home until after the baby is born. He did not elaborate, but he also said she has been depressed and he fears leaving her alone when he goes to work. He has asked his mother to take a leave of absence from her teaching position to come stay with them. He feels this is critically important considering Ann is in a bad place mentally and he fears what she might do if she continues to spiral downward. In her drunken state, she had even threatened to kill herself rather than remain in Atlanta living as they do in a tiny apartment in the city."

Beth interrupted to express her opinion. "There is no way Ann could deny being pregnant. This is another one of her ploys to gain attention and her way."

Walt confessed he had no answer. "I can repeat only what William writes in his letters. His present worry is Ann's continued state of drunkenness and its effect upon his unborn child."

Olivia was horrified. "Surely Ann would not deliberately try to kill her baby?"

Walt did not hold back. "Yes, she would! Ann is evil. She married William expecting him to provide her with the lifestyle she felt she was entitled to have. He has not been able to do so, and she blames him. Killing his baby is her way of punishing him."

Annie burst out desperately, "Walt, you have to go to Atlanta and bring Ann home. We may be able to prevent so tragic an ending for our daughter and her baby. It is a horrible act that Ann appears willing to commit."

Beth stared at her father in disbelief. Surely, he and his mother did not intend to have Ann return to High Point where she would undoubtedly create a living hell for all of them!

"Please don't bring her back here. There will be no peace for any of us. Moreover, I fear what the stress of her horrible behavior every day will do to you, Mama."

Walt and Annie sensed the fear in Beth's voice, and understood that her words reflected everything the two of them had already considered.

"We have no choice, Beth. Now go find Olivia and prepare the house for Ann's return. Her constant nagging and complaining about her lot in life and how her mother and I have failed her will not sit well with her mother and I fear it will only make Annie's condition worse. So, you will need to find a way to insulate Mama from her so that she doesn't suffer from Ann's ungrateful behavior. I'll leave for Atlanta first thing in the morning and return as soon as possible."

CHAPTER 47

That night, Olivia helped Annie get ready for bed. Then she tucked her in and ensured she was comfortable. Annie worried about Walt's trip to Atlanta but Olivia held her hand tightly, stroking it gently as she reassured her he would be fine. Annie had trouble falling asleep so Olivia opened the family Bible on the night table and read to her passages illustrating how God has a plan for everyone. After hearing these Scriptures, Annie was reconciled to leaving Ann's fate in God's hands. As Mama drifted off to sleep, Olivia quietly left her to find Beth. They had a heap of work to do before sunrise.

The following morning, Beth dropped a sleepy Olivia and the girls off at home. She and Olivia had been up all night and they were proud of their handiwork. As the girls toddled inside, she and Olivia lingered on the porch and recounted what they had achieved the night before.

With the help of two of the men in the Quarters, they had sectioned off part of the large parlor on the far end of the house to serve as Ann's sleeping quarters. The space would be a comfortable one and would provide Ann with the privacy she would crave while keeping her at the far end of the house away from their mother's suite.

After a few minutes, Beth hugged Olivia and left to return to High Point and some much needed sleep. Olivia was exhausted too, but renovating Ann's quarters set her mind in motion and caused her to think of John's difficult adjustment to moving into a home with two children.

For a long time she had given thought to John's having his own 'inner sanctum' where he could study his engineering manuals and otherwise escape from the whirlwind the girls often created around them. Now that his schedule would put him at home for three consecutive days each week, she would convert what had been Mr. Smith's study into a comfortable room for him. It would be a lot of work and cost money she probably could not afford to spend but she had an ulterior motive. "Having a sanctuary where he could escape the drudgeries of family life might not only help keep him from backsliding into his old habits of drinking, carousing, and gambling, but it would certainly provide stability for the girls and me," she thought. In other words, she could not afford not to create John's study.

.....

John left on the New Orleans run on October 15th and returned on October 19th. He was scheduled to be home for three days; and Jean, if not Kate, was excited to have him home. Upon his arrival, the girls greeted him, while insisting he follow them to see what they had accomplished.

John was uncertain why it was so urgent for him to see a room he had already seen many times before. When he finally walked into the room and looked about at the fresh paint and newly arranged furnishings, he was amazed. What was once cold and uninviting been transformed into a warm and welcoming space. It made him think of a sanctuary, a cozy retreat he could retire to at the end of a challenging day. Never could he have been prepared to have this testimony of the love his daughters had for him. Truly, he was blessed.

Jean tugged on his arm and directed him to sit at the desk. "Daddy... like it?."

John was overcome with emotion as he realized what Olivia had done for him. "Is this room really for me? If it is, then I like it mighty fine."

Olivia sent Kate and Jean to set the table for supper. After they left she shared with John her thought about his room. "Every man should have a place where he can be to himself, as a reprieve from the hustle and bustle of his shared life. This will be your place of refuge."

Then she took a key from her pocket and handed it to him. She cautioned him to safeguard the key; it was their only copy. The gesture was not lost on John. If he felt the need for privacy for himself or any of his things, there was a door with a lock to which he, alone, had the key.

Olivia went to join the girls while he remained in this room prepared just for him. He thought, "Although I risked immeasurable shame returning here from Florida where I have tried to hide my arrest and incarceration, I am so glad things worked out as they have. I almost missed experiencing the love of my daughters because I was such a fool."

. . . . .

Two evenings later, on October 21st, John poured himself a cup of coffee and prepared to retire to his room when he approached Olivia at the table.

"If you are not too tired I'll tell you about the message I received when I returned to Dothan. It confirmed the dates for my final six exams. I'll go to Memphis the second week of November and I'll not return until just before Thanksgiving. I just wanted you to know my schedule so you could make your plans for the girls."

He paused to allow Olivia to make any observation about what he had shared. She expressed her appreciation of his consideration of them all and then asked if he desired to hear news of Ann. He said he did and then Olivia gave him an abbreviated version of what was occurring with her. She mentioned Papa was due back that evening or the following morning and was bringing back a pregnant and likely soon to be divorced Ann to live at High Point. John was not surprised.

"I suspect I know much of what you have not told me so I'll not press you for more details. William has been unable to satisfy Ann's desires for an esteemed social status, so she wants out of her marriage and will raise the baby alone? I shudder to say it but no child should have Ann as a mother."

John knew Olivia would be anxious until she could determine how Ann's arrival would impact everyone at High Point, especially her mother. Thus, he suggested, "Why don't I take you there late tomorrow afternoon so you can welcome her home and provide a buffer for your mother? Perhaps your presence will ease the process of her settling in to her 'new' home."

Olivia thanked John for his offer while acknowledging her concerns for Mama's health. But she shared that she was more concerned over Beth's reaction to Ann's return. She worried Beth could not deal with Ann's tantrums she threw when things did not go her way or when she simply felt she wasn't receiving enough attention.

She stopped there and did not further elaborate on her anxiety. It would do no one any good and besides, she knew too well what Ann was capable of doing and did not doubt the length to which she might go to carry her point. She would stop at nothing to punish William for his 'sin' of not measuring up to the impossible role she had created for him to fill in her life.

John said he understood and asked if there were something he could do the next morning to prepare the girls for their trip to High Point while she settled the day's agenda with Martha. Upon considering the drama that might ensue, Olivia said it might be best to leave the girls at home with Martha. She thanked him for his thoughtfulness and started off to find some dish soap in the pantry.

Before she could move too far, John rose and placed his hand on Olivia's shoulder. "You know, there's something I've been meaning to tell you today."

"Yes?" Olivia answered looking up at him.

"I really like my study and I appreciate what you and the girls have done to give me my space. It means a lot," he said as he disappeared down the hallway and closed the door.

"You're welcome…, John…," she said, her voice trailing off.

Olivia washed and dried the dishes but forgot about putting them way the dishes. A Scripture lingered in her mind and she felt compelled to retrieve her Bible and read it. She turned to John 14: 1 and read silently to herself.

Let not your heart be troubled: ye believe in God, believe also in me. In my Father's house are many mansions: if it were not so, I would have told you. I go to prepare a place for you. And if I go and prepare a place for you, I will come again, and receive you unto myself; that where I am, there ye may be also.

Immediately, Olivia felt better. Her children, the bright spots in an otherwise dour existence, were safe in bed and she had reached a peace with John. Hopefully, she prayed, Beth, Mama and Papa were adequately prepared to deal with whatever baggage Ann would be bringing with her tomorrow.

Olivia looked at the back of her hands. She rubbed them softly and massaged the cuticles of her nails. It appeared everyone's mind had been elsewhere and as a result, her 30th birthday had been a quiet one. Whether they knew it or not, she had been surrounded by the two people she loved most. And that was all that mattered.

CHAPTER 48

When John and Olivia arrived at High Point the next morning, Gussie rushed out the front door exclaiming, "Miss Olivia, you best git in the house and hep with Missus Annie. For sho 'nuf all hell has done broke loose and Missus Annie is in a bad way."

Olivia rushed to her mother's room, leaving John standing on the porch with Gussie. Gussie hurried after her while calling back over her shoulder.

"Mr. John you needs to git in here and help Beth and her Mama and Papa for they is having a time with Miss Ann. I has done sent for Dr. James ifn it ain't too late."

Upon entering her Ann's room, Olivia discovered Ann on the floor in a state of acute distress, covered in blood and was having difficulty breathing. She saw Walt and Beth kneeling on the floor working fervently to staunch the flow of blood from her midsection. Olivia turned to Florabell and asked what had happened.

"Lordy Missus Olivia your sister is in a bad way. Best I know is Miss Beth went to check on her before she left for work and found her covered in blood and barely breathing. Then Mister Walt done come in here and yelled for me to go to the Quarters to fetch my Pa, and send him to town to bring back Dr. James."

Annie clutched Olivia's arm and pulled her close to her.

"Olivia, it is terrible. Beth found Ann and the baby she aborted. Beth was nearly hysterical as she yelled for someone to come help her. When Walt got to her, he found Ann's condition critical. Now, they are doing everything they can to keep her from bleeding to death.

When John arrived at their side, he looked upon Ann's grayish colored face. He understood it was doubtful she could live long enough to be helped by Dr. James. He tried to hide his alarm, but he was certain Walt recognized what appeared to be the futility of their efforts.

"What can I do to help you and Beth?"

At that moment Ann opened her eyes and managed a weak smile. Then with all the strength remaining within her, she declared in a weak voice, "I did it and I have survived. I'm in the land of the living!"

John thought he had known everything about the depth of Ann's wickedness, but hearing her expression of joy given her success in killing William's child, was more than he had imagined her capable of. He realized he had not been prepared to witness her methodical murder of her unborn baby. As he looked at the fetus, he realized Ann was evil personified.

.....

Walt questioned Beth about the afterbirth and she confirmed it had passed. "If I leave you, do you have enough strength to continue your efforts to staunch the flow of blood?"

She nodded and Walt took the tiny figure, wrapped it in a clean towel, and motioned for John to come with him. As they walked together, Walt was filled with remorse. Seeing his grandson who was never given his chance for a life, tears formed in his eyes. As he wiped them away, he asked John to go to the stables, collect a wooden saddle box, and meet him on the back porch.

John nodded in agreement and Walt went off to find a proper

burial garment for the baby. He wasn't going to have his grandson buried in a dish towel.

John found the box and carried it, along with a hammer, nails, and two shovels, to await Walt's return.

Walt knew Annie was too upset to assist him in locating suitable burial clothing so he resigned himself to find it himself. He simply would not stress her more. He went to her door and motioned for Olivia to come into the hall. She knew exactly where Mama stored the baby garments and blankets, and within minutes she returned with them. He had no need to caution her not to divulge what he was doing to her mother. Olivia agreed; her mother could not withstand more stress. When she returned to her side, she stilled her mother's questions with assurances that everything was being done that could be done.

She declared, "Mama we are at a point where we must rely upon God's will to prevail. Everything is being done for Ann that Beth and Papa know to do. Let us offer a prayer for her deliverance and for our willingness to accept whatever His will is for Ann and her baby."

Olivia's calm assurance of acceptance was exactly what Annie needed. She resigned herself, knowing that He was in charge.

Once John returned, Walt was relieved he had found all the equipment they needed to complete their solemn duty. As he took a shovel from him, he let John know his plan.

"If you'll help me dig the grave I'll bury him in our family plot with your brother-in-law Jim and the rest of our kin. And, if we have time, I'll show you another spot where we can bury Ann if she does not survive. Although it is often the custom when both mother and child die during birthing, I'll not permit my grandson to share a grave with his murdering mother!"

John nodded in agreement but said nothing else. Aside from the grunts the two men exhaled as they piled the black soil beside the widening hole, the only sound they heard was a whistle of the wind and the rhythmic hollow echo of their steel shovels piercing the tough earth. Before they were finished, their melodic symphony was interrupted by the sounds of an approaching auto.

CHAPTER 49

Walt turned to see Dr. James' car heading up the long hill. Beside him in the passenger's seat was Janie Green, whom he had commandeered to assist him. Although he was a sole practitioner, with a life hanging in the balance, another competent healer was a welcome addition. Walt motioned to John to go and meet them.

"Leave the rest of this to me. Go now and meet Dr. James and Janie Green and take them to Ann. I'll be there directly." John did as he asked.

After he dug the tiny grave, Walt tenderly prepared his grandson for burial thinking, "I could not put my grandson in the ground without dressing him and treating him as the human being he is. Hopefully this will ease some of William's sadness when he learns of his son's death."

On October 22, 1936, baby Bryant was buried at High Point among the kinfolk whom he would never grow to know about.

·····

Dr. James and Janie entered the parlor and found Ann in obvious distress with Beth kneeling over her holding towels firmly against Ann's midsection in an attempt to staunch the flow of blood. While Dr. James checked her breathing and pulse, Janie carefully pulled back the towels to determine the amount of blood that still flowed from her. As she did, she noticed something out of the ordinary. Under Ann's back lay a three-pronged serving fork covered in blood. There was no doubt in Janie's mind as to what Ann's intention had been.

"Doctor James this wasn't no miscarriage; this here was a vicious act committed by Ann to destroy her baby. I ain't never knowed a human to do to itself what Ann has done done. She sho 'nuf weren't gonna let that there baby live."

Janie pointed and Ann's midsection and Charles James removed his stethoscope and leaned over to see the wound.

"Oh Lawd, this girl is sho 'nuf torn up inside from stabbing so hard to break lose that there baby. She be a plumb mess. If we don't stop this here bleedin' soon, she ain't gonna make it."

Dr. James checked Ann's pulse and was alarmed at how weak it was. She had lost too much blood and was querulously close to expiring. He retrieved a vial, syringe and a needle from his traveling bag then handed Janie a bottle of alcohol and a wad of cotton to swab the injection point on her hip while he filled the syringe.

Once he had it filled, he injected Ann with a drug to increase her blood's coagulation rate. After a few agonizing minutes, the blood flow subsided and he began the slow procedure of suturing her internal lacerations. As her pulse returned, Ann stirred.

"Lie still child," Dr. James cautioned. "You have been through quite an ordeal, and you are not out of danger yet. If you overexert yourself, you could begin bleeding again and there will be a possibility of an infection. I'll leave you some medicine for the pain. It won't make it subside fully but it will be enough to take the edge off of it. Given your condition, it is all I can dare to risk."

Ann's eyes narrowed as she spoke directly at him. "Forget your weak pain medicine. What I need is a double jigger of some good whisky. Hell, the way I feel now even rot gut will do."

Her unexpected response left him speechless. At that moment,

Walt returned from the family burial plot and heard her crude response. The men looked at each other incredulously but neither said a word.

When he recovered from his shock, Dr. James closed his black bag and left hurriedly with Janie tagging along behind him. As they walked briskly, he instructed Janie on Ann's care over the next 24 hours. He even suggested that her herbal tea might help control Ann's bleeding. At this point no treatment, even home remedies, was out of the question if they even remotely could improve Ann's chances for survival.

"There is nothing more I can do for her now. Hopefully she has sufficient resistance to fight the infection. I'll come back sometime tomorrow to check on her."

Janie headed to the kitchen to put on a pot of tea and Walt followed Dr. James to his car. As he opened his door he stopped and turned to Walt, looking at him squarely.

"What in the hell did that girl do to her baby? In all my years I have never witnessed such a barbaric act. Is she mentally ill?"

He paused, awaiting some explanation, but none was forthcoming.

. . . . .

Janie returned shortly with a cup of tea for Ann to sip. Beth was exhausted.

"Janie, I am going to check on Mama and find out when Olivia and John will leave; they left the girls with Martha thinking they would make a quick trip here and back, and they need to get back home; I'll return shortly to relieve you."

As soon as Dr. James drove away, Walt went to Annie's room. She told him she knew what had happened and that she was alright.

He did not linger knowing the difficult task facing him. He was determined to write William to acquaint him with all that had occurred and to let him know how he had handled the burial of his son. He intended to insist upon William's immediate action to file for divorce. "Now," he thought, "He can free himself from this devil he has married."

As Walt left to write William, Annie urged Olivia and John to go home and take care of Kate and Jean. She assured them she would be well taken care of by Florabell. Beth left the room with Olivia and John and promised to stop by the next morning with news of Ann's condition.

As Olivia and Beth said their goodbyes, a look of horror came over Beth's face. Tears began rolling down her face as she reached out and hugged Olivia tightly and pulled an envelope from her dress pocket.

"I'm so sorry, sister. With all of the commotion around Ann's return, I completely forgot to give you this and wish you a happy birthday yesterday. Can you forgive me?"

"There's nothing to forgive, Beth. We've all been busy with Ann. I had forgotten it myself so that makes two of us. Thank you for the card. I will cherish it."

The girls hugged again and at that moment, John did an unusual thing. He hugged Beth's shoulders, telling her how greatly he admired how she had handled such a terrifying experience with Ann. Predictably he eyed Olivia sheepishly but made no mention of her missed birthday.

·····

Walt drove straight through the night from Nashville and made it home in time to join Annie and their family at Thomas' house to celebrate Thanksgiving, 1936. They spent their time giving thanks for their many blessings and especially for the blessing of Ann's improved health.

The weeks flew by and Olivia was inundated with orders for her Christmas themed cakes as well as for design and construction of evening dresses for women from Dothan, Geneva, and High Springs. The demands were more than she could meet. Several women attempted to have her prepare their dresses before completing others; but she would not accept the significant bribes they offered and held fast to servicing her faithful customers.

As John noted the many customers flocking to their door, he realized Olivia was turning down work. He walked into where she and Martha were busily working and asked them to give him a job to help out. His query could've knocked them both over with a feather.

Martha laughed at the idea of a jock like John Ward taking up sewing. Martha asked, "What did you have in mind?"

John reminded the two women he had seen one or the other of them spend time with people coming to pick up finished garments. He could relieve them of these disturbances. He pointed out Olivia spent a good bit of time writing out bills for collection of her fee which he could do from the handwritten notes she used to make out her invoice. And the times he had driven her to pick up supplies, whether sewing or baking ones, had given him experience enough to handle this chore alone as long as he had her lists

"Now tell me, do you ladies not think I could save you a lot of time doing piddling things when you could be doing things to make the big bucks I see coming to you?"

Olivia was excited at the prospect of having his help with these mundane chores which took so much of her time. "Do you really mean you are willing to spend your days off helping with these things? If so, then you're hired!"

John laughed at her excitement, it was unusual to see Olivia laugh, and it did him good to think he was responsible for it. "So I'm hired, but you haven't told me what you will pay for all my help. So, how much do I get?"

Martha looked at him with wonder. Was he going to charge for his help? She was just about to ask when Olivia responded: "You'll be paid with clean clothes and good food." Not waiting for his retort, she turned to make out her list for him to fulfill.

CHAPTER 50

As Christmas approached, Olivia was in a quandary. John had not been at home for Christmas for the past several years. Usually, she and the girls spent Christmas Day with her family at High Point where she managed the Turner clan's festive and bountiful lunch.

Gussie required specific instructions as did the women from the Quarters who had been recruited to assist her. This year was different in that Ann made it plain she did not want Olivia at High Point. Once Olivia heard about Ann's comments from Beth, she wondered how she could supervise Gussie and the other women and avoid Ann's foul behavior. It was ironic to her how Ann always viewed Olivia as a ghost until the time she needed something.

•••••

By late December, it had been nearly two months that Ann continued to be plagued with an infection. She grew progressively weaker, making little progress toward recovery. At the time of his last two visits, Dr. James expressed to Walt his conclusion that Ann lacked the will to survive. Until something in her life changed to cause her to want to live, he could do nothing more for her.

Following Dr. James's last visit and his admission that he could do nothing more for her, Annie sent for Janie and put Ann's recovery in her hands. Upon her arrival, Janie decided what Ann needed.

"Honey chile, it's time for you to get well. You done did away with that there baby, and now yous gonna take the easy way out and die. Well you ain't!"

Ann understood Janie would not tolerate her behavior. So, she swallowed the horrible doses of Janie's concoctions, broth, and soft food. Within a week Ann's fever left her and each day thereafter she improved. Within ten days she was sitting up, and within a few more days was strong enough to walk to Annie's room.

· · · · ·

John had fought the hill at High Point before and barely succeeded. Now, the stake bed truck easily overcame the ruts and holes that caused the drive from the main road to the house be be nearly impassable. Walt had meant to do something about that a while ago but he had never made the time.

As he and Olivia parked beside the side porch, they saw Papa with William Bryant down by the pump shed. Olivia hurried to meet them while John hung back. He didn't know the purpose of William's visit, but he suspected it was not a social one.

Olivia rushed to greet him, "I am surprised to see you. Welcome back."

Walt interrupted, "William is here because he wants to pay his respects at his son's grave, and he needs Ann's signature on their divorce papers."

After a few moments, John came forward. "William, I am so sorry for the loss of your son. I don't know if you are aware but Mister Turner handled his burial with love and care he deserved. I earnestly hope you find some comfort in knowing that."

William was unsure where this was leading but he could tell the sincerity of John's intent and he appreciated all John and Walt had done. As he spoke, there was a sterile nature to his words. He seemed detached and it was obvious to both Walt and John.

"Walt's action is no less than I would have expected of him and my family is grateful. Thank you your kind words. I wish I could stay but I need to leave without delay. I have an extremely large caseload facing me, which is a blessing. With the demands of work, I have no time to dwell upon this tragedy. Once my divorce is final, I'll not return to High Point again so let me thank you, Walt, for all you attempted to do before my marriage. I am aware you tried to spare me the untenable situation I endured with Ann this past year. It is unfortunate I did not heed your counsel. I'll file these divorce papers tomorrow. Ann should receive a copy within a few weeks."

William had an urge to vent his hatred of Ann and her barbaric act, but he refrained, not wishing to hurt Walt more. It was time for him to walk away from this tragic aspect of his life and close this chapter forever.

·····

Isaac was heading into town to pick up some supplies for the farm. Before he drove downtown, he stopped by Olivia's house to inquire if she needed a ride to High Point around lunch. He suspected she would want to check in on her mama and sister, Ann.

"I surely do. How could you have known? I need to go over last-minute plans for Christmas with Gussie."

"Good, I pick you up on my way back out of town and after I drop you off at your family's farm, I will run over to High Bluff and finish up some work on staining a table for Mister Ward. Then I'll meet you at High Point and carry you home before three o'clock."

After an afternoon visiting with her mama, Olivia and the girls Olivia rushed around gathering her things and barking at the girls to wait for her on the front porch so they could be ready to leave when Isaac arrived. She was normally patient with the girls, but today they were on her last nerve.

Amid the confusion, Ann appeared at the door, causing Olivia to wonder what she had in store for her. She knew Ann did not want to see her so she had given her a wide berth in the house. "Great she thought," I have to deal with fussy girls *and* a fussy sister. That is just what I need today."

Ann ignored Olivia and made her way to where the girls were seated in rockers on the front porch. She addressed each giving them a candy cane and telling them she would expect them to come back soon.

Olivia waited patiently as both girls rushed to hug their Aunt Ann, telling her they would be back for three days for Christmas. Olivia thought, "Perhaps the time for healing is at hand."

Shortly after they arrived home at four o'clock, Robert stopped by to ask Olivia if she would allow the girls to accompany him downtown to complete his Christmas shopping. He would, of course, buy whatever items remained on their lists. Olivia objected softly and hurried to explain she was teaching the girls that they should expect no one to hand them anything. If they wanted something, they had to work for it.

"We may not have much but we have principles. You must understand I shall not allow you to finance this shopping expedition. We have our pride and we would not welcome having you purchase things for us."

Robert understood too well the strictures Olivia put upon accepting 'charity,' and he admired her for it. "I agree with you. Now is it alright if I take the girls?"

Olivia said she did not mind and then helped the girls don their coats and ensured they were buttoned up. Robert waited patiently for the girls and based on Olivia's statement, he asked her a question that had been on his mind for a while.

"Am I correct in my understanding that John does not provide funds for the girls? And if I am correct, why not; and why haven't you told me before?"

"Mister Ward, this is a question you should ask John. You are correct, I receive no support from him nor do the girls. I don't ask him to account for how he spends his earnings or to help me; it is his decision to either do so or not. If you please, leave the matter alone. The arrangements I have with John are predicated on his respecting his daughters and me. It may not mean much to some but it means more than any money he could provide for us to me. Besides, with my renovations at Mrs. Smith's house my business has expanded to the point it is I who should be supporting John."

"But why are you so reluctant to spend a penny?

"Papa asked each of us to prepare our plan to survive the hardships of uncertainties such as war or the collapse of the economy could bring. Each one of us developed our on plan and has executed it. My family believes in saving for the worst of times. This is what I am doing and why I spend not one penny that is not necessary."

Robert expressed his fascination with the concept her father had taught her and asked her to tell him more.

"I have made my list and securing a teaching position is my number one objective. The second is to obtain a car so I may travel to a distant school if it is necessary and see my mother when I can. I am saving every penny to purchase one Beth knows is for sale at a cheap price. I just hope I can save enough before someone buys it. Also, the Southern Railroad Company now requires John to have a telephone so they can reach him quickly. You and Papa already have had one installed and I am saving to get one for us."

Robert made a few mental notes and thanked Olivia for sharing her father's ideas. As soon as he returned home, he would meet with Frank and Flora. Dark clouds, he knew, were on the horizon

CHAPTER 51

The clock on the wall struck five-thirty and John hurriedly signed the cashier's ticket to his charge account at his last stop. The afternoon with the girls had passed swiftly and Robert knew he needed to get them home soon. He intended to head back to Tallahassee later that evening but not before he made one or two stops at some stores. He knew Judy had shopped for Jean before she left, and instructed Joe to deliver her gifts to Olivia's on Christmas morning. And, if things turned out as they usually did, she suspected Kate had been an afterthought and would, as usual, come out on the short end of the stick.

At each store, he had stopped at the curb leaving the girls sitting in the warmth of the running car, and dashed inside. After several minutes at each stop, he emerged with armloads of mysterious packages which he unceremoniously dumped in the trunk. Joe would deliver them in his usual Christmas Day deliveries to Olivia, the girls, and various friends in town. Robert was particularly happy about Kate's gifts and he hoped she would be in for a big surprise. He had purchased the very toys the shopkeepers had told him she had admired and placed back on the shelf in each store.

Upon arriving at Olivia's, the girls ran inside to sequester their mother while Robert brought in the bundles of gifts wrapped in craft paper through the side entrance to the annex where Olivia's rooms used to be. The girls giggled uncontrollably as she teased them about breaking out of their 'corral' consisting of their tiny bodies they used to 'fence' her in life a wild stallion to keep her from seeing the gifts.

As Robert put away the last bundle, he called out to the girls to 'let 'em run now, yeehah!' The girls responded with a whooping noise as they 'opened' their imaginary gate to let their mother out. Then they ran straight to Robert and hugged him tightly thanking him for a wonderful afternoon.

At the door he donned his coat and hat but before he could leave, Kate asked him if he could stay for tea because as she said, "That's what the 'dults do after shopping." He looked at his watch and shook his head in mock disgust at himself. Of course he would stay.

"It is, after all, what 'dults do after shopping."

.....

Robert never made his train to Tallahassee; he had simply enjoyed his time with the girls too much to leave them. Besides, he had other business he needed to tend to before it was too late.

The next afternoon, Robert stopped in at the cannery to speak to Beth about the car Olivia had told him about. As far as he was concerned, when it came to things that were desperately needed for her family, it was time for Olivia to cease skimping as she did now. With a little luck, he wasn't too late to seal the deal and he hoped to provide Olivia and John with a genuine surprise for Christmas.

After walking the floor in search of her, he inquired with a foreman who advised she had gone home for the day. Thus, he headed out to High Point to see if he could catch her there. About halfway through his drive, he remembered Walt had a phone at the main house and he could have called ahead from the office phone at the cannery to see if she was there but he simply forgot.

His arrival was unexpected and as she invited him in, Beth wondered what brought him there. Surely he knew Papa was in Enterprise delivering some lumber. Beth welcomed him as Gussie took his hat and coat. Beth led him to the parlor while telling him as far as she knew, Papa was out of town and would not be home until Christmas Eve.

"Beth, I have come here tonight to see you and seek a favor from you. I have to be on my way to Tallahassee to be with Judy tomorrow and there is a matter I need your help on and I must not to leave unattended."

Once he explained his intentions about the used car, she assured him her friend had not sold it, and he could get it for a few hundred dollars. He signed a bank draft leaving the amount blank and not setting any limit on the amount she could write in on the draft. Having heard of his hardnosed approaches to several business deals, she was surprised.

"This is Christmas and as such is not a time that I would desire to have anyone treated unfairly, especially someone like your friend. So, I ask you to let your friend set a fair price for the car and in no way be shortchanged."

It was settled between them what Beth was to do and how she was to arrange for Joe or Isaac to pick up the vehicle and deliver it to John and Olivia on Christmas Day. Beth assured him she would take care of the car business the next day. Robert insisted he could see himself out and for her to return to look after Annie.

Ann had been watching and as soon as she heard Robert state he would see himself out, and after Beth left him to return to her mother's room, she rushed to meet him at the front door.

"Mr. Ward, could you spare me a minute? I heard you tell Beth you were in a hurry, but I need your help."

Robert knew from John how difficult it had been for the entire Turner family since Ann returned home and how they feared for her wellbeing considering the severe depression she experienced after her miscarriage. He was in a hurry, but he could spare time for this pitiful woman. "How may I help you?"

She came right to the point. "Mr. Ward I am a burden to my family and I am totally dependent upon them. I have to find some way to become more self-sufficient, and I was hoping you would help me."

Ann did not wait for his response but hurried on to enlighten him as to how he could help her. She explained that a few days before Beth had told her about a clerical job in the office at the cannery.

"I have a college education and am qualified to handle such a job. Although Beth is now senior secretary to Mr. David Anderson, Sr., I can't ask her to try to get me the job. So, I am asking, no I am begging you, to use your influence with him to help me get the job."

Robert's mood that evening was one of goodwill. Later he reflected upon his readiness to call a favor for Ann when he had not stopped to consider her past behavior. Without hesitation he had agreed to assist her as best he could with the understanding his influence was not great and much would depend on her behavior in any interview he could arrange for her.

Hurriedly, he promised to leave a note for David Anderson, asking him to consider her for the job. He suggested she get a ride into High Springs within the next two days and make personal application, for he felt certain David would be receptive. He explained he had a long trip ahead of him and took his leave.

On his way back to High Bluff, Robert suffered through his mixed emotions. For the first time he could ever remember, he regretted Judy and their obligations in Tallahassee. He longed to see Evelyn. The full-length mink coat Judy left for Flora to give Evelyn on Christmas morning would not be of much importance to their level-headed daughter. She paid little mind to material things. Rather, she yearned for attention.

Given her magnificent transformation into an attractive young lady by Olivia's hand, he knew an interest in boys, and they in her were not too far off in the future. With her thirst for any attention, no matter the source, he worried she might fall for the first boy she met. He would deal with that when it presented itself. Now though, he was relieved that Evelyn would be with her beloved brother John and his family whom, she preferred to anyone else.

CHAPTER 52

The next morning, Ann was dressed and waiting for Beth, for she intended to ride with her to the cannery and make her application as Robert Ward suggested. She just hoped Mr. Ward had kept his promise and Mr. Anderson was aware of the favor he was asked to grant Robert Ward. She never asked Beth for a ride to town. She simply announced she was going to ride with her to work and seek an interview with Beth's boss.

"Ann, I will not approach Mr. Anderson and ask any favor of him to give you the clerical job for I can't trust you to behave yourself or to stay sober enough to come to work should he be foolish enough to hire you."

Beth hoped her denouncement of her sister would put an end to her foolish notion of attempting to see Mr. Anderson. How wrong she was, for her sister turned, saying not a word and went to the car, got in, and closed the door. Beth was in a quandary as to what she should do. She could physically pull her out of the car and leave without her, but she knew if she did so she would leave Mama with a hornet's nest, and she knew she could not bring more stress to Mama.

"Alright, you can ride with me but don't expect any help from me; and if my boss asks me, I'll tell him he is crazy to consider you for any position."

Beth drove them to the cannery and upon arriving, left Ann and hurried inside her office, telling the receptionist she was not to be disturbed.

.....

On December 20, 1936, just two days before the Anderson Brothers' Cannery closed for Christmas and New Year's holidays, Ann Turner Bryant was ushered into David Anderson's office for her interview. It was not a surprise to those who knew her but in the space of less than an hour, Ann had captivated David Anderson only she knew how. She may have entered his office as an unemployed soon-to-be-divorced woman in search of a menial clerical position, but left with far more than she had bargained for.

Later that evening, Beth walked to her car only to find Ann waiting for her.

"Alright, so you duped the poor man into giving you the clerical job; I never doubted you would. You always have a way with getting your way with men," she said as she glimpsed Ann's dangling top button on her white blouse. "I know it will be awkward for you at first, but I am confident you will find the maturity to handle the situation at hand. Even though I will be responsible for overseeing your work in my role as Mister Anderson's senior secretary, I will not treat you with any less respect than I do the other girls under my supervision. Although… I will certainly have to review the proper dress code with you."

The ladies entered the car at the same time. Beth sighed in dismay, started the car and headed for High Point.

"Well Beth, I have good news for you. You won't have to worry about feeling awkward with my working under you. I told Mister Anderson you might feel weird supervising me so during lunch at Dallon's today we decided to eliminate that embarrassment for you. Come the first Monday in January, I will be taking the position of special assistant to Mister Anderson. I will oversee the clerical support staff so you see, from now on; I will be your supervisor."

.....

John arrived home to an empty house a few days later. He was pleased to have a little time to himself as he settled in. As he unpacked his bags, he noted the house had a festive atmosphere to it. There was a Christmas tree with gifts underneath and several aromatic evergreen branch wreaths adorned the door and fireplace mantle.

Shortly thereafter, Olivia came home followed by the girls and Isaac, who carried a load of wrapped presents from the trunk of the car. He greeted John and placed them under the tree while explaining to Kate and Jean that these presents were from their grandparents, Mama and Daddy Ward. Then he went back outside to grab another load. Olivia followed along to help him. As Isaac opened the trunk, Olivia was overwhelmed with the sheer volume of packages there.

"I was supposed to deliver these on Christmas Eve as Mr. Ward told me, but when Mama learned ya'll was gonna be at High Point, she told me it'd be best I deliver these here packages to you in High Springs this evening rather than taking them to the Turner's tomorrow."

Olivia thanked Isaac for taking time to bring her home. "Don't linger any longer on account of us. I can get these last few packages in the house by myself. I know tonight is always a joyous time of celebration in the Quarters when your father, Frank distributes the Christmas gifts Mister Ward arranges to have for everyone on Christmas Eve"

"You are right, ma'am but if it is alright with you, I have to wait until Joe gets here; he is riding back to High Bluff with me."

Olivia was surprised at Isaac's explanation and asked him to clarify his remarks.

"Why is Joe coming here?" she asked as they walked together back inside the house.

Before Isaac could answer, a car pulled into the driveway. John joined Isaac and Olivia on the porch and together, they witnessed Joe getting out of an unfamiliar vehicle. He approached the gawking group with a grin that stretched from ear to ear.

"Miss Olivia, Merry Christmas from Mister Robert and Missus Judy. This automobile if for you and ain't it a fine one?"

Joe's outstretched arm held the keys for her which she timidly took from him.

"And he had one more thing for me to tell you. He said tell you it is one item she can check off her list of things she needs in case of a war."

Isaac and John looked at her with puzzled looks but Olivia knew what Joe meant, and she promised she would explain it to them later. For now, though, Isaac and Joe left to finish their deliveries and Olivia went inside to pen a note to Robert and Judy, thanking them for their kindness. They had no idea how much her having reliable transportation would mean to the girls and her while John was away in New Orleans.

Inside, Kate sat apart from everyone else in a self-imposed solitude near the back of the Christmas tree. She had always known Jean would have a lot of gifts because that is how it was every year. She was happy for her sister, but as she read the tags on each gift, she was surprised to find so many with her name on them.

On the other side of the room, John and Olivia discretely watched her reaction and smiled at each other as they observed her excitement. It was something very uncommon for her and they hoped to hold on to every moment of it.

. . . . .

That evening, Martha joined them to enjoy a smorgasbord Olivia had prepared and to listen as John shared tales of his experiences in New Orleans. After an hour or so, Martha excused herself to go home. While Olivia walked her to the sidewalk, inside John helped the girls get ready for bed, reading them several of their favorite Christmas stories before hearing their prayers. As he shut their door, he could hear Jean's whispers to Kate about their bounty of presents. They could only imagine what they would discover to be their presents come Christmas Day.

In her thirty years, Olivia could not recall a happier Christmas season than this one. For the first time in a long while, she actually felt like she was a part of a family. Sure she knew how John felt about her and the girls, and their marriage, but at least it appeared he was making an effort to maintain a civility between them. The girls were happy and it appeared Kate might be getting over her standoffishness from her father.

Olivia hurried to finish work in the kitchen and joined John in the sitting room where they discussed plans for sustaining themselves in time of disaster or war. Papa felt strongly that all of his children be prepared for the worst of times and John, along with the other husbands, was expected to present their plan in two days, after the Turner clan's Christmas Day luncheon.

As they talked, it was apparent to Olivia how much thought John had given in preparing his plan. He had incorporated some suggestions from importers he had met in New Orleans. The believed war would impact individuals, families, businesses and institutions equally hard.

"From what I hear it will be difficult for importers to get

shipments of sugar cane and refined sugar from the islands. We can expect severe shortages, and probably some form of rationing. It will be necessary, Olivia, to plan to severely restrict, or cut out entirely, your baking. Due to shortages of supplies, it would be foolish for you to rely on that as a steady source of income. You must diversify."

Olivia listened and realized how smart John really was. She relayed the conversation with his father about the car and about the progress she had made in having a telephone installed in their home as he had asked her to do.

"We are on the list and within the next month or two, a two-party line will be installed."

She centered the remainder of her discussion with him on Papa and Mama's recent decision to have Aunt Pearl come to live with them at High Point Olivia believed having Pearl around would help keep up Mama's spirits, especially as her brain tumor continued to develop. When she had exhausted this subject, she thought about telling him about Ann's new job but decided he had heard enough for tonight. She would tell him tomorrow.

CHAPTER 53

It was a far from joyous Christmas Eve and John was fuming in disbelief.

"Hell, Olivia, David Anderson knows about Ann and her past. Has he lost his ever-loving mind hiring her? She has the morals of an alley cat, and what concerns me most is that David has opened himself to the Jezebel she is. Will your father intervene? He knows Ann is capable of creating a heaping scandal without an ounce of remorse for what it will do to all of us?"

Olivia shook her head. "I think Papa has realized he has no control over her, and it seems he is like the rest of us: 'just waiting for the other shoe to drop.' "

John couldn't stand it any longer. His first inclination was to hop in their new car and drive out to High Point to confront Ann about whatever nefarious plan she had up her sleeve. Then he realized the real idiot in the whole matter David Anderson, his longtime friend and former boss. Perhaps he just needed to drive there instead and knock some sense into him?

After a spell, he calmed down a bit and Olivia suggested that he try to get some sleep before their big day tomorrow. They would exchange gifts with the girls and then they would drive out to High Point for lunch. Then she reminded him of his presentation and how much she knew he wanted to impress her father with his plan. And, after all, he couldn't be really serious about fighting David Anderson, was he? She reminded him gently that he had only recently escaped the narrow walls and cold concrete floor of a jail cell and she couldn't imagine he wanted to experience that again anytime soon, especially on Christmas Eve.

John agreed reluctantly and Olivia sent him on his way while promising to join him as soon as she put out the girls' presents from them under the tree.

A half hour later, Olivia turned out the bedside light and got into bed beside John. She was uneasy, for it had been a long time since they had shared a bed. She was about to turn onto her side and away from him when he pulled her close to him and spoke.

"Tomorrow morning when we awaken, the girls will be excited to open their presents. I am ashamed I have not even thought of buying them anything. I know you have placed a present they will believe is from me, and I thank you."

John paused for a moment as he tried to find the words to explain the duality of his thoughts when it came to Kate and Jean.

"There are some things I must tell you; things I cannot leave here tomorrow without your hearing. I was free to come home a week ago, but I did not want to. The company is providing me living quarters in New Orleans, and I have met people with whom I enjoy sharing my free time. For the first time in years, I feel free of the burden of our marriage and of being a father."

He waited for Olivia to respond, but she lay still and quiet beside him with her arms tightly crossed against her chest. He could tell she was fighting to smother any emotion his words might cause her to feel.

"As to Kate and Jean, I don't know what to say. As I told you when I was released from jail, I wanted so much to win their love and respect but once I arrived in New Orleans, it was easy for me to forget them in favor of the euphoric feeling of freedom. Is it possible for you to grasp how a man could revel in vanquishing thoughts of his family in favor of temporary pleasure in the company of so many strangers? Please, tell me."

Olivia turned toward him and coupled his face in her hands, "No, John. I cannot grasp how a *man* could discard his family like a piece of unwanted trash. Nor can I understand a *man* denying his children in favor of experiencing some fleeting pleasure with a soulless woman."

John could feel tears trickling down her fingers and onto his checks as she spoke barely above a whisper. He knew for certain her answers were those couched in pity for him rather than for his daughters and her. She continued.

"I cannot accept a *man* who would make those choices. However, I can accept such irresponsible behavior from a selfish, immature *boy*. Only a *boy* would ignore the futility of his quest for freedom. There! You wanted it and now you have my answer."

She tried to turn away but he held her tightly. "Damn you, Olivia! I try to make it easier to go my own way, but there is always something that pulls me back to you. Right this minute I want to have you this last time, but I don't want you by force."

He felt her relax and he slowly released his grip on her. She slid back from him a bit but did not turn from him. Instead, she loosened her nightgown, wrapped her arms around him, and prepared to forget what she hoped would be her last night in bed with her husband.

MCMURTRY

CHAPTER 54

As though they had scripted their congenial behavior, John and Olivia shared their daughters' joy as they opened their presents on Christmas morning. Judy's presents for Jean were equally matched by those which Robert had purchased for Kate, who was overjoyed beyond belief. It had cost him the better part of an afternoon but making the rounds at all of the toy stores in Dothan to determine which toys Kate had most coveted had paid off in spades.

For Olivia, the most precious part was opening her gifts from the girls. She recognized Kate's thrifty personality had been the determining factor in selecting them for her. Kate would not use her hard-earned money for frivolous things. Olivia's gifts from the girls consisted of a new pair of heavy work gloves and thick knee pads for her to use as she pulled weeds.

Jean explained, "Mama I wanted to get you a comb and brush that didn't cost more than that old gloves and knee pad, but Kate said you wouldn't want us to use our money that way so we didn't."

John could not contain himself as he burst out laughing thinking how Kate would have explained her thrifty philosophy to Jean, and how her sister would have completely discounted such frugal thoughts.

Jean wasn't finished just yet though, "Mama what did Papa give you? I bet he didn't give you something to work in the garden with, did he? Papas are supposed to give stuff that smells good. At least that's what Aunt Beth told us."

Olivia explained their father's gift wouldn't be here for a month or so but it was worth waiting for because it was a telephone. Kate didn't say a word. She knew the telephone was for her father. She was with her mother when she had placed the order and explained how her husband's job required him to have a way to call in to the central dispatcher to check his schedule. Kate frowned a bit. She knew her father had not gotten any presents for her mother. "He's no good for her or for us. I look forward to the time when he will leave us and Jean, Mama and I can get back to normal," she thought.

Once the girls had opened their presents and played a bit, Olivia asked them to gather up their gifts and them away in room. It was time for them to get dressed for the drive out to High Point to open their presents from their aunts, uncles, and grandparents. They giggled with glee as they ran to don their winter clothes, strewing their gifts and wrapping paper shards behind them as they ran.

With the girls out of earshot, Olivia turned her attention to John. Last night, he had been clear as to his decision to leave shortly after breakfast today. Now, the time was upon them and she asked if he wanted to accompany her with the girls on their way to High Point on his way out of town. She said they could ride together as a family and he could drop them there in the farm truck. Either Beth or one of her brothers could drive them home later.

John said he didn't see the point in that. They had already said their goodbyes. He said there was no use carrying on like a family. He was leaving High Springs and would not return in the foreseeable future. New Orleans was his new home. Olivia shared a puzzled look. She knew John would not be back for a while but the word 'home' had thrown her off. John confessed with all the hubbub of the new car, opening presents, and everything else, he had neglected to mention a new development.

"Although I have only been certified and on the job a short while, I've bene offered and accepted a position as a new engineer trainer for the railroad. With everything going on in Europe, the company feels like there are strong prospects of war on the horizon. To prepare for that, the company must position itself to transport materiel and troops across the nation which means recruiting and training engineers at an increased pace. I've done so well in my practical and written exams, my bosses want me to prepare my students in the same way."

He paused to gauge Olivia's reaction but she was stoic in her thoughts so he continued, "The last few days has been a welcomed distraction for me. I have enjoyed spending time with the girls. I wouldn't mind doing that again for a few days if you and the girls are up for it. I mean, I guess I should try to come back once in a while just so Kate and Jean will know they have a father. What do you think? I will agree to whatever you best see fit."

Olivia had remained silent until now but did not hesitate with her answer and she came at him with both barrels, "John, you have chosen to exclude your daughters from your life and you will have to live with that one day. Why would you even consider returning here only to have them face being abandoned time and time again? No, absolutely not. It is best for you to walk away and not look back. It is far easier to explain to the girls that you are gone and will not be back than it is to explain why you continually leave them. *That, is the situation as I best see fit.*"

Shortly, the girls emerged from their room and were ready to open more presents with Mama and Papa Turner. Before they could say anything, Olivia grasped both girls' arms and quickly ushered them to the car. As they sat back in the rear seat, Olivia started the car and began to back from the driveway. Neither girl noticed their father's absence until they were around the corner. Then it was Jean who asked if they had forgotten him. Before Olivia could answer Kate spoke.

"Jean, on your next birthday you will be five and you are old enough to understand the simple truth. Our father is neither coming with us now nor is he ever coming home to us again. You just need to accept that there will be just the three of us from now on."

CHAPTER 55

At High Point, Walt and Annie, along with Beth welcomed family to the gathering. Olivia shifted nervously as she forestalled answering questions she could tell each was dying to ask. The children were out of earshot so she decided to take the bull by the horns and get it over with.

"I know you are all wondering about my husband, John so I will tell you what I know and ask you not to question me further."

Now she had everyone's attention and Annie moved beside her and wrapped her arm around Olivia's shoulder to comfort her in advance of the news she suspected was coming.

"John is headed back to New Orleans where he has a job training engineers with the Southern Railroad. As I have expected for some time, he has informed me his move is final; he will not be back to High Springs. His reasons are those he has harbored for as long as I have known him. He cares for his daughters, Kate and Jean, but not enough to share their lives. As for me, he cannot endure the thought of having to live with me for his lifetime. John has discarded his unwanted burdens and there is nothing more to add. I ask you not to offer your sympathy or show your pity, I need neither."

She then quickly turned and headed to the kitchen before any of her family noticed the tears she was trying desperately to hold back. Surprisingly, it was Ann who followed her.

"Olivia, I don't pity you, but I do want to admit to you how wrong I have been toward you and apologize for my selfish behavior.

As you spoke just now, I imagined it could have just as easily been I standing in your shoes today. I have been a terrible friend to you and an even worse sister. I am truly sorry for my actions toward you these past few years and I hope you can forgive me one day."

Ann turned to retreat to her suite when Olivia spoke, "Ann, I forgave you a long time ago. My hope is you will not dwell on my misery, but rather find some happiness for yourself. I will be fine. I am always *fine*."

.....

After their noon meal, the children exchanged gifts and shared toys and games while the adults huddled around the massive dining room table sharing their separate disaster plans.

When they concluded all of the presentations, Walt pulled a small notebook from his jacket and spoke.

"Aye they are all good plans ye have put together. Although he is not here, there is one more that I feel the need to share with ye. It is John Ward's and it is the most comprehensive plan of all of you combined. The boy might be a scoundrel when it comes to my daughter and granddaughters but he certainly has a mind for planning and I suggest ye all listen and incorporate his key points."

Then, he called their attention to John's scribbled notes, detailing actions to be taken and during what timeframe. A point he emphasized about John's notes was having each family acquire a telephone to facilitate fast communication amongst them. Another key point was his observations on supply management. The Turners and other families had to find a way to wean themselves off of certain supplies that would not be available to them due to likely shortages caused by delays in shipping. Some things, they would have to learn to make on their own.

"It's a good plan he's made here. His absence doesn't make it any less so. It is a pity as brilliant as he is it has been impossible for him to accept and be content with the hand life had dealt him. But alas, we all move on in this life one way or another."

. . . . .

It was well after supper time by the time when Olivia and the girls left High Point to return returned home. It had been a difficult visit for Olivia, her first Christmas with the family since she had been unceremoniously banished from their midst nearly six years ago. She was exhausted from the angst she had suffered under the weight of John's decision to abandon them, and she needed to make a place for her beloved Evelyn to sleep while she was there.

Upon arriving home, she fed the girls. Then she placed a pot of poinsettias on an end table, and admired it beside the day bed Isaac and Joe had made to fit inside the bay window area in Mrs. Smith's front room. As it turned out, it looked very welcoming.

When he picked up John to carry him to Dothan, Isaac had dropped off Evelyn and her presents from her parents at Mrs. Cox's house where they listened to Christmas carols and visited until Olivia arrived home with the girls. As soon as she saw Olivia drive by, Martha Cox walked Evelyn over.

Now that their party was complete, Kate and Jean took charge of the stray gifts, arranging them around the Christmas tree along with their gifts for Evelyn. Both girls were excited to see their aunt and to watch her open the present they each had for her. As Evelyn sat at the kitchen table listening to Jean tell about her present, she was aware of Olivia's tension.

Olivia suggested it was time for the girls to open their presents from their grandparents and give Evelyn hers. She deliberately waited until the last present to open was the one from Kate and Jean because it was such a delight to watch their excitement in expectation of her learning what their gift was. At last she opened a long slender box, and inside laid a dainty gold heart on a chain. The heart opened to show a place to put a picture of each girl.

Jean excitedly explained she and Kate thought Evelyn might want to have pictures of them in her room. "The only problem, Evelyn, is we don't have any pictures of either of us, but I'm going to ask Mama Ward to have one made."

With complete sincerity, Evelyn hugged each girl and told them she liked their present the best of all, including her full-length mink coat.

Olivia had the girls clean up the wrappings and get ready for bed. Jean wanted to know if Evelyn would read them a story as their father had done when he came home to visit. Evelyn read not one but two stories before Olivia came in to say prayers with the girls.

Jean was first. "God, I don't know why Papa left without telling us goodbye, but I want you to watch over him. And, God, please make him change his mind and come home to be with us some time. Amen!"

As she got up from beside her bed she looked at Evelyn and asked, "Why doesn't Papa love us anymore?" Evelyn had no answer so Jean crawled into bed as she awaited Kate's prayers.

"Lord our Papa is so unhappy. I ask he be at peace. Don't let Jean miss him too much. Amen!"

Evelyn looked at Olivia who knelt beside Kate and bowed her head. "I know You have a plan for John and I kneel before You praying he will let Your plan come to fruition in his life. I earnestly pray he may find relief in his decision to move on and away from all he resents here with us. Amen!"

Olivia stood and kissed each girl and wished them a good night.

Then, she and Evelyn left them and went to the sitting room. There was no doubt in her mind the girls' prayers had raised questions Evelyn would want answered.

Evelyn sat quietly soaking in all she had heard and thinking about the meaning of their prayers. Olivia considered how to keep her promise to John not to comment on his actions to Evelyn.

"Olivia, will John be home tomorrow? Or, ever again?"

This was what Olivia feared. Evelyn would not be satisfied until she learned the truth, and so she began.

"John has moved to New Orleans where he has accepted a new job. He was anxious to join his friends for the holidays and said he would write you."

Evelyn was concerned for the girls and Olivia. "What plans has he made to have you and the girls join him?"

"We will not join him. He has longed to find a way to free himself of an unwanted wife and two daughters he merely tolerates. I know it sounds harsh, but there you have it. He has abandoned us."

Evelyn loved her brother with all his faults. Long ago she had recognized how John had sought to escape the realities of his life. She had witnessed him transform from a strong individual to one easily led by others, and it frightened her to think of him living in New Orleans and being accountable to no one. Although Robert may have been worried when John did not come home on the weekends that he was off, Olivia remained uncertain.

"In the last few months, your father has expressed his concerns when his friend at the Southern Railroad dispatch office in Dothan mentioned on at least two occasions that everyone in the dispatcher's office expected John to be back in Dothan for his extended time off but no one ever heard from him."

Olivia wished she could tell Evelyn something to allay her fears, but she could not.

"Evelyn, although I have no influence with John, I was foolish enough to believe he would want to share his daughters' lives. I was wrong. I know how you love him and want him to be happy, but there comes a point, and it is now, when you have to cease worrying about him. There is nothing to do but pray for John to find peace and happiness with the life he has chosen. Then, you must get on with the business of your own life of which high school, college, and a career in medicine await you. Do not fall prey to the demons that have plagued your brother. Do not let anything or anyone deter you from your objectives."

"I won't, Cotton. I've witnessed firsthand the chaos that has surrounded John and I am determined not to be drawn into that. I promise."

CHAPTER 56

New Year's Day 1937 was an exciting one for Ann. The following morning she was set to begin working at Anderson Brothers' Cannery and she could hardly wait. While Ann was elated at the prospect of making a new beginning for herself, Beth remained disturbed as she considered a multitude of scenarios she might face with Ann as her supervisor. She shared her fears with Papa and asked for his advice.

"Papa, I have worked hard over the past few years to position myself to be selected as Mr. Anderson's senior secretary. He's the only person I have ever worked for there. Yet, he interviewed Ann for a clerical position and now I am told she is being hired as his special assistant and will be my supervisor. It just doesn't seem fair."

Walt could appreciate Beth's concern. From what she said, her close association with David Anderson would be changed. He knew, too, she worried Ann would pull one of her tricks and jeopardize both their jobs. Walt considered decided to take the bull by the horns and confront Ann. He wanted to understand how she planned to manage her sister and how she expected to behave toward her co-workers and David Anderson. He was, after all, a married man.

Surprisingly, Walt found Ann eager to talk about the position Mr. Anderson had created for her. While Mr. Anderson was impressed with her overall attitude and drive to accomplish goals, he was concerned about her lack of experience in business. But, he felt like her personality would be beneficial in meeting with other businessmen and in ensuring the clerical work was completed timely.

"Papa, you are a businessman and you deal with many people. Do you have knowledge of what a personal assistant is expected to do for the president of a company? And do you understand the difference between Beth's job as senior secretary and mine as personal assistant? Please believe me when I tell you how much I want to succeed in this job, and just as importantly, I do not want to harm Beth's position."

Walt considered the plight of his daughters, and was relieved to learn Ann understood how any ill-advised actions on her part could adversely affect Beth. He believed Ann. It seemed she had truly turned a page. He would answer her questions based upon his experience. Hopefully she would gain an appreciation of how she could succeed in her work and support Beth. He shared his recommendations and noticed that Ann listened intently to his counsel. Later he shared with Beth his belief that she and Ann could work together in harmony; he emphasized his belief that Ann would not create a problem for her.

What neither appeared to consider or ask their father about was the reaction of their co-workers. Walt elected to let the matter resolve itself, although he suspected there would be expressions of hostility. He was certain they would face the anger of some who questioned the decision of David Anderson to place Ann in a position some felt they had earned the right to fill.

Although Ann would be the primary target of hostility, Beth would not escape some of its effects simply because she was Ann's sister. While Walt anticipated the strained relations from the workers, he was unconcerned about any negative impact on Ann. He smiled to himself when he thought of the outcome. Ann was a tough one, and those who opposed her would rue the day. She would prevail with ease, especially considering none of her would-be- adversaries understood her cunning nature, her intelligence, and her ability to excel in whatever she put her mind to accomplish.

. . . . .

The following morning, Ann and Beth were met with hostile stares from a few of the clerical employees as they entered the offices of Anderson Brothers' Cannery. Ann proceeded to the rear, where Mr. Anderson's office was located, and Beth walked to her desk which was adjacent to his office. Beth could detect some degree of Ann's anxiety, but others could not. To the casual observer, Ann appeared at ease, greeting each person as she passed, and exuding an air of supreme confidence along with an unmistakable swagger that said, 'don't mess with me!'

Beth was proud of her little sister, and without conscious thought allied herself with Ann.

"Ann, don't pay any attention to those girls up front. Lord knows I went through the very same treatment for the first two weeks after Mr. Anderson selected me to become his senior secretary. Every one of them expected to be chosen even though my work was far superior to theirs and I had never gossiped or shared information I had access to during my work here. I know Mister Anderson recognized this and I think it was the deciding factor in my selection."

Ann asked if she should go on in Mr. Anderson's office or should she wait for Beth to announce her.

"Before I let him know you are here, listen to what I have to say, for it may make it easier on you these next few days. Your absolute loyalty is what he will expect and what he will value most. As his personal assistant, you will take over some of the duties I have performed for the past year, and you will have access to his personal information, and some of his family's. Be complimented he trusts you to handle his personal needs and guard all you are exposed to. Don't let others learn anything about his business because you let something slip or you shared something with someone you thought you could trust. Know that anyone associated with this organization would give anything to gain inside information Mister Anderson's business and personal life."

Ann took in everything Beth told her and was grateful she was willing to help her understand what to expect. Knowing how she had treated Beth in the past, she realized Beth could have be justified in leaving her vulnerable and unaware of the pitfalls she would likely encounter.

"Finally, Ann, don't let anyone pull the wool over your eyes. Come to me if you are unsure how to handle a matter and I'll share with you how I have done so in the past. The 'busy bodies' we work with don't understand what they are up against when we two Turner sisters put our heads together. We'll give them as good as they send."

Ann's her heart was filled with genuine affection for her sister who was willing to do battle for her.

"Beth, I have fouled up royally throughout my life here in High Springs, and I know it would be better for you not to align yourself with me. But with you standing with me, I say come on and sock it to me, but be prepared to dodge what is hurled back."

Beth laughed at Ann's choice of words. They were so unlike her.

"That's the way to go; make them understand that words won't break your bones, but the power you are being given is a mighty force they will have to endure. Let me tell Mr. Anderson you are here and see how he wants us to begin training you."

. . . . .

The morning went well with Ann working closely with Beth, learning to handle multiple duties which were now hers. As the morning passed and Beth observed Ann's handling of information and implementing instructions, she was astounded at Ann's intellect.

She was smart. Beth realized Ann possessed something she did not: the confidence and poise of a professional woman who could handle any problems she had to work through.

Lunch time came and Beth was prepared to share the lunch she had made for the two of them. However, Mr. Anderson came to Beth and told her to look after the office while he took his personal assistant to lunch. What a mistake. By mid-afternoon the rumor mill was in full operation as several of the office workers had observed Ann and Mr. Anderson having lunch together at Dallon's Diner. Again.

Before the work day ended, Beth had heard enough to know her co-workers were busy speculating on how Mrs. Anderson would react to her husband selecting Ann as his personal assistant, considering her reputation. Beth went into Mr. Anderson's office and closed the door behind her.

"May I have a word with you?"

David Anderson expected her to be a little put out with him at his hiring her younger sister to fill a position to which she now answered, but he did not anticipate the grave expression on Beth's ordinarily unflappable face.

"Are you here because of the job I gave your sister?" he asked. "I observed you two this morning and you seem to make a great team. I'm pleased how you willingly showed her the ropes. So, what is it which makes you look like you swallowed a sour pill?"

Beth smiled at his description of her expression.

"Well, if you must know, I feel like more like a tiger than a sour puss just now, and if I were not the genteel daughter of Annie McGee Turner I would probably go knock together a few heads before I left this afternoon."

"Wow, you really are the feisty one some have talked about. Are you going to stand there the rest of the afternoon or are you going to tell me what has caused you to be so riled?"

"Mister Anderson, as soon as you get home this evening you need to tell Mrs. Anderson about taking your young and attractive personal assistant to lunch today. The 'Gossip Girls' in the clerical pool already have you and Ann labeled as co-conspirators in a torrid love affair. I am serious. This is what is circulating because one or two of the girls saw you with Ann at lunch again."

David heard it in the tone of her voice and realized Beth was serious, but could not help laughing at her pained expression as she delivered her warning.

"Honestly, Mr. Anderson, how could you have been so dumb? Excuse me for calling you dumb, but you have to admit it was a dumb thing to do. She is young, pretty, and as much as I am embarrassed by it, a tarnished reputation in High Springs. My sister values this job and looks at it as a way to prove she can overcome her checkered past and have a good life here in High Springs again. She can't achieve that if everyone in town thinks you two are committing 'Hanky Panky' in the storage room I am sorry but that is what they think."

Beth waited, not knowing how he would take what she had shared with him, especially her suggesting that her boss and the owner of the company were dumb.

His response was measured, "I know all about Ann's past including the tragic circumstances of the loss of her child and her divorce. Before she moved to Georgia, I was privy to more gossip about her untoward behavior than I cared to hear. I considered all of this when I hired her, in addition to information I gained about her from several of my friends in Gwinnett County. Their reports were filled with complimentary statements about her behavior as a genteel woman who was a credit to her grandmother, and who conducted herself in an exemplary fashion."

"Oh," Beth responded with a hint of surprise. "I had no idea you knew about Ann's time in Georgia. Everything Papa heard was as you have said. She worked to conduct herself in a manner to be accepted in grandmother's select circle. Actually, Papa and Mama were proud of her and our grandmother doted on her."

"Beth, have you ever known me to act without careful consideration of the facts? You don't have to answer, for you have not. In the case of your sister I acted on the basis of her behavior in Georgia and factored in the fact that people can change. So it was when she interviewed for a job with me."

He paused to allow her to digest what he had said.

"At the time I interviewed Ann, I made the decision to act on what I knew of her behavior in Georgia and not on petty gossip that prevails in High Springs. I hired Ann because her demeanor was what I desired in my personal assistant. "

It seemed Mr. Anderson was dismissing her, and Beth hurried to thank him for giving Ann a chance.

"Your advice was good although a little late. Last evening, I shared with my wife my intention to take Ann to lunch today. Within the next week I expect my wife to invite Ann to have lunch with her. I want them to become closely acquainted because of their interactions, now because Ann is my personal assistant. As such, she will be responsible for handling many of my wife's requirements. The gossips will not succeed in undermining Ann's position or in riling my wife, even though I suspect that after meeting Ann, she will remind me constantly that I am already taken."

Thinking she had overstepped her bounds, and anxious to escape from Mr. Anderson's office, Beth gathered some file folders from a nearby side table and made for the door. But, she found, David Anderson wasn't finished with her quite yet.

"Hold on there, Beth. You need to hear this. I admit it; no reasonable person can meet Ann and not be impressed with her. One would have to be blind not to see her beauty and be enticed by her schoolgirl charm. Certainly, I see all of that in her, but what interests me most is her keen mind and ability to quickly and clearly articulate her thoughts. Ann is more than an attractive woman. She is an extremely talented one who is going to make my job running this cannery much easier."

Beth agreed in principle and suggested they call for an all-staff meeting tomorrow morning. It was best to aggressively get out in front of the gossip before it took hold and she felt he had some strong words to deliver the staff needed to hear.

David agreed saying, "It is important every employee understand how I shall react to spurious, unfounded gossip about myself, my family, and any of my employees. There will be no tolerance of malicious untruths. I plan to tell them first offenders will have to seek employment elsewhere. Do you agree this will put a lid on the current gossip?"

Beth was nearly giddy in her agreement, but said she really did need to leave for the evening. She told him she was in a hurry to help her sister, Olivia prepare for her sister-in-law, Evelyn's thirteenth birthday.

As Beth turned out of the cannery parking lot, she wiped away the 'fog' on the inside of the windshield and the thought occurred to her that much of life was the same way. "Sometimes the angst inside you clouds your vision to a greater degree than influences from the outside. That certainly has been the case with Ann and I pray this new opportunity for her will wipe away her inner turmoil and allow her a clearer vision for the future. Only time will tell but for now, I will celebrate Evelyn's maturing into a teenager. She, like my sister Ann, is intelligent beyond her years and I am confident she won't let anything cloud her future. Olivia simply will not allow it."

EPILOGUE

It was not until the end of the decade of the 1930s that millions of jobless workers were able to find employment due to President Roosevelt's creation of the Civilian Job Corps program and with it the emerging WPA.

Although Roosevelt's programs provided job opportunities for many, it did not provide farmers in the South with sufficient economic relief to forestall the loss of their homesteads and farming equipment to foreclosure by banks and individual holders of their mortgages, like Robert Ward. Tragically, most of these farmers were never able to regain ownership of their land and became tenant farmers or sharecroppers on their former farms. Or worse, they became itinerant day laborers.

Businessmen such as Walt Turner and Robert Ward benefited from the federal WPA program which produced contracts for goods and services, as well as an environment in which those with money financed crop loans that could not be repaid by many farmers. The multitude of contract awards to both Robert and Walt through the 1930's enabled them to prosper and also to provide work for many of the citizens of Geneva County.

Olivia Turner Ward faced these challenging economic conditions as she worked tirelessly to find ways to support her young family. Her determination, strength, and faith in God enabled her to survive these desperate times. However, High Springs, like so many small Southern towns, thrived on the gristmill of gossip; and Olivia had thus far unable to overcome the long-standing censure of herself and her daughters. Their crime? Being born to a father resented far and wide as the boy who had the world by the tail and had given it all up in the name of Greed, Lust, and Slothfulness. His daughters were guilty by their association with him and neither could ever hope to redeem themselves without taking drastic measures.

.....

Partnering with Mr. Adkins in their venture to service outlying farms with a rolling store, John Ward found his own redemption, although temporary, and in doing so elevated his standing among his fellow citizens of High Springs as a businessman. Even so, his discontent grew as he struggled with his forced life as a husband and father. He attributed every moment of his "captured" existence to Olivia for what he considered 'his ruined life.'

.....

The premature birth of Jean, the youngest daughter of John and Olivia, had altered the dynamics of the relationship between Judy Ward and Olivia from one of adversaries to compatriots.

Surprisingly, Walt and Annie Turner became indebted to John. He had succeeded where they had failed in persuading Ann, their youngest daughter, to go to live in Georgia with her grandmother and aunt. Ann's behavior had caused her to be viewed as being beyond the pale in their small town and with her move to another state, Annie and Walt dared hope their youngest child would take advantage of her opportunity to turn over a new leaf in her book of life. Redemption, it seemed, was destined for those who least deserved it.

.....

A light rain tapped gently on the tin roof of the porch as Olivia sat back in Papa's rocker and surveyed the grounds. It was hard to believe it had been seven years since she had been exiled from her family home. Aside from the physical changes in her mother and father, little had changed around the farm. The trees and bushes were taller and the wood on the outbuildings was a little more weathered. But still, it felt like home.

After much struggle, Olivia had either sidestepped or outright overcome many of the aforementioned barriers to her success. Now she felt she could move forward and make a life for her daughters without John. Because of a shortage of teachers, Olivia secured her teaching certificate and actively sought a position in a school where she could teach young children as she had with Joe and Isaac, and Kate and Jean, since their birth. Hopefully some intuitive principal would overlook her lack of formal education and the heavy burden she carried as a social pariah in Geneva County and give her the opportunity. She prayed for this nightly and had faith He would provide for her.

John remained in New Orleans leading his Hedonistic lifestyle without regard for how it might affect his employment. He lived two lives: that of absentee father and abusive husband, and that of carefree bachelor recapturing the youth he felt he lost with his forced marriage at age eighteen to a woman who was seven years his senior. As each day passed, he strayed further and further away from redemption. Sad as it may seem, he was just fine with that.

. . . . .

Nothing changed in Ann's demeanor during her stay in Savannah. Always the master manipulator, she goaded her grandmother Amelia and aunt Pearl into introducing her to a lifestyle of a debutant. Although she was often regarded as a prize catch and the belle of the ball, she was still the same cruel, cold, and calculating person she had always been. With Papa funding her extravagant lifestyle, she took Savannah by storm. When he signaled the end of his largess, she settled on a suitor with a socially acceptable job, William Bryant. Although she loathed his 'menial' position and an attorney for the city, Ann seduced him into a hurried engagement and wedding, and an early pregnancy. Dissatisfied with his social standing, modest lifestyle, and lack of rapid upward mobility, she aborted her baby in a gruesome manner, nearly costing herself her own life in the process. By the time the ink on the divorce papers were dry, she was hired into a prestigious position at the cannery where Beth worked which gave her the impetus she needed to regain acceptance within her family and the community.

·····

For Flora, Frank, Joe, and Isaac, life remained much the same. Although the world around them continued to be difficult for colored folks in the South, they were insulated from much of the prejudices prevalent in Southern society as long as they lived at High Bluff. Robert continued to see that the folks in his Quarters were safe under his wing while becoming cognizant of the drastic cultural changes which appeared to be on the horizon.

·····

Walt and Annie grew older, and because of her terminal diagnosis, Walt prepared himself for a future that did include his beloved Annie. He didn't know how he would ever go on without her, but knew he must for Kate and Jean. Once viewed as a blight on his family's reputation, Kate had grown on Walt's curmudgeonly disposition and he found he adored her. He could not wait to see her grow into the woman he knew she would become—a sort of second coming of his beloved Annie.

·····

After surviving a near takeover of their clubs in Florida by the Chicago Mafia, and John's resulting incarceration for illegal campaign 'contributions,' Robert and Judy continued to expand their empire while coming to terms they had failed both their children as parents. They couldn't put their finger on it but John's release coupled with

Evelyn's emergence as a debutant and Kate and Jean's presence caused them to finally accept Kate at least marginally. This was a significant culmination of events for Olivia who had always sought to ensure her girls 'had a name' that put them at least on equal footing with their peers in High Springs.

.....

After moving back to High Springs after graduating from the University of Alabama, Paul had settled into his position as vice-president at the bank. There he worked closely under his father who was president. Unfortunately Paul was caught in several predicaments: dealing with his father who had an unhealthy sense of always being one-upped by Robert and John Ward, and an untenable marriage to his wife, Sandra who loathed the social and political trappings of a small town in South Alabama. Their marriage had hung by a thread for several years and his only respite was flying. Although he had begun flying in college as a hobby, with war looming in Europe, several new opportunities presented themselves to him to supplement his income by training pilots. As the situation in Europe deteriorated, he felt an obligation to ensure his work on behalf of Triangle Aviation prepared as many pilots as possible for any future war effort.

.....

After *planting* the seeds of their families, Walt Turner and Robert Ward tended their businesses as they watched and waited for their families to *grow*. Both men knew that with love, attention, and dedication they would witness the emergence of some of their offspring pushing upwards and outwards in many directions, while others would wilt and die in the rough untilled terrain they had chosen for themselves. Both patriarchs eagerly waited for the fruits of their labor to emerge.

COMING NOVEMBER 2019

"A HARVEST SEASON: THE COTTON
CHRONICLES VOLUME THREE"

BUY YOUR COPY AT:
WWW.THECOTTONCHRONICLES.NET

PLEASE LIKE US ON FACEBOOK AT:
BETTY COTTON MCMURTRY – AUTHOR

PLEASE RATE AND REVIEW "A GROWING
SEASON" ON AMAZON.COM AND
GOODREADS.COM

MCMURTRY

356

ABOUT THE AUTHORS

Betty Cotton McMurtry grew up in rural Geneva County, Alabama. After attending college at Auburn University, she set out on a life of a civil servant, management consultant and NFL player agent. Betty resides in Auburn, Alabama where she enjoys her two grandchildren and five great-grandchildren.

Ford McMurtry was born in Columbus, Georgia. After high school, he attended Auburn University where he was a walk-on member of the football team. In addition to becoming a successful coach at the high school, college, and professional levels, He counts NBA Hall of Famer Shaquille O'Neal among his most accomplished players. Ford's career included stints as an NFL agent, sports journalist, business owner, and auto insurance claims director. He resides in Auburn, Alabama where he enjoys spending time with the family and dog, Missy.